THE ILLUSIONIST

John E. Poulson

THE ILLUSIONIST

DOUBLE DRAGON

A DOUBLE DRAGON PAPERBACK

ISBN 978-1-78695-458-9

Double Dragon
is an imprint of
Fiction4All

Published 2020
Fiction4All
www.fiction4all.com

Chapter 1
Inspector Ashton

"What a miserable day to start my new job?" Inspector Ashton thought as she drove through the pouring rain.

It was early, she was trying to beat the rush hour; she had left at seven o'clock; the sun wasn't up yet, not that it would show its face today, the forecast was for rain, and more rain.

At thirty she had not had a fast rise through the ranks, but she had made steady progress, and her prospects were good. The move from Manchester to London was a good move, but she knew just how bad the traffic could be, and she had left early to try, and make a good impression.

Julie Ashton was a good-looking woman her black hair tied back in a ponytail hanging between her shoulder blades, a trim figure well proportioned, and a smile to melt any heart.

"Yes Madam," the desk sergeant said smiling a welcoming smile.

"Good Morning Sergeant, Inspector Ashton reporting," Julie said handing over her papers of introduction.

"Morning Inspector, the chief isn't in yet, you are a bit early. Jones, show the Inspector to the canteen. I don't suppose our excuse for coffee is any better than the stuff you are used to, up north," he said smiling at her.

"Probably not," she replied, smiling back.

Julie didn't have to wait long, in the staff canteen, before Jones came for her to meet the

Chief Inspector, again it was amiable, and friendly as you might expect. He suggested that to allow her to find her way around there were just two, as he put it, straight forward cases for her to look into. Jones was called, and he showed Julie to her desk.

Julie sat down after being introduced to the other detectives, and looked at the first case.

It was very simple; an argument had reached a crescendo, and a neighbour had called the police. They arrived to find the husband stood over his wife with a blood-soaked knife in his bloody hand, and his wife lying in a pool of blood.

Julie smiled wishing all cases were so simple, this case just needed her to cross the T's and dot the I's, a confession would add icing to the cake.

The husband was in custody, so she decided to go, and have a chat with him.

"Sergeant, can you have PC Jones bring Mr. Higgins to the interview room please, I want to have a chat with him?" Julie asked him.

"Jones is due on a break soon, will it take long?" he asked.

"No, it is more a matter of sign the confession, rather than an interrogation," Julie replied.

A detective showed her the way to the interview room.

"Good morning Mr. Higgins, I trust you slept well?" Julie asked him.

"Hey, what?' he asked confused.

"The accommodation was suitable, the bed comfortable, and every room is en suit. How was the breakfast?" Julie asked amiably.

"Yu, erm who are you, what the hell are you on about, it was a fucking prison cell, are you stupid, woman?" he asked confused and angry.

"Yes, indeed, allow me, I am Inspector Ashton, and beside me is Detective Sergeant Williams, by the door is PC Jones. Now we all know each other, shall we begin? The red light lets us know that this little chat is being recorded.

First of all, what was the argument about? We know this because a neighbour rang us to complain about the excessive noise, like an argument. Let me give you a clue. Was it because she wanted to buy some food, for a meal, instead of the Heroine you wanted to buy?" Julie asked being glib.

"Fuck you, I didn't do it," he shouted at her.

"Mr. Higgins, there is not a cat in hell's chance of that. With regard to being guilty or not, shall we look at the facts? One, you were arguing with your wife. Two, you were found holding the bloody knife, with blood all the way up your wrist, arm and across your chest. This is called blood spatter from a stab wound. Three the look on your face was outrage, etched with anger, and directed at your wife.

If I were you I would go for diminished responsibilities, because of drug abuse.

Just one more little thing, we all know that according to the prison population they are all innocent, but the courts rely on two things evidence and facts. Evidence we have, the bloody knife with your fingerprints on it, and you were found standing over her lifeless body with her blood dripping from your hand. Oops, big mistake, hey what? A little overzealous in the stabbing, weren't you? What was

7

it? Seven stab wounds, but I will have to wait for the coroner's report before knowing exactly how many times you stabbed your wife. You were slow to think about being caught red handed in more ways than one. Was that because of an abused childhood, or are you just thick?" Julie asked demeaning him.

"Look, look can we do a deal, I, I, well, she was screwing around?" He asked bleating.

"Ah I see, jealousy, you know that is quite a common motive for murder, along with money, so what deal? This is England, and not America, we do not tend to plea bargain. The name of your supplier is not enough to get you off," Julie said calmly.

Her soft approach, calmness, and factual statements were confusing him, his mind was not quick enough to counter her accusations, and faced with overwhelming evidence he was close to confessing, Julie knew this, and sat back smiling at him, she had him.

"I, I don't do drugs, but I do know who the main supplier is around here," he said uneasily.

"I have here your arrest record, three arrests for possession, what was it, icing sugar? Have they really started selling icing sugar by the gram?" She asked in a mocking tone.

"No, no, I was a user, but I am clean now, and have been for six months. What have I done?" he asked, and slumped in his chair sobbing, "I didn't mean to kill her," he added.

"No, I am sure you didn't. It was just the heat of the moment. To find out that your wife is being unfaithful is a nasty shock, and your actions are understandable, if regrettable. Now you just write down exactly what happened, and Sergeant Williams will get you a nice cup of coffee. Do you take sugar?" Julie asked, not so much belittling him, more mothering him.

Julie got up, and left with Williams, leaving PC Jones in the room to watch over him whilst he wrote his confession.

"I have never seen that approach before," Williams said when they were outside the room.

"He is not a full shilling, probably from the drug abuse, but bullying tactics, hardnosed shouting would only make him retire into his shell, and cower in a corner fearful, mothering him, being friendly, but firm; helped him open up.

I am sorry to inform you Sergeant, but you lack two assets to make it work," Julie said looking down at her breasts, "I had him sucking on them, metaphorically, he is a lost little boy that threw a tantrum at being hurt, but as an adult, it killed. You would have known this, if you had read his sheet, and the psyche report from the last time he was arrested.

He is not unlike me actually, I have two sides to me, but I control both sides, he cannot. In there I was his mother cuddling him with words to get him to tell me what was troubling him, and it worked. Then there is the other side I let out rarely, the Bitch, and boy is she a bitch. Sergeant even you, as big as you are, do not want to meet her.

I joined the British army to see action, and spent a lot of time in the barracks or on exercises, so I applied for, and got into the SAS, but again I seemed to be barrack bound, a spell in Iraq where we were more of a police force, little, or no action.

It did give me the idea to join the police force, and I have never regretted it. I use my brains and occasionally my abilities. The courts tend to frown on catching a criminal and slitting their throats, pity," Julie said, and looked into his eyes, she laughed, "The look on your face Sergeant was a picture.

I don't deny that on the one and only foray into a Taliban nest, I was called upon to slit a throat or two, I had been trained to do it, and the mission called for surprise. I took out two guards before we went in shooting. Iraq was where I became a bomb disposal officer. I would hate to say expert, but I have defused a couple of bombs, under supervision, erm, successfully as you can see, ten toes and fingers, quite an achievement.

After the mission I went back to the barracks, and cried my eyes out, being soft, not on your life. I would not be normal if I could kill without regret. I leave that to the psychotics. I am proud that I did, it proves that I am a normal human being, doing a dirty job efficiently, and effectively.

Being glib about it, is just my way of coping with the trauma, and horrendous sights I have witnessed, passing it off so lightly makes it seem less traumatic, somehow. We all cope in different ways, my granddad was in the D day landings, and he never spoke about it, even when asked. I sometimes wonder if that contributed to his mental state as he grew older, bottling it up, all those years," Julie told him.

"You may have a good point, a very good point. A few years ago I was diagnosed with PTSD after attending an explosion, picking up all those body parts turned my stomach. As you said it was just a job that had to be done, but it does play on my mind, and talking to the councillor helped me, so perhaps your way of being glib, is effective. An undertaker I knew laughed and joked all day long, disrespectful, no he was very respectful, but again it was his way, of coping," Williams said thoughtfully.

"We have had a chat, and now my friend in the interview room is waiting for the coffee I offered him, and asked you to supply. Oh I can feel the Bitch rising, I do so hate it when people do not do as asked," she said.

"I am on my way, Inspector," he said smiling back at her smile.

"After you have done that I want to take a walk, and look around at the area, find my feet as it were, and settle in," Julie told him.

"Shall I get a pool car for us, ma'am?" He asked.

"The car, a means of getting from point A to point B, efficiently, but useless when wishing to converse with the locals, they can't run fast enough, so perhaps not, on this occasion," Julie replied giving him a look.

"Right, Ma'am a walk, as you said," he replied, and went to make the coffee whilst Julie went to her desk, and opened the other file.

The file was of a mugging that had gone horribly wrong. The assailants may not have known that he was on the waiting list for a pacemaker to be fitted, there were several bruises to his chest, and abdomen from hard punches, which caused his heart to fail; killing him, therefore it was classed as murder.

"Inspector, I believe you got him to confess, was his solicitor present?" the Chief asked.

"You seem to be under a misconception Chief. I merely went to have a little chat, and he decided to make a full confession, to ease his conscience, I suppose. I followed protocol in having a detective sergeant with me, and a PC on the door, and I recorded the chat as per the guidelines, but at no point did I push him to confess, or use forceful means by strong questioning to get him to confess. It was just an amiable chat, to help me understand his mental state. In my humble opinion he is psychotic, and may not be fit to stand trial. He is incapable of understanding what he has done, and I believe he does not know what he has done; the period during the attack is blank; he was in such a rage that he acted without thought, or memory, but I am a humble police inspector, and not a psychologist, so my opinion does not count, does it, Sir?" Julie asked him, smiling her got you smile.

"I was told about your, erm, not so much disrespect for authority, but disregard, and your effective if unorthodox methods. Fortunately for you it has proven to work, according to your success rate, but be careful, I will be watching you," he said.

"Thank you for the compliment, and I will be careful. Whilst you are here Sir; this file, are there no witnesses? It was broad day light when he was attacked, yet no-one saw anything, not even some yobs running down the street? I am going to go out with Sergeant Williams, I want to take a look

12

around, and visit the scene. Shall we see if my unorthodox methods can work a miracle?" Julie asked him, adding a smile to lessen the words.

"Has nothing I have said sunk in, Inspector?" he asked.

Julie knew that he was pleased with her so far, but had to make the point about her methods, which as he indicated, were questionable, but effective.

Sergeant Williams caught up with her at reception.

"Ma'am, where would you like to go?" He asked.

"Home, but I am on duty, so how about down the High Street, and taking in some of the side streets, and alley ways, and in particular where he was mugged, Sergeant?" She asked, and turned to the desk sergeant, "Chase up on forensics and the autopsy report, please. All I have is that he was mugged, and is dead. I need to know how? What was the case of death, definitively, was it caused by a fist or some sort of weapon, and if so what type?" she asked him, and thanked him, and then left with Sergeant Williams.

They walked down the main street towards the centre.

"Well Sergeant, I am waiting," Julie said.

"Waiting Ma'am, what are you waiting for?" He asked.

"What are you, six two, one hundred and seventy pounds, good looking, late twenties early thirties, apart from that, I know nothing," Julie said.

"Where to begin, I have a degree in philosophy, and joined the police, I have a wife, and two lovely children. I enjoy helping people, and woodwork. What else is there?" He asked.

"Have you arrested anyone, broken up a bar brawl, chased a suspect down an alley?" Julie asked him.

"Of course I have, apart from breaking up a bar brawl; once I enter they seem to stop. Once whilst on the beat I caught a man beating on a woman, and got stabbed for my efforts, he got away, but I got him three weeks later, he's now doing time," Williams said.

"Good, I now know that I don't have to protect you," Julie said.

"Ma'am, really," He replied shocked.

"Just kidding," Julie said laughing, "Wait; hold up a minute, what is that?"

"What Ma'am, erm, a dress shop," he said querying his answer.

"Yes, yes, I know that, the dress. What do you think? It's in the half-price sale, and red suits my complexion," Julie said.

"And like a red light warns of approaching danger," he said glibly.

"Oh, you do have a sense of humour," Julie said, and laughed.

"Stop, stop!" a woman exclaimed.

Julie and Williams both turned to see a youth running towards them clutching a handbag. Williams tensed ready to catch the youth Julie just stood there waiting. The youth saw Williams tense and dodged to his left.

"The dress over, oops, sorry, did I hurt you?" she said to the prone figure lying on the ground at her feet.

"Clumsy bitch," he retorted.

"Well really, such course words from a young man. By the way, I am Inspector Ashton, and I moon-light for the fashion police, and really don't you know that accessories should match. I mean bright green trainers with a red handbag, is so bad, red and black, you can get away with, but two so distinct colours.

You don't mind if I take a look inside your handbag, do you?" she asked and snatched it from him.

By this time the woman had arrived puffing and panting, Williams blocked her path.

"Let me see now, my oh my what have we here, you know I think the shoulder length blonde hair suits you much better, and the lipstick yes a nice shade of red, but a deeper red, to match the handbag, like I said all accessories should match. Green eyes, are those contact lenses? In the picture on the driving licence the eyes are blue. Maybe this is not your handbag, in which case, why do you have it?" Julie asked him. Her foot firmly planted on his chest holding him down.

"Erm, erm, well, erm," he said lost for words.

"I am Inspector Ashton, and my sergeant is Sergeant Williams.

Sergeant, will you please contact the station, and ask that they send two nice police officers to our location, and take this little boy for a nice ride. What's your name, and how old are you?" Julie asked.

"Billy Sutch and I am thirteen, so you can't arrest me," he replied.

"Billy, why do all criminals think they have a law degree, I can, and I have. Now Billy listen carefully to me, I am arresting you for theft, and anything you say will be taken down in writing, and can be used against you in a court of law. Do not say anything you may later rely on in a court of law. Do you understand?" she asked him.

"Yes," he replied.

"Good, now when you arrive at the police station they will put you in a room with a pen and paper, and I want you to write me an essay telling me all about this afternoon, and most importantly, recent events. Will you do that for me? Oh, and who told you to steal? That is very important, you don't have the brains. I mean a bright red handbag, I saw you snatch it from over there, over a hundred yards away, not very bright," Julie belittled him.

"Madam, will you please make a statement, your handbag I believe, from the photo on the driving licence," Julie said handing the handbag back to the woman.

"Yes and thank you, Inspector," She replied.

"May I suggest a clutch bag is perhaps not the best handbag to take shopping?" Julie advised her.

The officers arrived, and took Billy away, and Julie with Williams continued on their walk.

"Ma'am, what just happened? It was a good collar, but I never saw you move, and a bit excessive on a thirteen-year-old, don't you think?" Williams asked.

"Most people tense when about to make a move, and he probably saw you, and went for the softer target, the female. I just waited until he was committed, and raised my arm locking my elbow.

16

The energy he used in his attempt to escape could have pushed me over, except that I made half a step back to ride the impact, moving my centre of balance to ride the impact, and then planted my foot on his chest.

I studied martial arts, and I mean studied, not just the practice although I did. I actually read books and asked questions, the main thing I learned, is not to exert energy, but to utilise the energy of your opponent. In a fight black belt against black belt it isn't easy, but to a thirteen-year-old kid, hitting my arm at full speed was like running into a brick wall dazed, but no real injury. Now lesson over, did you know he was thirteen, or like me did you think he was much older, he is a big lad, and looked to me about seventeen, eighteen, now, where, is this alley?" Julie asked him.

"It is at the end of the next block Ma'am, this end is as you can see onto the main street; it is the other end where the muggings take place. It leads onto a much quieter street Ma'am, and yes he was a big lad, and I would have to agree with your assessment," He informed her.

"Interesting, it is clear at this end, but there is a multitude of rubbish bins at the other end, well away from the main street, I presume that is for appearances. We can't have our crap on the main street, can we?" Julie asked him when they arrived at the alley.

"Most of the shops take their rubbish away so as not to have to enter the alley. We don't know this, but the butcher takes a knife with him, and I for one do not blame him," Williams said.

"You may not, but the courts will if he kills one of them," Julie said.

"It would be self-defence, surely Ma'am?" Williams suggested.

"A knife to a fist fight is never self-defence Sergeant, and you know it that, is premeditated," Julie scolded him.

"I don't understand you, one minute you are well soft and cuddly the next hard as nails. I am not uneasy with you, I just don't understand," Williams said.

"No-one does, soft as a pin cushion, and then I hit you with a concrete block, surprise and confusion, my best tools. Mind you the pins in the pin cushion are tipped with curare," Julie said and laughed.

"Why does that not surprise me?" Williams asked rhetorically.

"So this is the scene, no cameras, quiet, secluded yet visible, and no-one saw anything. It doesn't surprise me that they didn't; I can imagine the locals running across the opening, after what you have told me. Even now, at lunchtime the closeness of the buildings means it is well shaded, hum, these guys are not stupid," Julie mused.

"The council have deliberated about a camera, or street lighting, but budget cuts mean that it is talked about only," Williams offered.

"Yes, just like putting officers in cars, we have become reactionary rather than pro-active. We attend crimes instead of trying to prevent them. The beat bobby was a form of prevention, raising awareness, now there isn't a policeman, to ask the time," Julie said and chuckled.

"Ma'am I didn't know you knew about that, my dad told me, even so I could never find one when I needed directions," William's said light heartedly.

"Are you inferring that I am old, Sergeant?" Julie asked a wicked smile on her lips.

"Indeed not Ma'am, I just wondered who had told you?" Williams asked light-hearted.

Chapter 2
The Crime

It was a hot July afternoon, with temperatures reaching twenty-nine degrees centigrade. Mid Sunday afternoon and the pub garden was full, seats were available, but it was very busy with people taking a cooling beer, and chatting in the summer sunshine.

She entered erect, a demure female, attractive with a well-defined figure her cleavage on display, but not overtly. Her clothes expensive tailored and fitting snugly. Her make-up was clean and applied with care, and paying attention to detail. Her stiletto heels clicked on the paved area as she seemed to make her way deliberately to a table at the far end. She presented as a well to do woman, knowing what she wanted and was able to get it, aristocratic almost in her stance, and walk.

Arriving at the table she tucked her skirt neatly under her, but allowed her Camel coat to hang down the back, and sat down. She smiled and chatted for a few moments, and then there was a pop, and she got up and left, just as demurely as she entered.

One hour later the phone at the police station rang.

"What is your emergency" The operator asked.

"Police, I, I think there's been a murder, he hasn't ordered a drink in over an hour, and has not taken a drink from his glass, and there is blood down his side I, I think he has been shot," the nervous caller said.

"The police are on their way, what is the address, exactly, and what is your name?" the operator asked.

"Oh, erm The Dog and Duck, erm, on the A1, erm C, Colin Masters," the caller said.

"Please stay on the line until the officers arrive. Are you the manager of the pub, or owner?" The operator asked.

"Oh erm, no, I, I am just the relief manager, he is away on holiday, I can hear the sirens," he said as the wailing noise of the sirens became audible to the operator.

"Thank you Mister Masters, an ambulance is also on its way," she informed him, and the line went dead as the officers entered the bar.

"Mister Colin Masters?" A pretty lady asked him.

"Y-yes, I am still shaking I-I have never seen a dead body before, excuse me," he said put his hand to his mouth, and ran off towards the toilets.

"You two secure the crime scene, Sergeant take a look at the body and make sure the coroner is on his way. I will wait here to speak to Hughie, Mister Masters, when he has finally stopped talking to the big white telephone," Julie said organising the officers, in a matter of fact way.

"S-sorry about that," he said upon his return.

"Don't worry about it, seeing a dead person for the first time can be upsetting. I suggest you get a glass of water, it will help take the nasty taste away, I will be sat here," Julie said with empathy.

He left her and got a glass of water took a sip and returned.

"In your own words what did you see, start at the beginning, please," Julie asked him.

"I-I well erm, I didn't see anything. I-I was busy serving, we have been very busy with the heat and all, and I left the bar for a fag, and she was well she looked a million dollars, as they say, she walked towards the table. She sat down, and ordered a drink, and then I went back behind the bar. Later on I went out, and she was gone. I asked the lad clearing the glasses about the man, because I noticed that he had not taken a drink, and I thought it odd that it was at the same level. I think I looked at him because I was hoping to see that woman again, boy was she good looking, a beauty, and she knew it, well the lad collecting the glasses, said that he had not ordered, and he had not seen the guy take a drink even, he just sat there, as if asleep.

So I decided to check up on him, and as I touched his shoulder he slumped onto the table, and I saw the blood. I came back, and rang you," he said.

"Have you ever seen the man or this woman before?" Julie asked him.

"No, never, as I said I am a relief manager, and last week I was in Chesterfield, and before that I was in Bognor for a month, until they found a new manager, this is my first time here," he told her.

"I see, so you have no idea who he or she is, interesting. How long are you here for, then?" Julie asked him.

"It is my first day, they are in Spain for a week's holiday, so till next Sunday, unless I ask to be moved, it is very distressing," he said meekly.

"Yes, it is, but I will need to speak to you again, so please stay here, and then I may need your new address," Julie told him.

Julie got up, and went out to the actual crime scene; all the patrons had now been asked to leave after their names and addresses had been taken and a brief statement.

"Well Sergeant what do we have?" Julie asked.

"Not being too obvious, a dead male, late fifties, well dressed, with a hole in his side, and burning around the hole, but insufficient for a close contact shot, I think. I usually leave that to the coroner, and forensics," he said.

"Let me see, you are correct in your assumption he has been shot with a point two five calibre bullet from the size of the hole, and at close range, but insufficient gunshot residue for a contact shot, yet not spread out enough for a distance shot, interesting. How can you get a contact shot, without gunshot residue, and burning, interesting," Julie said.

"The time of death will have to be confirmed, but he ordered his last drink at three this afternoon, the lad clearing the glasses was going on his break at that time, and cursed because he saw all the empty glasses, and knew he would be in trouble if he didn't get some cleared, so he checked his watch as the man was walking towards the bar. A quick whip around, and then he went on his break," William's informed her.

"And it is now four thirty, so we have just a one-and-a-half-hour window, less because the body was reported at four o'clock give or take a minute or two; we can get precise times later. What do the people sat around here have to say?" Julie asked him.

"In a word, nothing, they all saw the woman, it was as if she wanted to be noticed; even the women saw her, most women well my wife only notices when I look at a woman," William's said.

"You'd be surprised, we notice, but are just not as obvious as you males. So we have a male sat drinking at a corner table, a very attractive female joins him, and has one drink and leaves. An hour later he is found dead, shot at close range, but no gunshot residue, well not sufficient for a contact shot. It's as if the woman shot him, and wanted us to know she had, this is very odd. Who in their right mind leaves a trail right back to them?" Julie asked her hand to her chin in thought, "A penny for them Williams?" Julie asked seeing his eye brighten.

"What if there was a barrier between the gun and him? No, just think about it, sorry Ma'am, I didn't mean to be rude. Like all women she had a handbag what if the gun was inside the handbag?" He asked.

"Then the initial residue would be inside the handbag, and not on him, possible, very possible, but that is assuming that she shot him, and even a twenty-five would go right through the soft tissue, yet it wasn't a through and through. How do you explain that, sergeant?" she asked smiling at him.

"Ma'am, you are the one trained in guns, I am just guessing to make the facts fit the scene. He was shot at close range, but there is no gunshot residue, how else?" Williams asked.

"I guessed that it was close range, what if it wasn't? The woman made a show of herself, and as you said, 'Only a fool, would do that.' There is the tree line close by, and our shooter could have hidden there, hence the lack of gunshot residue, not the best place to take a shot with a pistol, for accuracy that is, but possible," Julie said.

"A point two five sniper rifle, is that possible?' Williams asked.

"Yes, there are several on the market, the French use one for their snipers, and the longest kill shot was about 2.5 kilometres, roughly a mile, but that was by a highly trained military sniper, and begs the question, who was the sniper supposed to shot; him, or the woman. Now take into account the tree line, what is behind it, and how, can a sniper shoot someone between the third and fourth rib from anywhere, apart from being sat beside them, or on the actual tree line. Of the two, the tree line is perhaps the best option, because when seated next to a person, their arm well the upper arm, is in the way, most of the time.

It takes a sniper a few moments to get set up; they usually have to build the gun. They do not want to be seen carrying a sniper rifle on the bus, sorry, just being glib. Then they have to sight the rifle, adjust settings to give them the perfect shot. Then they have to aim and all before they squeeze the trigger.

They would have to know that he would be here, and sat at that particular table. From my military experience, there are too many things that could go wrong. I think we can discount a sniper in the tree line, it is my belief that the woman who made such a show of herself, shot him, which is odd in itself. Who walks into a crowded bar garden, and shoots a man, and hopes to get away with it, it beggars belief," Julie said, shocked.

"Because she was elegant, tall and had expensive clothes on, and she was a very pretty, blonde hair, shoulder length. That is the best description, apart from a male who added she had big tits. You know Ma'am that fits you, perfectly," Williams said with irony.

"You are almost right Sergeant, apart from the fact that, my clothes are basement bargain. Being on the meagre wages of a police Inspector, I tend no, have to wait, for the sales, and I have long blonde hair, but I do get your point. It fits probably eighty percent of the female population, everyone is pretty, to someone," Julie said with irony.

"Scene of crimes has arrived Ma'am, with the coroner," a constable informed her.

"Good, well Doctor what can you tell me?" She asked as he arrived eager to get started.

"At this moment in time Inspector, there is a dead man sitting there, but even that as yet has to be confirmed. If I may examine the body, first?" he asked.

"Yes, he is dead, I will write the death certificate as of 16.52, and from a cursorily inspection of the body it would appear that it was caused by a puncture wound to the thoracic cavity, between the third and fourth rib. The lack of blood suggests that his heart stopped immediately, and that would lead me to believe that the bullet will be found in his heart, or there about, seeing as there is no exit wound," the coroner told Julie.

"Just what I need, a comedian for a coroner," Julie said, as her and Williams left the scene.

"You did ask him before he had even seen the dead man, Ma'am. I have always found him to be thorough, but slow. It will take a good week for him to send his report, Ma'am," Williams said.

"I want that bullet with forensics within twenty-four hours, or I'll dig it out myself. Let's assume for the moment we have two options, a sniper from the tree line, and the woman. So get the PC's to do a search on the tree line, they are looking for flattened grass, perhaps a tripod mark in the dirt and a shell casing. Two officers half an hour should be enough; it is a relatively small area to search.

The other option is the woman, did anyone notice any blood on her perfect clothes, even a close range shot or perhaps because of a close range shot there would be blood spatter on her clothes, surely someone would have noticed that," Julie said aggravated by the lack of reasoning to this case.

Chapter 3
Analysis and Questions

"Sergeant, you drive, I will evaluate. We start with what we know, we have a dead male," Julie began.

"One Andrew Johnson, of fifteen Melrose Avenue and he was fifty-three," Williams added.

"Ok, he died from a sharp force trauma, via a bullet, which penetrated his thoracic region between the third and fourth rib, and that is it. So now we go to probabilities, or assumptions.

From my experience in the field, the field of battle that is; I know that it was a point two five bullet; a fifty calibre makes one hell of a mess, trust me.

Again from my experience, the woman sat next to him, shot him. There are just too many things that can go wrong if he was shot by a sniper in the tree line. She is the one, I am sure of that," Julie said organising her thoughts.

"Ma'am, surely there are more things that can go wrong in a public place like that; I mean so many people, any one of them could have seen her shoot him, surely?" Williams asked her.

"You would think that, one she could have made an appointment to meet him at that particular table, because she could only be seen by a few of the customers, being a corner table, which also means that she has been here before, to case the place. They could also have met there regularly, a lovers tryst?" Julie said questioning her statement.

"So they knew each other?" Williams said.

"Not necessarily, but possible, a proposed business deal, erm, any number of things, which I can't think of right now. Like a job opportunity and that was a first interview, erm, say double glazing salesperson, an amiable chat, I don't know.

Like I said these are just assumptions, but what I do know, is that she killed him, let me think about this. What if she put her hand on his opposite shoulder to pull him back say, to hold him upright, when dead?" Julie proposed as a rhetorical question.

"And her coat would have shielded the gun it was just draped over her shoulder; a woman commented on her coat, and I quote, 'A Camel coat on a hot summer's day, did seem a little odd.' It didn't register until just now, Ma'am," Williams said.

"Interesting, hum, a Camel coat; was she sat on it, or was it draped over the back of the chair?" Julie asked.

"Sorry Ma'am, I didn't ask," Williams replied.

"Pull over, I need something's, I have an idea as to how she did it," Julie said.

Julie got out of the car, and went into a clothing shop, Williams stayed in the car whilst she shopped.

After she had bought the things she needed, they went to the station in silence, and entered the main office.

"Sergeant, do we have a bench? If not, put two chairs next to each other, as they were at the crime scene. We are going to re-enact it," Julie told him, and left him setting up the chairs, he even put a table in front of them, for effect.

"Right you two sit at that desk, and you two sit at that one, you are in a pub beer garden enjoying a chat, joke, and a nice cooling beer," Julie told them.

"Will you provide the beer Ma'am, for authenticity?" Officer Jones asked.

"Yes, here it is," Julie said picking up four mugs and placing them on the desks with a smile for Jones.

"It would be more authentic if they were full, Ma'am," Jones said smiling.

"I am sure it would be, but I am just an under paid Inspector, now sit, I do not want you to watch, but to see what you see, paying attention to your partner, not us. Sergeant you sit there and I will sit here just as they were in the garden.

Julie walked up to the table, and sat down, she made sure her coat was behind the back of the chair, then leaned over slightly, put her hand to his shoulder, and her other hand into the shoulder bag. She stuck her finger into his ribs, and gave the sergeant a kiss on the cheek, then said, "Pop."

"Now what did you see?" Julie asked them.

"Sergeant, she kissed you, and you a married man," Jones said laughing.

"Well Sergeant, you can stop being dead," Julie said.

"I didn't see you kill him," Jones said, somewhat shock that he had missed it.

"No, you didn't, all Magicians use it, and it is very simple. They make you watch here whilst they do what they need to do, here. The kiss was a theatrical act, to stop you seeing, what I was doing.

Gunshot residue would be caught in the bag, more or less, there would be some, but minimal, the burning associated with close contact shootings, again would be inside the handbag. She now had about sixty to one twenty seconds to make her escape, plenty of time. I heard a witness say that she marched in a long stride, moving fast without running, so when she left using the same stride, no-one would think anything of it, as they would, if she ran.

What colour where her gloves? What drink did she order, do we know, we should do?" Julie asked.

"Ma'am I have been here just a month, and I am still learning so can I ask you why what colour, and not if she was wearing gloves?" Jones asked.

"Keep it up that is a good question; if I were to ask was she wearing gloves, most people would say yes or no, almost immediately, they would not think, just answer, but if I ask what colour, they were, the witness would stop, and think. Thinking that I knew she was wearing gloves, making them think, and that is all I want them to do, think. I want them to delve, to try and remember, not give me an off the cuff answer. By delving they may remember something else. Likewise the drink, did she have one, yes or no, but to make them think, I ask, which one, did she have?

I have a bet for you, a fiver," Julie said putting a five pound note on the table, "She entered the bar, and stood close to the till end, where the empty glasses were, and smiled at the barman, it would not work with the barmaid, just the bar man, and my bet is that he served her out of order. She did not want to stand there for too long. A nice sexy smile and he would drop everything to serve her, add to that the expanse of cleavage, and he would notice her, as they all did," Julie said.

"Ma'am, I am confused, why would a killer want to be noticed?" Jones asked.

"For that answer we need to catch her, and ask her, as you say it confuses me, but there is a reason; we just have to work out what it is," Julie answered him.

"She is definitely a pro, to commit a murder in a public place, and walk away is a true professional," Williams said.

"Indeed she is, the coat hid her actions, the kiss distracted any on lookers, the gloves stopped any fingerprints, and I bet her glass had already been washed before anyone knew he was dead. How, you may ask? She would have returned it to the glass collector, or bar on her way out, or taken it with her, she left nothing to chance, no fingerprints, and no DNA," Julie said.

"Then how are we going to catch her?" Jones asked.

"With perseverance, that is how, unfortunately it may well be after another death, or a few deaths, but we will catch her, I am conceited enough to say, because I am on her case. Are you conceited enough to join me?" Julie asked them.

"Yes, Ma'am," they said with enthusiasm.

"To begin with who is this Andrew Johnson? What does he do? Is he married? What is his job? What phone calls has he received recently? I am confident that the meeting was arranged, I am confident that I know how the murder was committed, and how it was, but I need to know why? Talk to his friends and work colleagues, his neighbours, get me as much information as you can about the victim that, is where we start, he is one half of the equation, and it takes two halves to make a murder, the victim, and the killer," Julie told them.

Julie left the station with Williams, and went to the victims address.

"This is the worst part of the job, and I need to bolster my strength, shit, I hate this part," Julie admitted.

"I think that is what we all feel, I mean there is no easy way to say your beloved husband, is dead, it seems so cold," Williams agreed.

"It is cold, dead cold," Julie said with irony.

They walked up the path, and rang the doorbell; it was answered by a young woman.

"Yes," she said.

"Hello, I am Inspector Andrews, and this is detective Sergeant Williams is Mrs Johnson in, please?" Julie asked, not assuming that the young lady was his wife.

"Mum, there's a couple of coppers to see you," she shouted.

"Well invite them in; I will be with you in a moment. This dinner will be ruined; I'll kill him when he gets home, he promised he would not be late. Just a couple of pints, like hell," the voice from the kitchen shouted.

"Mrs. Johnson?" Julie asked when she appeared from the kitchen.

"Yes, sorry to make you wait, the dinner is cooked, and I needed to turn the pans down, to stop it burning. Andrew, has anything happened? The look on your faces, oh, god no, no, no," she screamed, and almost fell into the armchair sobbing and shaking, her head in her hands.

"I am very sorry, but I have to tell you that your husband has been murdered, and I need to ask you a few questions, but they can wait. Is there anybody close by that can come in? I realise it is a great shock to you, a relative perhaps?" Julie asked, her own heart being crushed at having to relay the news, and seeing the distressed state of Mrs Johnson.

"Angela, turn the pans off, and the oven, I-I," Mrs Johnson said in a moment of calm.

"Mum, what's happened, mum?" Angela asked and cuddled her mother in her arms, and began weeping.

"I will turn the pans off, perhaps a neighbour can come in, Sergeant Williams, will go and ask for you, is there someone close by that can come in?" Julie asked a little more forcefully.

"Two doors down, Amanda White, she will come," the daughter said between tears.

Julie went into the kitchen whilst Williams went to ask Mrs White to come to the house. Julie came back into the room, and stood there desperate to ask a question, but somehow unable to.

"Put the kettle on Tom, and make us a tea," Mrs White said taking charge. Julie followed Tom into the kitchen.

"Mister White, I need to ask a few questions, but Mrs Johnson is in no condition to answer, so perhaps you can help me. Did Mister Johnson work, and if so where? What was his job?" Julie asked him, as he busied himself making the tea.

"Andrew, worked from home, he was a manager erm, sales manager for one of these energy firms. He had I think six or seven teams going around, trying to make customers change their supplier," he answered.

"Thank you, he was with a young woman at the pub, do you know why?" Julie asked him.

"Not what you are implying, he often interviewed potential salespeople at the pub, he didn't work from an office, that could be why, sorry, probably was, he was a decent person, and loved Mary very much," he said.

"I was implying nothing, just asking. Like my next question, which I have to ask, did he have any enemies?" Julie asked.

"Good god woman, enemies! Across the road there is an elderly woman, she is house bound, and every Sunday without fail, he takes her lunch across, Mary cooks for her as well as the family, and he delivers it. How the hell can a man as kind as that, have enemies? And he is the first to take the tin around for poppy day, their son was killed in action, in Dessert Storm," He said angrily.

"Are you sure, Dessert Storm was from 1990 to 1991 that would make their son about 45 and Mister Johnson say seven, when he was born," Julie queried.

"Erm, no, I meant the aftermath, we are still there you know, cleaning up and training, it was a roadside bomb three years ago; he was just twenty-one, at the time," Tom told her with a solemn expression.

"It seems to have hit close to home?" Julie asked.

"Our son was with him, they were friends, the best of friends. My son was lucky, he just lost a leg, Andrew came around as soon as my son came home, and handed him a folder. He told him that he needed to get a job, make himself useful, and to go down the street, and show the residence how much they could save by changing energy suppliers. 'I know you can do it,' he said encouraging Simon, our son, and took him down the street. My son is now one of his team leaders, and makes more than I do. What kind of bastard kills a good man, like that?" Tom asked her.

"I don't know, all I can promise you is that I will give one hundred per cent to catching them, and putting them where they belong, behind bars," Julie said with compassion.

"They rob her of her husband and income, and now she has to pay to feed the bastard, it's all wrong," Tom said.

"I agree with your sentiments, but that is the way things are, and now if you will excuse me, I have a bastard, to catch," Julie said trying to lighten things a little.

"Mandy, plate a meal up and I will take it to Mrs Crawford, Andrew would have wanted us to do that," Tom said to their daughter.

"I have to go, but I will need to come back to ask you a few questions. I will leave it for a couple of days," Julie said her hand on Mary's shoulder for comfort.

"Sergeant, I just do not get it; according to Tom White, Andrew was a saint. Why on Earth would anybody want him dead, he wasn't in a government position, or military post that could put him in

36

danger, he was just a manager of several teams of door to door salespeople. He had a decent job, and earned a good living, but he wasn't a millionaire by any means, and robbery was not, the motive.

Sergeant, hit me hard, knock some sense into me, this does not add up. Apparently there is no motive, no reason whatsoever to kill him, so why do it?" Julie asked angrily, once they were in the car.

"Ma'am, if I may suggest, we have had a long, hard day, perhaps a good night's rest will give us some inspiration," Williams offered.

"Ha, my foot it will, we have a saint, killed by an elegant woman with a point two five bullet. I have never had so little, to go on," Julie replied adding, "But until we have more, there is nothing we can do, so I agree, back to the station, and then home."

Chapter 4
Forensic Reports

Julie spent the next week pacing up and down the station, or so it seemed, she regularly walked the alley way, in the hopes of seeing something, or someone to help with that investigation.

"Sir, my presence in the alley way has stopped their activities, there is a house for rent in the street the alleyway goes to, and with a good view of the alley way. I am asking for surveillance. Not for this week, allow it to cool down a bit, say one week from today, for a month?" Julie asked the chief.

"Have you seen the wages bill, the costs I have to argue about? Inspector we have to catch criminals, but within a budgeted figure. I do not have an open cheque book," he argued back.

"I appreciate that Sir, but how much does it cost to investigate these muggings, with no return by way of a conviction? Every time we have to send two police officers to the scene, forensic officers, and then after collecting the evidence, much of it useless, we process it. One month's surveillance equates to one mugging investigation, with all the ancillary processes. Don't forget Sir, there is not only police time, but also the ambulance to take the victim to the hospital, the doctor's time to treat them, the nurse's time, and the bandages, stitches whatever else they use. The victims are beaten, not just robbed," Julie argued back raising her voice.

"Inspector, I realise how passionate you are about catching criminals, but you do not raise your voice, to me. What you are asking is to mount an operation that will cost thousands, in the vein hope that we may possibly catch someone. You cannot guarantee that they will attack someone in the next month, bring me something with a guaranteed result, and I will support you," the Chief said angrily.

"Sir, apologies, but I am female, and always have the last word so, screw you, respectfully, Sir," Julie said, and walked out.

Julie smiled as she walked back to her office, and wondered if he was also smiling, he would no doubt also be shaking his head, in dismay.

"My you look hot under the collar, Ma'am," Sergeant Williams said as he entered her office.

"Does the chief have a sense of humour, I hope so; I just told him to get screwed. He counts the pennies whilst some old woman is being beaten and robbed of hers. All I wanted was to mount a month's surveillance on the alley; there is a house for rent in an ideal position,' Julie said, not thinking.

"How is the hotel? You are still there, aren't you?" Williams asked her.

"Yes, but not for long, I have two weeks left to find accommodation, but I pay the rent, and don't eat, or have to move so far away it is impractical," Julie replied.

"Ma'am, I know the owner of that house, and shall we say I have erm, a contact for things like a camera, linked to a computer. For a friend of mine, he would be well willing to say, reduce the rent to a more, reasonable, level?" Williams suggested.

"You want me to become the guardian of the alley way?" Julie asked.

"He owns several of the properties, and has a high turnover of residents, and finds it hard to let them, but with a police officer on site, it would help him, and he is willing to compensate them," Williams said.

"I had a nice three-bedroom semi in Manchester, and now you are offering me a two-bed terraced house in a bad area. I am beginning to wonder if I have moved up the ladder, or down? OK, arrange a meeting to discuss the rent," Julie said with an ironic smile at her good luck, and misfortune.

"No need Ma'am, this is his house," Williams said pulling up at the end terrace.

Williams introduced Julie, and they did the deal, it was a good offer, and she accepted it, and agreed to move in over the weekend. Williams was true to his word, and arrived with the camera and computer which he set up in the front bedroom, to watch the alley way. Julie moved in over the weekend with the help of Williams, and by Monday she was established, and settled in.

Monday morning Julie arrived at the station to be greeted by the desk sergeant with two folders.

"Morning Ma'am, the forensic report, and the autopsy report," He said in greeting.

"Thank you Sergeant has," she began, as her mobile phone rang, "I was just about to ask where you were Sergeant?" she asked.

"On my way to the alley Ma'am, we have the blighters, send help will you, please?" he asked.

40

"Sergeant, send two squad cars to the alley, silent approach, Jones you drive, top speed, silently, you're with me," Julie said making for the door with Jones.

Jones used his siren to clear a path for them, and then switched it off as they arrived at the scene; he turned into the alley to see Sergeant Williams in the middle of the melee. Julie didn't wait for the car to come to a full stop, exiting it, as it slowed.

She ran and grabbed an assailant by the arm swung him around and punched him, he fell and lay still, whilst she grabbed another, a third turned to attack her, but she saw him, and dodged the fist, only to land a well-timed and perfectly aim kick to his groin. Two down, and the one she had grabbed was now flailing about, as he flew through the air, and he crashed into the brick wall. By the time Jones had stopped the car and made his way to the fight, baton out, the six assailants were on the ground moaning, and Julie was attending to the Victim.

"Jones, call for an ambulance, you are safe now, just lie back the ambulance is on its way," Julie said comforting him.

Ambulances arrived and extra officers, to escort the assailants to the hospital under arrest.

"Sergeant you go with them, and get checked over, there appears to be a nice black eye developing, and I am sure bruises, but nothing too serious. Wait, have you been stabbed?" Julie asked shocked.

"I think so, in my back," he replied with a grimace.

"Then go, what are you waiting for? Get out of here now, Sergeant, we can cope," Julie said.

Julie turned to the officers, "I want that knife found, even if it takes all day, you find it," she told them generally.

The officers formed a line, and moved forward on their knees inch by inch so as not to miss anything, and Julie went back to the station.

"I believe you have caught the assailants from the alley, well done," the chief congratulated her.

Julie ignored him, and collected a file putting it in the filing cabinet, and slamming the drawer.

"I have heard from the hospital, Detective Sergeant Williams will be just fine, it was deep, but not fatal, six stitches I believe, and they sent him home. Inspector, I am talking to you, show some respect," he ordered her.

"Respect is earned, a good officer is injured; an elderly man is in hospital, why, because you counted pennies. Had you done as I asked there would have been two officers to call for backup, not a brave lone officer, who did call for backup, he rang me, because he was afraid it might affect your precious budget," she said angrily.

"That is very close to insubordination Inspector, be careful; I will ignore it this time, because you are upset, justifiably, with your partner in hospital, but be warned, I will not if you ever disrespect me again," he said, and now it was his turn to slam the door closed.

Julie sat down breathed heavily for a moment or two, and picked up the file, it was the autopsy. It read that Mister Johnson was killed by a single gunshot wound to the thoracic region the bullet lodged in his heart stopping it immediately.

There was a lack of gunshot residue, which led the Coroner to believing it was fired from a distance, yet there was a circular impression which contradicted this finding, leaving him of the opinion that is was a close contact shot. The depth of the wound indicated that it was fired from a distance, because a bullet fired from a close contact position should have gone through all the soft tissue it would have come into contact with, therefore the findings were contradictory and he could not give an accurate report.

The bullet was as he and Julie had originally suspected, a point two five which he had sent to ballistics, for their report.

Apart from that, he was a healthy 53-year-old male with blood alcohol consistent with the two pints of beer the bar man had served him with.

'Interesting, close contact yet only penetrated to the heart. Close contact circular pattern, yet little or no gunshot residue,' Julie thought as she read the report, 'Close contact without gunshot residue, impossible, what am I missing? Close contact, and no residue, just isn't possible, think bitch, think,' Julie thought as she walked up and down her office.

"Dam, dam, dam," Julie shouted in frustration and banged her fist on her desk.

"Are you all right Inspector?" The desk Sergeant asked her entering her office.

"Yes, fine it just does not make sense. Look Sergeant; come here now my left hand is a pistol. I put it here like so, and pull the trigger, bang, now where would you expect to find the bullet?" she asked him.

"I'm not trained in ballistics Ma'am, and I have had no firearms training, so I could only guess, on the floor over there somewhere?" he said with a question mark in the answer.

"Even with your lack of knowledge you guessed right, if it missed the ribs on the other side, flesh has a tendency to change the trajectory of the bullet as it tumbles through the body. So with my experience, I know that you are correct, or it may be resting against the rib, because of the change in trajectory," Julie told him.

"What else would you expect to find?" Julie asked him.

"Erm, well I am not sure, but what is it called, Gunshot residue, is that the term Ma'am?" he asked.

"Precisely, when a gun is fired the spent powder exits the barrel with the bullet leaving a shower of carbon, and from the spread of the powder we can determine approximately the distance from the gun to the person. Gunshot residue is light, and can't travel very far, so depending on the gun, but an average of say three to five feet is as far as it will go. So because there is no gunshot residue, I would have to assume that the gun was fired from a minimum of three feet away.

Yet we have a circular pattern on the wound, which would suggest that the gun was pressed up against his chest. Close contact shots will rip, and burn the clothes of the victim, yet we don't have any ripping and tearing, which suggests that it was not, a close contact shot, so why the circular pattern? It is unmistakably the size of the barrel of a point two five gun. It would be like me slapping you on the face, and leaving finger prints, but not slapping you, it just cannot happen," Julie explained in the hope that something would come to mind, "Also for the bullet to have traversed the chest cavity, nicking the lung, entering the right ventricle and lodging in the left ventricle of the heart, means that the gun was fired from a lot further away than, five feet even. Sergeant, this murder breaks all the known laws of physics and ballistics, it is just impossible. Now Sergeant, do you have any pearls of wisdom?" Julie asked him with an ironic smile.

"Ma'am, I wish I did, Ballistics was never my strong point, and I'd better get back to my desk. Just one thing, before you try using the brick wall and your head, instead of your fist, and the desk. Why don't you have a nice cup of tea?" he asked her, giving her a smile.

"Your suggestion is noted, and I will act upon it, thank you," Julie said.

Julie followed him out, and went to the canteen, and ordered a nice cup of tea, she didn't think she had got one, it was too weak, but it helped, even if only to relax her, it had been a fraught morning.

Chapter 5
Interviews

"Sergeant, I need a car, I need to speak to Sergeant Williams, and then to some of the witnesses with regard to the murder," Julie said entering the front office after her break.

"Ma'am, do you require a driver, I can send PC Jones with you, if you like?" He asked her.

"Hum, oh yes, sorry I was miles away," Julie replied.

"Ma'am, if I may suggest? To find out how a magic trick is done, you need to ask the magician, or another magician," He offered knowing why she seemed so distant.

"The stupid part about this is that I am that Magician, I should know the answer, but it eludes me, for some reason," Julie said absentmindedly, concentrating on the problem.

"Again I sometimes forget the problem, and the answer comes as if by, magic. The harder I think about it, the further away it seems to go," he suggested.

"Yes, you are right thank you, I will forget the problem, and concentrate of Williams, I will take his statement whilst I am there, thank you, Sergeant," Julie said lightening up.

Jones drove her to Sergeant Williams' house on the outskirts of the town.

She knocked at the door, and an attractive lady answered her knock.

"Hello, Inspector Ashton, I'd like to see Sergeant Williams, please, is he in?" Julie asked formally.

"Inspector, please come in, go through he is in the lounge," the lady told her.

"I thought you were to be kept in for observation, twenty-four hours the wound wasn't that deep, but elongated. So tell me why, I find you at home?" Julie asked him bluntly.

"Inspector, Ma'am, I-I well I have a nurse for a wife, and they said I could go home. How can I thank you, you definitely saved my life?" He asked.

"By being in the office tomorrow, it was a flesh wound, and I am at my wits end, how the. Mrs Williams, I was telling your husband how much, we miss him," Julie said smiling her inane smile.

"Alex, I would like you to meet the human tornado, Inspector Ashton," Williams said.

"Julie, please," Julie said, holding out her hand.

"The knife missed his Superior Colon by half an inch Inspector, it was not just a flesh wound," Mrs Williams said.

"I was under the impression that it just nicked the skin, but was long, I had no idea it was so serious. Oh, here a present," Julie said handing him a six pack of beer.

"I would however like to thank you for saving his life, a moment later, and he very likely, would be dead," Mrs Williams said, with a genuine smile for Julie.

"Alex, you should have seen it. I mean the car had not stopped and she was, sorry the Inspector was out, the Inspector ran full tilt, and I heard two yells, almost at the same time, one rather high pitched, I thought, and then another fell, and another flew through the air, the one next to me disappeared, and I managed to punch the one to the other side. It was as if they had been hit by a tornado, bodies flying everywhere. What did the chief say?" Williams asked her.

"Not much, but then again he only knows that we caught them, and that you were injured. He did however threaten to suspend me for insubordination, when I told him you were in hospital because he was too tight to do the job properly, or perhaps it was because when he told me to respect him, I told him that he had to earn it, he wasn't happy, I can tell you that much.

Now Sergeant I need to take your statement, and less of the human tornado, if you please?" Julie asked him.

"I was proceeding along the High Street in an easterly direction, when my phone bleeped, and I saw an elderly man being attacked in the alley between Jack's butchers and Muriel's House of Fashion.

We had set up a camera which was activated by motion, in the end of the alley way, which came out in Edward Street, the particular part under surveillance.

I rang Inspector Ashton to inform her of the attack, and asking for backup.

I parked my car, and rendered assistance to the elderly man, by pulling the attackers off him, and stating that I was a police officer. They then attacked me, as well as the elderly male.

After a few moments an unmarked police car pulled up, and Inspector Ashton got out, and ran towards the melee.

Inspector Ashton disabled two of the assailants, and then tackled a third, whilst I fought with the other three. Inspector Ashton then tackled one of three attacking me, and rendered him out of the fight, and as she took hold of the one to my left, they surrendered, and at that point in time, reinforcements arrived. The assailants were arrested, and those in need of medical care were taken under escort, to the local hospital, as was the elderly gentleman. Having been stabbed, I was also taken to the hospital.

Inspector Ashton deserves a medal for her timely intervention, it saved my life," Williams said.

"You may not have noticed, but the last sentence was not included, I did my job, aiding and assisting my fellow officer. Thank you for the tea Mrs, sorry Alex. One more thing, I know what your nick name is, so be careful, one comment, like Tornado Julie, and it will be well known, Desperate Dan, was what the source informed me, OK?" Julie asked him smiling.

"My lips are sealed, but seriously, I saw you like fall out of the car and then one of them was screaming in a rather high-pitched voice, and another was literally flying through the air. I never saw you running towards me, nor what you did, enlighten me?" Williams asked.

"It is never to be repeated, OK?" Julie asked him.

"My lips are sealed, honest," he replied.

"Ok, as I told you, I used their energy against them, quite simply I ran in, and timed my kick to the one on the left, he saw me, and came at me, so I kicked him in the scrotum, not hard, but, added to his energy very hard, down, and out rolling around in agony. I grabbed the arm of the other one coming to his aid, and assisted his charged, by grabbing his arm, and adding to the impetus, so that he collided with the brick wall to my left, two down and out.

Now Sergeant whilst you are sitting here, you can do some reading for me, the autopsy report, and the forensic report. How can you have a circle etched in the chest of the victim from the barrel of a gun, when the ballistics says that it was fired from over three feet away? You have time to research it, I don't. Thank you for the tea, it was just what the doctor ordered, and goodbye; I can see myself out," Julie said, and got up to leave.

"The whys and wherefores are not important to me, just the fact that you were there, is what matters, thank you for being there to help Dan," Mrs Williams said.

"He is a big lad, but that can work against him, making him slow and lumbering, and he is an easier target, because there is more of him to hit. That said, I can't think of anyone I would rather have by my side in a fight. Six to one, and he has some bumps and bruises, that takes some doing, he defended himself, very well," Julie told Mrs Williams at the door.

Julie left, and Jones drove her home. She had something to eat, and then went for a walk in the town, it helped her think. She was still concerned over the gunshot wound of her victim, it just didn't make sense.

Julie was ready, when Jones knocked on her door to take her to see one of the witnesses.

"Hello, Detective Inspector Ashton, and PC Jones," Julie said when the witness answered the door by way of introduction, "I have read your statement, and something caught my eye, may we come in, and have a chat?" Julie asked him.

"Yes, I don't see how I can be of any more help, but if I can, I will," he said allowing them to enter.

"Muriel, Detective Inspect Ashton, and PC Jones have some more questions for us," he introduced them, and after being offered some tea they sat down.

"Mister Collins, you saw the couple, how did they appear to you, like a loving couple, or just friends? How close were they?" Julie asked.

"Well, just like another two people sat having a beer and a chat, as we were," he said.

"Mrs Collins, you said that she seemed odd, in what way, everyone said she was elegant, and had an aristocratic air about her, is that what you meant?" Julie asked her.

"No, yes, sorry, that was part of it, but she also seemed, well effeminate. I can't explain it, I mean she was female, but it also seemed put on. Like erm, well, look at me, I am a woman; her actions seemed too good to be true," Mrs Collins said. "Like say a model, over emphasising her appearance to show the dress off, she is wearing. I don't know. Her stride was not right, I mean like who walks up to a friend sits down has one quick drink, and then gets up, and leaves. It was too quick, but she obviously had her reasons. We know why now, but at the time it struck me as odd; who goes to meet someone says, 'Hello, nice day isn't it, goodbye,' it just didn't seem right," Mrs Collins added as if confused.

"Interesting, can you tell me anything more about her, what about her face, can you describe it to me?" Julie asked her.

"No, her hair covered most of it, I did notice that her lipstick was a deep red, it was as if she didn't want to be recognised, but she wanted to be seen, does that make sense?" Mrs Collins told her.

"Yes, and no, it makes perfect sense, in that everything about this case is contradictory. There was only one glass on the table; did you see what happened to the other glass?" Julie asked her.

"She picked it up, which again seemed odd to me, and then put it on the tray the glass collector was carrying, I think. You don't think she stole it, do you? No, I did hear him say thank you Ma'am, which I presume was when she put it on his tray, and a glass with her colour of lipstick was on the tray when he collected ours, but that is an assumption," Misses Collins said.

"Thank you for your help, it adds to the confusion, but also clears up one thing, what happened to the glass? I believe you are correct in that she placed it on the glass collector's tray, destroying any chance of a DNA sample. Was she wearing gloves did you notice, and the colour?" Julie asked as she rose to leave.

"Now you come to mention it, yes she was, and that was something else that seemed odd, a Camel coat in thirty degrees, and gloves, they were black leather ones, the type worn by drivers with holes in the back," Mrs Collins told her.

"Thank you again for your help, Good evening," Julie said, and Mrs Collins showed them to the door, and they left.

"Jones, find me a nice hard brick wall I can bang my head into. We have a woman who looks odd in some way, her stride perhaps. She is wearing a camel coat in thirty degrees and driving gloves. She shoots a man close contact, without leaving any tearing to the clothes or burning and without gunshot residue, she wants to be noticed, but keeps her features hidden. There is a haystack over there, go find me a needle, it would be easier," Julie said frustrated.

"Ma'am, it strikes me that the case is so odd that it is the perfect murder. Is it worth asking other stations if they have also had the perfect murder? If she is a gun for hire, an assassin, what are the chances this is her first or only job?" Jones asked.

"You have a good point Jones, and an excellent suggestion, and try Interpol as well; this may not be just local. Who else was in the garden, has she made her first mistake, was he the target? It seems very unlikely that someone would hire an expensive gun for hire, to kill a nobody. He was not linked to the government or military, not what you would call a high-profile target, so why, yet another contradiction? Find out if a member of the government or local council was at the beer garden," Julie said, brightening up a bit.

"The bulk of the people were what you would call ordinary citizens, builders, factory workers, and two business men, shop keepers, all with their families and friends, the chairman of ICI was not amongst them, Ma'am, nor was the Prime Minister," Jones told her cheekily.

"I don't suppose they would be," Julie said and laughed, "OK here's what I want you to do, go nationwide with the details to see if anyone has a similar situation, and contact Interpol. She is that good, she may have worked abroad."

"Yes Ma'am, where would you like to go to now, the station?" Jones asked.

"No, take me home, and you go home, take the car with you, and pick me up at eight o'clock. I have some testing to do," Julie said.

Chapter 6
Repercussions

"Come in and sit down Inspector. We are here yet again, aren't we? I have just had a very upsetting phone call from the commissioner. Apparently there are several of the attackers in hospital, which they say was because excessive force was used to detain them. It appears to me that you do not know your own strength, and from the look of you, I do not know you, at all.

What are you some sort of demon like the Hulk? Do you turn green and grow in size exponentially? It has to end, we are not here to destroy an enemy force, our job is to protect the public, and arrest criminals, detain them, and not brutally beat them up. What do you have to say for yourself, Inspector?" he almost shouted at Julie.

"Well Sir, I have but one pair of hands, so I can detain, and restrain one person that would I agree reduce the amount of attackers beating Sergeant Williams by one, and then he would only have five, to contend with. I did not use excessive force, I am more than capable of breaking their scrawny little necks, but I did not. I just broke a couple of arms putting them out of action, whilst I assisted Sergeant Williams clearing the other assailants from the attack, on him. I will however admit that the welfare of my fellow office was of more importance than that of his assailants," Julie said, as if contritely, but it had a forceful edge.

"Yes, yes, Inspector, I have to agree, but I am under orders to control your erm, enthusiasm, for breaking bones. I have to put on your records a reprimand for the use of excessive force.

That said, I want to thank you for saving Sergeant Williams life. What the people upstairs don't always realise, is that there was not an army of officers in attendance, it was one injured officer, and you. They play the political game, appeasing the 'do gooders;' we are in the front line, even so do you know just how many, you injured?" He asked her.

"Sir, I don't keep count, I put four out of action, and must assume that is my tally," Julie replied.

"One broken arm, one dislocated shoulder, one broken cheek bone, one broken jaw, and last but by no means least, one pair of testicles, missing," the chief told her.

"Tell the surgeons to check the chest cavity; that was one very well-timed kick, and I did not do all of that, Sergeant Williams did his fair share," Julie objected.

"Not according to him, he said that he kept them occupied, whilst you reduced the numbers. Jones said that he tried to help, but there were bodies flying all over the place, and couldn't get into the battle, so he handcuffed one of the assailants," the chief told her.

"Sir, I am playing the fight over in my mind, the first guy came at me, he swung a fist, and I ducked, and then landed a nice elbow in his jaw, one broken jaw, a second came at me with a baseball bat, I grabbed it, and twisted causing a spiral fracture to his radius and possibly a dislocated elbow. I was engaged with him when another attacked me, and he is now speaking in a high-pitched voice. As I said, Williams played his part, as well, I did not break a cheek bone, I am sure of that," Julie said.

"Well either way, on a personal note, well done. Now what about the murder, how is that investigation going?" He asked.

"In a word Sir, crap. We have a female that looked odd, how, we don't know, a female wearing a long winter coat in the heat of summer, a gunshot wound fired close in, so close it left a circular bruise from the barrel where it was rammed into his chest, yet there is no gunshot residue, tearing of his clothes, or burning from the shot being fired, meaning, it was fired from a distance. She had her hair and coat making it that she was seen, but not notice, sorry wrong way about, I think?" Julie said.

"A misnomer, everything is apparent yet it isn't, so what are your plans to catch this female?" He asked.

"I did think I might ask Google, they say everything is answered there. Apart from that, I have contacted Interpol, and sent the details nationwide to see if this is a lone case. If it is then I am up the creek without the proverbial paddle. She had the means, she also had the opportunity, even if created, but I am at a total loss as to the motive.

He has a daughter, and a wife both of whom seem to have no reason to want him dead, he was not in debt, and did not have a job that would put him at risk. I say that, because she was just a killer, and not someone who wanted his money, or was having an affair with him. She was a professional killer. Think Sir, would you hire a professional killer, highly paid, to do a job, a local yob, could do? The normal motives just don't exist, I am missing something," Julie said.

"Have you considered that he may not have been the target, she made a mistake, was that the mistake we have been looking for?" he asked her.

"No Sir, he was the target, she sat by him, spoke to him, kissed him, such close contact she would have known if he was the wrong target, and made her excuses," Julie said, half thinking about the case as she spoke.

"Then the only thing we can do is wait to see if the nationwide check and Interpol come up with anything. Thank you Inspector, and try and use less force if there is a next time, please, it would make my life so much easier," He said with a smile.

"Yes Sir, I will try, and not break as many bones, if there is a next time, Sir," Julie said cheekily with a smile, and left his office.

Chapter 7
Reports

Two days passed, and Julie was no further forward, she was beginning to think it would go unsolved.

"Ma'am, Humberside police have just sent us this report, it is of a local by election, where one of the candidates was shot and killed. They didn't make the connection at first, until a detective read our report properly, and the gun used was a point two five," Jones said eagerly.

"Read it to me," Julie said, and got up from her desk, and walked up and down, listening to the report.

"He was stopped at a red light, a car pulled up alongside, and as the lights changed, the car turning right pulled away, but he didn't. It was only after three changes of the lights that the man in the following car got out angrily, and went to the car. He found the driver dead, shot in the temple with a point two five," Jones read.

"That was the abridged version, I hope?" Julie asked.

"Well, I didn't think street names mattered as yet Ma'am, it was more the action, again a random shooting. I mean, how did she know he would be stopped at those particular lights, and that she would pull up alongside him, to shoot him? No-one saw her, sorry the shooter, we don't know if it was male or female, but I have a feeling it is the same woman, it fits. She was driving a Range Rover in a bright

Yellow, noticed, but not seen, around the corner there was a car park, a multi-storey, which was where they found the Range Rover parked, forensics found nothing. A passing car said that he thought she was wearing a hood, but wasn't sure. Ma'am the car park was three hundred yards away up the street. She went in there, and drove out in a different car, timed to perfection. She made sure she was noticed, but not seen, as such," Jones told her just as eagerly.

"Your enthusiasm does you proud, but we rely on facts. I admit it does have all the hall marks of our killer. The only way we can be sure is the bullet, does it have the same striations?" Julie asked.

Jones thumbed through the papers, and then smiled, "I am not sure Ma'am; it could be the same gun was used in both cases. We have a link, there were no striations, the same as our shooting," Jones said eagerly.

"Jones, curb your enthusiasm, we just have two deaths, by probably the same gun, probably the same person, but no clues as to who the person is, just more confusion. You are correct, how could the shooter have known the lights would be on red at those particular lights? And that they would be next to that particular car? Our killer seems to leave things to chance, yet she is so particular and fastidious about detail, leaving nothing to chance; just another contradiction," Julie said.

"Sir, sorry to trouble you, but I want to go to Humberside, there has been a shooting, and it is very similar to ours, and I need to see the crime scene to form my own assessment, and ask some questions to make sure it is the same person, and to make sure they have asked all the people, that is between you and me, Sir, so with your permission I will leave in the morning?" Julie asked him.

"Similar, perhaps, maybe, not good reasons for you to go traipsing off to Humberside are they, Inspector?" the chief asked her.

"Sir, the whole case is built on contradictions, and only by going will I know if it is the same woman. This time there is motive, to reduce the competition, so I need to go to find out if that is the case, and have they looked at that side, I'm sure they have, but to what degree. Sir, it will take me out of your hair, or would you like me to walk the streets for a couple of days, who knows how many bones I can break, arresting the criminals, Sir?" Julie asked him smiling.

"Two days Inspector, and was that a threat?" He asked her.

"Oh no Sir, shall we call it, a reminder, Sir?" Julie asked him, being cheeky.

"Two days only, and no steak dinners," he said, and laughed.

"Thank you Sir," Julie said.

Julie took the train, and as arranged was met at the station by a local Sergeant.

"Inspector, welcome to Humberside, where would you like to go to, first," he said holding out his hand.

"Never mind that, I need thermal comms, is it always this cold? I'm a Manchester lass, but I don't remember it being this cold," Julie said.

"Not usually, but the wind is from the north east, and that is a cold wind, and what we call a lazy

61

wind, it goes right through you," he said with a chuckle.

"Last month it was a heat wave, and now the depths of winter, English weather, baa. I need to see the scene of the crime, and then, the reports if, that is alright, with you?" Julie asked him.

"That isn't a problem; we go past the scene on the way to the station," he told her.

"Who is in charge of the investigation?" Julie asked.

"My Inspector is, but he is down with the flue, which is why I picked you up. I am fully conversant with his investigation," he told her.

"From what I have read, you have a car and a bullet, and sod all else?" Julie asked.

"In a nutshell that is it. The windows were tinted, so the oncoming traffic couldn't see the driver, and they must have been wearing full cover overalls with hood, there are no finger prints, or DNA of any description, it is as if the driver went to a showroom, jumped in the car and drove off, killed the victim, and then vanished without a trace. I have read your file as well, thank you for sharing it with us, at least you got a description," he said.

"Ha, a description, tall, elegant, but looked odd, blonde, deep red lips, and one you will like, big tits; his description, not mine," Julie said miserably.

"This is the scene, not the busiest street in town, but busy. We are baffled by how she knew he would stop at these lights, and that she or he would be alongside the victim," He offered.

"Being alongside is quite easy, it is two lanes, and so the killer came along side, and stayed there, it wouldn't look odd, like these two cars coming

62

along now, almost side by side. Getting the victim to stop at these lights is much more difficult. Are the lights timed, to keep the traffic flowing?" Julie asked.

"Yes, but there is a long gap between the last set, and these and not all the traffic makes it, sometimes," He said.

"Really, so if the killer knew about this, could he delay the victim, I use he, loosely?" Julie asked.

"I don't see how," the Sergeant queried.

"The victim was well known, a prominent figure, I believe?" Julie asked.

"Yes, he has done a lot of charitable work, and his face has been in the papers for his work," the Sergeant offered.

"Interesting, possible, but needs good timing, and skill. Now we know the killer is very skilful, and is a perfectionist, timed to the second, military precision. The victim's next appointment had been advertised, so I believe, he was to speak at a meeting, after having lunch with a dignitary. This is the best route from A to B; I am assuming here, I don't know the area that well." Julie said.

"Yes, you are right, and he would know again, I use he for ease, what time the victim would leave, and could time his actions to be in position, but that does not tell us how he knew the victim would stop at these lights, does it?" the Sergeant asked.

"The victim was seeking support, and to be rude would not be advisable, so let's say that I wound my window down, it was a warm day, and spoke to him between these sets of lights, he would slow, not brake just ease the pressure on the accelerator, to smile at me, being complimentary, delaying him just enough, to miss the lights. Sergeant, it is just a theory off the top of my head, but hum, possible?" Julie asked.

"Possible, but risky, what if the victim didn't slow down, and made the lights, or surged at the last minute, and ran through them on amber. That is a theory with holes, if I might say so?" He asked her.

"You can, but do you have another one?" Julie asked giving him a smile.

"Erm, no inspector, I don't," the Sergeant said.

"A theory with holes like a colander is better than no theory. I agree it would be chancy, but our killer seems to understand human behaviour. The victim wants every vote he can get, so the probabilities are that he would slow, to at least smile, at, I again suppose, the compliment, and offer of support; I know I would do, wouldn't you?" Julie asked him.

"I have to agree, the victim would not feel threatened, especially if it were as in your case, an attractive female who smiled at him, and said she would be voting for him, one, two seconds, and just enough to miss the lights, which we know he did, but how does that help us, apart from clearing up a minor mystery?" The sergeant asked.

"The events leading up to the murder didn't begin here, they began back at his last appointment, his lunch, take me there. I believe it was more central, and I am hoping there are surveillance cameras, I want to see this woman, she may have got out of her car, some chance; she didn't take chances.

Sergeant, at some point in time, she has got to have made a mistake, something very small, perhaps. One comment that has been bugging me is that she seemed odd, her stride. Which I found odd, no-one else commented on a limp, or any form of impediment, yet this one woman said her stride seemed odd, but couldn't tell me in what way. Perhaps she left the car, and walked a bit, so that I can see her stride, a million to one chance perhaps, but what else do we have?" Julie asked him.

When they arrived at the scene Julie began to look up, and around, there were no cameras. She entered the shop next door to the hotel where he had eaten.

"Hello, Detective Inspector Ashton, do you remember a yellow Range Rover being parked close by here last Wednesday, around lunch time?' Julie asked the shop assistant.

"Yes, and no, I didn't see it parked, but, I heard the beep of a car horn, and turned to look, as a Yellow Range Rover had pulled out in front of a car, and he piped at it," she told Julie.

"I don't suppose you saw the driver, did you?" Julie asked.

"No, but I did hear a man say, women drivers," she told Julie.

"Thank you very much that, is a big help," Julie said and joined the Sergeant talking to the door man.

"The stupid cow drove right into the lane without looking, too busy putting her lipstick on, I guess," the doorman said angrily.

"Ignoring that sir, can I assume that you saw the driver, and can identify them, as female?" Julie asked him.

65

"Well, erm, I didn't actually see them as such, but who else would pull out without looking?' He asked.

"A stupid male not awake, as most are. The car was just there, and you perhaps were too asleep, to see the driver?" Julie asked raising her eyebrows.

"Erm, well sorry Ma'am, the windows were tinted, which I thought was illegal these days, all I really saw was a shadowy shape, there was no neck, so I guessed it was female, with long hair hiding her neck," He said blushing.

"Like mine say, shoulder length so that the figure is perhaps, shapeless," Julie offered.

"Yes Ma'am, if I may, you see Sergeant, it is flat, no shape; the hair hangs straight down, hiding the neck," he said uneasily, having been caught out.

"Thank you Fred, you have been a help, we didn't know if the killer was female, or not," The Sergeant said.

"We still don't, males have long hair as well these days, but I agree it is the same killer, and most probably, female. She turned right, and you found the car parked by the side of the road, on yellow lines, and she was nowhere to be seen. How long after the shooting were you on the scene?" Julie asked.

"Oh, half an hour perhaps, the car behind, let three changes go before doing anything, apart from pipping his horn, and then we had to drive here, after he had made the call, so half an hour, at best," the Sergeant said.

"Is that the first on the scene, or you personally?" Julie asked him.

"A patrol car was first; they landed at say ten minutes after the shooting. An eight-minute response time is good, it may even have been seven minutes," the Sergeant told her.

"It may not have occurred to you, but the response time is not that important, apart from that was the time she had to escape, so it is very important. Let us assume that it took as long as the shooting to be reported, as it did for her to drive to this spot, two minutes you said, which gave her eight minutes to get away. The officers would have come down the main road, it is the quickest way, so she would not leave that way unless, she was in a totally different car, or walking, to throw us off the trail.

Now where was the car parked, exactly?" Julie asked.

"I am not sure to be precise, but it was above the third set of pillars so about here, Ma'am," Sergeant Millar offered.

"Right, now walk towards me at a fast pace, use a long stride, and into here, we add. Was the car locked?" Julie asked.

"Erm, I don't know," He offered in an uncertain voice.

"See every second counts, now it took you thirty seconds to reach me, five seconds say to lock the car, two minutes to reach her destination, and then she would have to walk into the car park, unlock her car, get in. Start the engine, reverse out of the space, and drive to the entrance, before she was clear of the scene, and as you said in the shortest time, seven minutes.

This by my reckoning means that as you arrived on the scene, she would be turning to leave the scene, making her get away. I am sure the first on the scene would have seen her, they would not know it, but they did, of that I am sure. Sergeant, when you get back to the station, ask them for the details of any car they saw coming out of that particular street? I believe she was on the street or at the junction, when they arrived on the scene, from that little exercise," Julie said.

"Yes Ma'am, can I ask what you are going to be doing?" He asked her.

"Yes, I am going into the parking area to have a look around; pick me up in say, one hour, and please accept that I am losing my marbles. Why on earth I expect to find anything, when she is so meticulous I don't know, but I have to look, to be sure," Julie said frowning in disbelief.

"We did not think about that, assuming she had, had a car waiting for her next to the car, she had used," he told her.

"No, double yellow lines, she would not want to risk a ticket, or arrive whilst the warden was writing a ticket, no, she will have had her getaway car parked in the car park. Is there any kind of warden on the car park, if so find out if a car was parked overnight? Our killer leaves nothing to chance," Julie said ruefully.

Julie walked the car park, not knowing what she might find or indeed what she was looking for. The wind had not abated, and cut through her like a knife. Even though the supports sheltered her once inside they seemed to do little to reduce the chill, she felt. Huddled she walked down the first aisle, then up to the next floor scanning the floor with her keen eyes, a toffee paper fluttered in the breeze.

'*No, fool, she would not leave even a toffee paper,*' Julie thought.

On up to the top floor, now she felt the full effect of the wind as she carefully surveyed the floor for anything amiss.

Julie slowly walked back to the entrance, and then walked to where the car had been parked, and looked at her watch. She set off at a brisk pace, and walked for three minutes, which took her to the second-floor level; she back traced her steps for thirty seconds, and looked around.

'*Right Bitch, you turned right, and parked up; that would take about the time it took to alert the police, including locking the car, why lock the car? Was it locked? Bitch, I am beginning to question my own thoughts. OK, accept that it was, so now you have seven minutes to make your escape, allow two minutes to reach the lights, and make the turn, so the car has to be parked within two and a half minutes walking distance of where you parked the other car,*' Julie thought cursing herself, and checked her watch, and made her way back inside for two and a half minutes exactly.

'*Right, somewhere close by to this spot, the car was parked.*' Julie decided, and got down on her hands and knees thoroughly searching the area, she didn't miss a speck of dust, until a car horn made her jump.

"Bloody stupid place to be on your hands and knees woman, just up the ramp when we gun the engine to get up it," A man shouted leaning out of his car window.

"I know, but I have lost my contact lens, and I can't see a thing without them," Julie said blinking at him.

"You my dear are in luck, I am an optician. Allow me to guide you to my shop just around the corner, and I will fit you up with a temporary pair," he told her beaming.

'*Just my bloody luck, of all the people that could have piped at me it has to be an optician. How the hell do I get out of this*?' Julie thought.

"No, no don't trouble yourself, I will be fine, my friend will be here in a few moments, and I have a spare pair at home, I know I should have them with me at all times, just in case of an accident like this, but I was in a rush, and forgot them, thank you for the offer, I will be fine," Julie said, still blinking and squinting, as if to try and see him.

"Think nothing of it; we have an offer on, two pairs for the price of one, please, let me help you," he said holding out his hand for her.

'*Where the hell are you, Miller*?' Julie thought, "No seriously, my friend is on their way, and if I am not here they will worry, so please. I am fine, and you don't want to be late for work, thank you, goodbye," Julie said trying to push him away.

"Well if you are sure, it isn't a safe place to be alone, and a, if I might say pretty, young lady, allow me to escort you to the entrance then," he offered.

Julie considered her options, there wasn't much else she could do here, the killer was just too meticulous to have left a clue, and she didn't want him to know she had been lying, so she smiled, and held out her arm to him.

"We are going down the ramp, mind your step," he was telling her.

'*I am pretending to be half blind not an idiot, then again only an idiot would end up in this predicament,*' she cursed herself.

To make matters worse Sergeant Miller pulled up just as they reached the entrance.

"Inspector, are you all right?' he asked concerned.

"Yes, yes just lost a contact lens I have a spare set, take me to the station; will you Sergeant?" Julie asked him.

Her embarrassment was not over, as the gentleman opened the car door, and ensured her head was inside safely, before closing it.

"Contact lenses, I didn't know you wore contact lenses, Inspector? Do you have a spare pair?" Sergeant Miller asked her with concern.

"Sergeant, do you value your life? If you do then I will hear no more about this, do I make myself clear? For your information I was on my hands and knees looking for a clue, because the car park had not been declared a crime scene, which it should have been. It was open and the gentleman came up behind me, I needed an excuse, and used looking for my contact lenses, just my bloody luck, he was an optician, and a keen salesman. Now the subject is dropped, did anyone see a car leaving, back to business," Julie said.

"No Ma'am, contact lenses, seriously, and him an optician," Miller said and guffawed.

"Sergeant, I will have you know, I have twenty, twenty vision, and with one punch I can render you speechless, for at least one day now would you like me to hit you, or is this over?" Julie asked him trying hard not to laugh.

"Mum's the word, Ma'am," he said with a titter.

"I decided that she gave herself two and a half minutes to get to the car, and that happened to be at the top of a ramp, an ideal spot for her. She likes to put things on view, display them even, yet keeps everything hidden. Where better to hide the getaway car, than at the top of a ramp where everybody can see it, yet ask anyone what the car was as they topped the ramp, and I bet no-one will know. They notice it, but do not see it. She is flaunting herself under everyone's noses, and not leaving a clue, not a hint, as to who she is," Julie said thinking out loud.

Miller drove her to the station, and into the chief inspector's office.

"Good afternoon Sir, and thank you for extending this courtesy to us, it is more than a baffling case. We now know she is an assassin, a killer for hire, the cases are unrelated, apart from the killer, there is no serial comparisons. The victims came from totally different back grounds and business operations. One was a wealthy industrialist, campaigning to become a member of parliament. The other a manager of six teams of door to door salespeople, ergo one prominent the other just an ordinary person. One was a red head, the other black haired, one was fifties the other mid-thirties, it is not a serial killer in the normal sense, but she will kill again, and again, unless we can stop her.

She is very clever, she likes to be noticed, but not seen, she walked through a packed beer garden, shot and killed a man, and walked out again, and no-one can give us a description, apart from she was tall, elegant, aristocratic perhaps, red lipstick, and wore inappropriate clothes, for the day.

On that subject, the clothes were ideal if I might say so, for her job. They hid her actions, so as I said noticed, but not seen. You on the other hand got even less, yet there is a similarity. Why pick a bright yellow car to shoot someone from? Again if I may, noticed, but not seen. The car distracted them from seeing her, her actions, and the number plate, again drawing everyone's attention to that particular car, and not what the driver did.

A person of his stature, usually has a driver, why was he driving himself?" Julie asked.

"He was not the easiest of people to work for, three secretaries in the last twelve months, yet the public liked him, and he was tipped to win the election. We have as a matter of course, spoken to his nearest rival, well all the candidates, as part of the process of elimination. The interviews were not entirely successful, and we are waiting for a search warrant, for their bank accounts. The accounts for the election from their offices have been served, and we have scrutinised them, it is the ones for their personal accounts, we are having trouble with," The chief told her.

"I can understand, a rival trying to reduce the odds; that does make sense, but my guy was anything but, a key person. As far as I can see, no-one stood to gain anything from his death. Thank you for allowing me to poke around; it is never a wasted trip. I now know her better than I did, but that has as yet, not helped me solve the crime. I will stay overnight, and return tomorrow, can Sergeant Miller drive me to the station, please?" Julie asked.

"I can see no reason why not. Please, keep us informed will you, as a matter of course?" He asked.

"Yes, I will, and thank you once again Sir, for all your help," Julie said.

"It wasn't much help, there is very little for you to take back with you, Inspector," the Chief said.

"Indeed, very little information, but a clearer picture, and a chill; that wind of yours is so cold," Julie said, and laughed, he smiled at her.

"You get used to it, the secret is not to stop it, and allow it to go right through," He said laughing.

"Does that work?" Julie asked.

"No," he said, and laughed with her.

Miller drove her to her hotel, and as she entered the reception, she saw a male bending down as if to pick up a handkerchief.

Julie was quick, she walked up to him, and gripped his ear twisting it to his yells of pain, she moved in close.

"Drop the purse back in the lady's bag, and turn and walk out," she told him calmly, and quietly.

"Mrs your hurting me, let go, this is argh," he yelled.

"Drop the purse, and the pain stops," Julie said.

"OK, OK," He said pained.

"Let go of the purse, and I will let go of you," she told him, and gave his ear another twist.

He dropped the purse, and Julie let go, she bent down, and picked up the purse, and handed it to the lady.

"Yours I presume, may I suggest that you put the bag beside you, on the other side, it is so tempting for itchy little fingers, where it is currently," Julie suggested with a smile.

"Oh, oh yes, thank you miss, I didn't see him," she said.

"No you wouldn't, it is very simple. They drop the handkerchief whilst you are talking, and then bend down to pick it up, with their right hand, whilst their left hand relieves you of your purse, from inside the bag. Drawing your attention to the handkerchief, and away from your bag," Julie told her.

"Excuse me Ma'am, this boy is accusing you of assaulting him, he says to tried to rip his ear off, is that true," the security man asked her.

Julie smiled, "Hello again, I would assume that you are about sixteen, and stealing a purse is theft, now a sore ear, or six months in prison, which would you prefer, be careful how you answer, it might mean six months, and a sore ear?" Julie asked him.

"He was trying to steal my purse, and this young lady stopped him, and made him put it back," the woman said.

"He didn't tell me that part, sorry to have troubled you. You get out, and don't come back," the security man said, leaving them, with the lad in tow.

Julie had a couple of drinks in the bar, and then went to bed; she had an early start the next morning.

Julie was up, dressed, checked out, and had breakfast before the sun was fully up. Miller had said he would meet her, and take her to the station, by ten she was getting into the car with Sergeant Williams, and on her way to her police station.

"Was it worth the trip?" He asked.

"That all depends, I got away from you for a day, and the chief," Julie said laughing.

"I had a restful day as well, without you, nagging at me," Williams said.

"Nagging, me nagging, that was below the belt. I do not nag; I just smack them if they don't do as told, the first time of asking. To be honest no, it was a waste of time, yet it did confirm our suspicions. Again she used a yellow car, bright yellow, and very noticeable, and left it on double yellow lines. It was the magician's trick again; follow the yellow car, whilst she escaped, in an ordinary one.

I estimate it took them fifteen minutes from the shooting to them finding the car. They agree it was two to three minutes after the shooting before the police were informed, and then seven to eight minutes to get there. Then they had to set up, and ask some questions before they found the car, so fifteen in total, ample time for her to make her escape.

The police would in all probability still be measuring, and asking basic questions when she drove past them, and she had to drive past them, the entrance to the car park was on a cul-de-sac. She is one hell of a brazen sod," Julie said angrily.

"Do you want to go home to unpack?" Williams asked her.

"No, the station, I will unpack when I get home tonight. What have you been up to, whilst I was away, anything?" Julie asked giving him a smile she knew he would not have lazed about.

"Yesterday a report came in from Interpol, of a shooting three months ago," Williams told her.

"Oh, and?" Julie asked.

"A witness to a major crime family's activity was shot dead with a point two five rifle, they know it was a point two five, because they have the bullet, otherwise he may as well have just dropped dead, they don't know where the shot came from, no-one saw anything suspicious, but there was one glib comment of an elegant female striding past, he noticed her because of her breasts, they looked odd. When pressed, he just said odd," Williams told her.

"Tell you what Sergeant; I am glad to be back, the wind up there is bitter. They call it a lazy wind, it blows right through you, and believe me it does, and of course to work with you," Julie said with a smile.

"Ha, you can't get around me that easily Ma'am, I am cut to the quick with your earlier comment," Williams said, and laughed with Julie.

"So we have odd breasts, and an odd stride, on a very elegant female, wonderful, if only we knew what, was odd? At least Sergeant Miller, the guy assigned to me up there, and I, managed to put a sex to the driver. All they had was a yellow car, and a point two five bullet; they now know it was a female who murdered him. So it was not entirely wasted from their viewpoint, for us, it was, we already knew it was a female," Julie said disheartened.

77

"Ma'am," the Desk Sergeant said, as they entered the station, "Interpol have just been on, they wondered about your request, and have now linked several murders to the same gun. They apologised, because it is of little help, really. A shooting in America of a witness, by a point two five bullet, no-one saw or heard anything; two floors of a skyscraper were searched, to no avail.

Hamburg, a politician was gunned down, an elegant female was seen leaving the area, and the witness assumed she was hurrying to get away from the scene to safety, as others were. Then there is the Paris shooting and ours. That makes it to date five shootings, by a female; we must assume it is the same person, with a point two five weapon. Ballistics, are comparing notes, and Interpol are checking other open files," he told her.

"This just gets better and better, a female and a point two five weapon, with at least five murders to her credit. She has an odd walk and odd breasts, which are also big. Wait, did the Hamburg police get the size of breasts, to say they were odd is one thing, but here he made the definite comment that they were big, check, will you?" Julie asked.

"Sorry Ma'am, but breast augmentation as a disguise? Surely not, I mean A, B, C, or D, will not make that much difference to her appearance, will it?" Williams asked her.

"No, yet yes, in the sixties an actress Barbara Windsor, was noted for her bubbly personality and expanse of breast. They were not big, which surprised a lot of people; it was her bra that lifted them, and formed them. Now how many males could tell you the colour of her eyes? Not one I bet, but they would all say she had big breasts. Now apply that to our female, the master of deception, she makes people look one way whilst she is doing something else.

The males will notice her breasts, not her eyes. She already has half the population looking where she wants, and not where we want. Look at the descriptions, tall, elegant, females notice these things, and expensive clothes, but not what colour her eyes are, male observations, large, odd breasts, and long legs. No-one has said that, perhaps the size of her breasts, distracted them from looking down there, but an odd walk, again a female observation" Julie said, and stopped, "Sorry I was just thinking, America, Hamburg, and Paris, no-one saw anything then Humberside, and here she makes a show of herself, why more so here?" Julie asked of no-one, and everyone.

"I see what you mean, who would want to be recognised as a murderer? We don't have much, she is very good at making people look at her, and not see her, if you know what I mean, like a bright yellow Range Rover," Williams said.

"Yes, and whilst the police, and forensics were all over it, and questioning people about it, and obviously the person who got out, a bog-standard Fiesta drives past, unseen. If we are going to catch her, we will have to up our game, and by a long way. She is laughing at us. She knows we have no description, and no forensic evidence. This may work in our favour, she is getting cocky, and is about to make a big mistake.

We have three on the political front, and one witness, and our guy; he can't be a trial run that, comes before the main event, not after it, he remains an anomaly, he just does not fit, so why, why, why?" Julie asked.

"Lose thinking Ma'am, could he be a mistake, did she shoot the wrong guy?" Williams suggested.

"Point one, she is too meticulous, point two, she was up close, and personal, she knew he was her target, she made sure," Julie said.

"Not if she was committed before, she realised?" Williams offered as a question.

"Hello, can I just make sure it is you I have to kill, today? Come on Sergeant, she walked up to him, and she sat down next to him. She ordered a drink; she drank it, she talked to him. Don't you think he might just have said something, when she asked if he was her target?" Julie asked frustrated.

"Not if she said something like, 'Oh shit, the wrong guy, sorry about this, bang,' that works for me," Williams said.

"Sorry, but no, she is just as I said, too meticulous. If it wasn't the right guy she would not have been there, she targeted him, why?" Julie asked.

"He was the only one sat alone reading the paper, and he was expecting someone," Williams said.

"There you go again, who was he waiting for? No-one else came to see him, he had an appointment with death, he just didn't know it, but that is what it was. The meeting was arranged, what was it his wife said, something about an interview, a new salesperson. Alone in a room with a woman can suggest things that are not entirely accurate, so where better to meet than in a pub beer garden?" Julie asked.

"That I have to agree to, even so, does he not have an office? I once tried that, and I was interviewed at the guy's home, his wife was there, there was no question of impropriety, why not there?" Williams asked.

"He wanted his Sunday pint, as simple as that," Julie offered.

"Ma'am, there has been another shooting," Jones informed her, "Seven Oaks are asking for the details of our case," he told them entering their office.

"Hold back on that, I want to see the chief," Julie said and marched out of the office to his, and knocked.

"Yes," the chief said in an irritated voice.

"Sir, there has been another shooting in Seven Oaks. They are asking for our details for comparison, I need to take them, Sir, I need to see the crime scene, and talk to the witnesses, and I need to be there. Will you arrange it for me, talk to the chief there, please, Sir?" Julie asked him.

"Do we not have enough crimes here for you to solve, instead of racing about on wild goose chases. What did you gain from your trip to Humberside, nothing," he said angrily.

"Not quite so Sir, I didn't bring a clue back, but I did bring a better picture of the woman, her traits and actions Sir, it was not wasted," Julie argued.

"Traits and actions are not admissible in a court of law, Inspector, just evidence. What evidence did you bring back, nothing? No, I will not call the chief there, and it is a waste of time. Get them to send their report," he said in temper.

"Then I must ask for my leave days, I have four due to me, and I want them as of tomorrow, Sir," Julie demanded abruptly.

"Denied, now get out of my office, and catch the criminals we have on our books," He shouted.

"Oh, oh my gut, I think I am coming down with a dose of food poisoning Sir, excuse me," Julie said, she put her hand to her mouth and ran out of his office.

"Dam you Inspector," he shouted after her, "Twenty-four hours, and not a minute longer, and then I want the jewellery robbery sorted. You have a suspect, bring them in," he added.

Julie went back to her office.

"Jones, who is the suspect, in the jewellery theft? I eliminated the one he came up with?" Julie asked him.

"That is the only one as far as I know, but when you questioned him, he had an alibi," Jones said.

"Which you, Sergeant, checked up on, didn't you?" Julie asked him turning to look at him.

"Yes Ma'am, he was at the dog track with three of his mates, they all verified the fact," Williams said.

"So it was a four-man team with the driver, Jack Jones, is that for real, Jack Jones?" Julie asked.

"Yes Ma'am, he has spent the majority of his life behind bars. The last time he was caught was just two days after being released, Ma'am," Williams informed her.

"So, a team of four and the main suspect is at the dog track with three mates. Did anyone else see them, or was it just the four probable suspects?" Julie asked.

"Ma'am, it is solid, they had betting slips, and they won on race four, and the bookie verified it," Williams told her.

"Interesting, a team of four at the dog track win on race four very conveniently, and the bookie pays up giving them a reason for the cash they have from the robbery. The chief is astute, and he knows the villains so, Williams ask him about this bookie, will you?" Julie asked him, "Jones get me a list of the winners, and starting prices. Give me an hour or so, and then bring the bookie in for questioning. At the dog track, my eye," Julie said.

"Ma'am the chief says that the bookie is a fence, as well as a bookie, but he has not been active for some time, the chief was the last copper to arrest him, two years ago, and he has been straight since then. He did six months, for receiving, but gave the robbers up, and had his sentence reduced," Williams informed her.

"Then our crew did not do it, and did not sell their goods to this particular fence, or they are stupid, knowing that he gave the last lot up," Julie mused.

"Bert Blackthorn is in the interview room, Ma'am," Jones told her.

"Good afternoon Mr Blackthorn, I am Inspector Ashton, and as you already know this is, Sergeant Williams. Thank you so much for coming in to help us with our enquiries," Julie said.

"I didn't have much fucking choice, did I?" He asked.

"Yes, under arrest for fencing, or willingly that was your choice. You see I know that you have a record as a fence, and I know that you work at the dog track as a bookie, so I would like you to cast your mind back to last Wednesday, the fourth race to be precise, and tell me the winner?" Julie asked him.

"You what!" he exclaimed, "There were twelve races that night and six dogs per race, and you expect me to remember one of them?" he asked raising his voice.

"No, not all the dogs, just the winner of the fourth race, there would only have been twelve winners wouldn't there, so just one in twelve, it would stick in my mind. What about you Sergeant, would it stick in your mind?" Julie asked him.

"Definitely, I would remember paying out so much cash," he said.

"Oh, oh yes, the fourth race, yes that does stick in my mind, it cost me a bundle," he said.

"I thought it might, let me see now five to one, were the odds so how much did the winner bet?" Julie asked him.

"I had three winners on that race, which one do you mean?" He asked.

"My, three winners, so how much did you have to pay out?" Julie asked him.

"Oh nigh on twenty thousand," he said, "Nigh on twenty thousand, one guy bet a thousand to win on the nose like," he added.

"A thousand on the nose, do you normally take such large bets?" Julie asked him.

"Not usually, but he was a regular, and I laid it off," he said.

"What about the other fifteen thousand, at five to one; they must have bet over a thousand each, to win so much. Yet you don't take bets of a thousand, usually?" Julie asked him.

"Well erm, no, but you see the odds started at ten to one, and moved up, and it is when the bet is placed that fixes the odds," he said.

"I see, interesting, but even at ten to one, they must have bet a thousand or there about, yet you don't take such large bets. Did you know the people, were they also regulars?" Julie asked.

"Yes, yes, that's it, they were," he said eagerly.

Julie slapped a piece of paper on the table, and a pen, "Then you won't mind giving me their names, will you? Being regulars you must know their names?" Julie asked him forcefully.

"No, it is cash, and they produce their slips when they win, so I don't know their names," He told her.

"Sergeant, put him in a cell, the peace and quiet may help his memory," Julie said.

"Y-you can't do that, I have done nothing wrong," he bleated.

"I never said you did, just that the peace and tranquillity of a nice cell may, assist you in remembering a name.

You see Mister Blackthorn, I don't believe you; you will know such a good regular by name, one who drops a thousand notes on a bet. You may not wish to give it to me, but you know it. Now we can keep you for forty-eight hours, then we have to release you, tomorrow is Wednesday and you will miss the dog races unless of course your memory begins working.

On Thursday we will release you as we have to, but what will happen next Wednesday, another forty-eight hours? I suggest you try very hard to remember," Julie said leaning in close for effect.

"OK, OK, Alan Toms, he gave me a thousand notes at ten to one odds, that was the biggest loss, to me that is," he said.

"Alan Toms, now where does that ring a bell? Ah yes, he was suspected of committing a robbery, but he was at the track betting with you, yet only his associates and you, can confirm that he was there. He was with a Jack Jones, did he also bet a thousand pounds with you. That is what I find odd, very odd. I am also interested in where he got so much money; he is on the dole, isn't he, as is Jack Jones?" Julie asked him.

"Look if I tell you, will you keep me out of it?" He asked.

"Can we say it is the word on the street?" Julie asked.

"Yes, yes that's it; the word on the street is; that the shop owner is in financial difficulties, and he staged the robbery, mind you, who did the job I don't know, but the bet was paid by the shop owner, and the second hand jewellers on Waterloo Road, is where they were fenced, so I hear, don't hold me to it, as you said it is just the word on the street," he said.

"So the shop owner gave you ten thousand pounds to pay Mister Toms to rob his shop, creating his alibi. Hum, I should really lock you up for aiding and abetting a criminal act, but I won't, this time," Julie told him.

They let him go and Julie organised a team to raid the second-hand jewellers shop; all they needed was one diamond with a serial number on it, to seal the conviction.

She then went to the chief, "Sir, I have information that leads me to believe that the jewels from the robbery are at the jewellers on Waterloo Road, the second-hand shop, I will need a warrant to search the premises," she said.

"Inspector, how long have you been doing this job? You dam well know that I believe, does not get you a warrant of any kind, the judge needs evidence," he said.

"It is from an unreliable source, the word on the street Sir, in the form of Bert Blackthorn, but that is between you, and me, Sir," she said.

"He rolled on them again?" the chief asked surprised.

"No Sir, he just heard that it was the shop owner who organised the robbery, being in debt, and that he had fenced them, at that shop," Julie told him.

"Not the most reliable source, as you say. I got confessions, but it has always troubled me that it was such a big job, ten million in gems, and a clean get away that; was what made me wonder if they took the fall, for someone else. What is the going rate to spend time in prison for a crime you did not commit? First time offences, they helped the police, they pleaded guilty, but one got away, and he had the diamonds. Inspector, it has always played on my mind that we did not catch the thieves, merely stand-ins," the chief admitted.

"I remember the case; they tunnelled into the jewellery warehouse, and took just the uncut diamonds, the ones not etched with a serial number, untraceable. It is a long time ago now Sir. I was in camp with the SAS when it made national news, a couple of years before I joined the police, so what is that now, six, no seven years ago. You were an Inspector then, and in charge of the case," Julie said.

"I was, and yes six years ten months, they all got ten years, and are out now, I wonder where they are, and just how much they were paid," he said ruefully.

"It is nice to reminisce, but I have a robbery to solve, then I can get to Seven Oaks, as agreed so, about the search warrant?" Julie pressed.

"Get me evidence, and I will get you the warrant," he said smiling at her; he was not to be budged.

Chapter 8
Delays

"Jones, bring the shop owner in, now," Julie said angrily.

"Arrest him, or just ask him, to come in?" Jones asked.

"Jones, do you want to be a PC all your life? If not, use your discretion. Sergeant, in the yard there is an old table, have it put in the interview room, and remove the one in there, will you, please?" Julie asked him.

Ten minutes later she was looking at the shop owner through the one-way mirror.

"Is he sweating enough do you think? He knows we suspect him; you made that very plain, the last time. Stay in here, I am going in alone," Julie said to the Chief, and smiled at him, and left him.

"Mister Greenwood, thank you for coming in, we seem to be at a bit of an impasse, everything points to you as the inside man," Julie began.

"Hold on a minute, I have money problems, but so do a lot of other people, there is a slump you know? As I told you the business is up for sale, it is my only option," he said with force.

"Yes, you did, and it is, but they entered through the only window without bars on it. Too small for someone to enter through, I disagree, I could get through it. They have been removed for painting, one night, and they would be back. One night Mister Greenwood, one night, the very night

89

you were robbed. How did the robbers know that they were to be removed that particular night?" Julie asked leaning on the table in close and uncomfortable.

"Now look you, I had nothing to do with the robbery, and it was just bad luck. They must have been planning the job long before and spotted the bars missing, and seized their chance," he said.

"They climbed the rear wall, where the cameras didn't work, just another coincidence? Just to see if you had removed the bars so that they could break in. Look I am losing my patience with you, you organised the robbery, admit it, now," Julie yelled and smashed her fist into the table breaking it in half, "Oops, I don't know my own strength, when I am angry, and standing before a fool who is stupid enough to believe that I am an idiot. I know you organised the robbery, to get out of debt, and when I get the search warrant for Waterloo Road which is on its way, they will tell me what I want to know. They have brains, they will realise that the game is up, and I have won. Do yourself a favour, and own up now, and tell me, who did you hire? I want names, and I want them now," she yelled, and again smashed a section of the table with her bare fist.

"OK, OK," he said quivering at her ferocity, "A bookie at the dog track gave me a name, I owe him two grand, and he said he would sell the debt to a rather nasty man, who breaks legs, for fun," he said still quivering.

"You are lucky, I just break tables. Start at the beginning, let me get a table first," Julie said and left him.

"Right, clean the mess up, and put a table in with a recorder, this should be good," Julie told Williams.

Quarter of an hour later he was telling his story.

He owed Bert two thousand pounds, and could not pay him, so Bert suggested that he get in touch with Alan Toms to get the money via the insurance, or he would sell the debt on, as the shop owner, had told Julie.

"A signed confession enough evidence, Sir," Julie asked the chief.

"It is, as long as it was not obtained under duress, Inspector, which I would like to believe? I have ears, and there is the old table missing from the yard, how many pieces, is it in?" He asked.

"Oh that one Sir, some lads are collecting early for bonfire night Sir, and I let them take it; it was rubbish, wasn't it, Sir?" Julie asked him amiably.

"In June, my that is early, one of these days your cavalier approach will bite you in the backside Inspector, make sure the confession holds," he said, and organised the search warrant.

Julie liked to be at the front, and she burst into the second-hand shop waving the search warrant.

"I have here a warrant to search these premises, OK lads, strip it and find the jewellery. You are under arrest for receiving stolen goods, handcuff him, and take him out to the car," Julie told them.

"You can't do this, I have done nothing wrong," he objected.

"Hold it; what do we have here, a Ming vase, imitation of course, but stolen from a house last week, that is all I need, you are booked," Julie said smiling at him.

"I-I have all the details about that vase, it was brought in by a woman, I have her name and address, I bought it legally," he objected.

"Don't worry we will take all the details down at the police station," Julie said smugly.

"Ma'am, we have found a cloth bag with diamonds in, they were not in the safe, but hidden under a drawer in a secret compartment, Ma'am," an officer said.

"Read him his rights, and take him away now, before I get angry that usually leads to broken bones," Julie said happy with the outcome.

It was just a matter of one and a half hours before the officers under Julie's direction had the gang all rounded up, and in the cells, and before she was again in the chief's office.

"There we go chief, I have the robbers, and the fence in the cells. It was very simple; he removed the bars to a rear window to have them painted. The robbers knew what night that window would be unguarded, pre-arranged, and the second-hand shop took their loot, as it were, and paid them, the shopkeeper then made an insurance claim, and got back certain items. Bert Blackthorn made out a ticket, as if a bet had been placed, and only after the race did he enter the winner. The second-hand shop then gave Bert the money, with which he paid the robbers, creating an alibi for when the robbery, took place.

This means that I am now free to go to Seven Oaks, having caught the robbers, as you requested," Julie said, not letting him off the hook.

"Very close to the wind Inspector, one of these days it will capsize your boat. OK, I have already warned them of your arrival," the Chief said.

"Don't you mean informed them, Sir?" Julie asked.

"No, warned fits your approach, much better," he said and laughed, "Well done with the robbery, but don't let it go to your head," he said laughing.

"I will do my best to be lady like, Sir," Julie said giving him a sideways glance and a smile.

Chapter 9
Seven Oaks

It was a typical summer's day in England, the heavens had opened and it was pouring down. Julie had her windscreen wipers on full power to try and clear away the rain.

She parked in the car park, and got out locking her door with the electronic lock, and ran into the station.

"Morning Sergeant, Inspector Ashton for the Chief. It is typical English summer, hose pipe ban then torrential rain, but it will be the wrong type, so the ban will remain in place. I can never understand that. When I went to school, water was H2O, what other kind, is there?" Julie asked shaking her coat.

"I think it has to do with the force, softer rain soaks into the ground this just bounces off," he said taking her warrant card.

"And where does it bounce to, down the hill side into the reservoir, it may not wet the land, but it does fill reservoirs, or does it bounce all the way to the sea?" Julie asked, and laughed with the Sergeant.

"Morning Ma'am, the chief is expecting you, please, follow me?" He asked her as he led the way.

The exchanged greetings and then got down to business.

"There is very little I can tell you, from what I have read about your murder it is almost identical. An attractive female, elegant almost aristocratic walks up to a local politician, she sits down, and speaks to him, she puts her arm around him, gives him a kiss, and walks away. Another person, male actually, sat down with a bump that was his word, and the dead guy landed on his lap.

She was wearing a camel coat, heavy for this time of year, long blonde hair to her shoulders, and breasts," he said.

"Interesting, you said breasts, not large breasts or odd breasts, which I have heard before, here they are breasts. Apart from the description matching eighty per cent of the female population, it matches my killer. I presume the bullet was a point two, five, and lodged in his right ventricle?" Julie asked.

"No, the left ventricle, he was shot from the right, but as with your report, no gunshot residue, burning or tearing, but the impression of the barrel on his right side between the third and fourth rib.

There is one difference, the handbag she had with her was over her left shoulder, in your report it was over her right shoulder," the Chief told her.

Julie got up, and walked up and down the room her hands clasped behind her back.

"What are you thinking?" He asked her.

"My guy was shot on his left side, so her right arm was around his shoulder; your guy was shot on the right so her left arm was around his shoulder. That I find very interesting, it means that she is ambidextrous; she cannot have shot him with the same hand, if the opposite hand is holding him to her. The coat hides the gun from view behind her, her handbag covers it from the front, yet it leaves no gunpowder residue, interesting.

In my case they could not be seen from the front, but on a bench in a park they could, so that is what the handbag does, but how does she get the gun. In my case she had trousers on witnesses think, but here she was wearing a dress. You are sure about that, it is important?" Julie asked the Chief.

"I can only tell you what the people saw. We were lucky in that there were some people left after the shooting who saw her arrive. Two women in the children's play area were there when she arrived, and when the body was discovered, and a man having a pint outside the pub. Without his statement, we would not know she had breasts," he gave an ironic laugh.

"Trust a male to notice that," Julie said, still walking up and down in thought.

"I need to see the scene of the crime," Julie said, and glanced at him as he blushed, "Sorry, have I said something bad, erm untoward Sir, I didn't mean to."

"Erm no, it is just embarrassing for us, please, look out of this window down there, at the park. I don't suppose we will ever live it down; right under my window, she killed a local politician, right under my window. My officers come and go all day, and not one saw her, or him. He had been killed a good hour before he was discovered, how blind are my officers to walk past him, dead, at least six if not eight of them walked past a dead man, and didn't know it. I am just waiting for the backlash," he said ruefully.

"If it is any consolation she is very, very good, and poses her victim. The arm around the shoulder holds him up to stop him slumping forward, his head may loll, erm drop, but it just appears that he is asleep, resting in the afternoon sunshine. His jacket, which I presume he was wearing, hides the blood, which because his heart stops immediately doesn't spurt, or spray; if there is, it is trapped inside his coat along with just a trickle, which is soaked up by his shirt. Sir, there are no visible signs that he is dead, just sleeping. It isn't done to go around waking up everyone asleep in the afternoon sunshine," Julie argued.

"Ha, I just hope the Chief Super feel's the same, it's a long time since I handed out parking tickets," he said ruefully.

"I don't think it will come to that, mind you they are looking for a Chief Inspector in the Outer Hebrides," Julie said and laughed, "Sorry Sir, I think you are making a mountain out of a mole hill. What has me puzzled, is how she drew her gun unseen, a lose coat would hide it in her belt at the back, but then she would have to put her hand behind her to bring it to the front, and there would be two seconds perhaps when the gun was visible. I am missing something, and why didn't he make a move, when she went for the gun? He could have cried out to alert the people close by, even you Sir, but he didn't, he just sat there, and let her shoot him, why?" Julie asked.

"A total stranger walks up to you say, they sit down beside you, and they talk to you, and then shoot you. What can they possibly say, to keep your attention?" The Chief asked.

"That part is easy, do you mind if I sit here? What a lovely day? Is the opening, but she says more than that. What puzzles me also, is she kisses them on the cheek, now that, has me perplexed.

97

Why kiss them, apart from distracting onlookers from what she is doing?" Julie asked.

"That is as much as I can tell you, which you could have read from the report we sent," the Chief said.

"It isn't always about the report Sir, our chat has not told me who it is, but has helped me form a picture, more of a better script, to her play.

The setting is wherever she wants it to be, but she orchestrates it. The character is an elegant, aloof woman, well dressed, if out of tune with the weather, but she uses that to hide her intentions. She is mid-thirties, pretty, long blonde hair, and well made up, and she is using make-up as a distraction, and attraction. It makes people notice her, but hides her facial features, as does her hair.

She is slim with a large bust, again something to notice, yet I think it is designed to hide her, men just see the bumps, women notice them, but don't really look; most women are not interested, as such. She is an illusionist; she makes you look here, whilst she is doing something over here. Finally, she is a perfectionist, she leaves nothing to chance.

How else could you kill a prominent person in day light, and in a public area, without someone noticing? I am beginning to wonder if she was even here, that is how good an illusionist, she is," Julie said, frustration creeping into her words.

"Well Inspector, I can assure you she was. You did miss out that she is Caucasian and English," the Chief pointed out.

"White, but English could be a second language; she obviously speaks it, but is it her native tongue? Apart from the fact that she could be

American, Canadian, Australian, or from New Zealand, who all speak English as a first language, may be that is it, she isn't English, which attracts people to her accent, and why they talk to her. See, another titbit of information, or theory, it isn't always the evidence, but a fresh mind that helps me, it makes me think on a different plane, Thank you Sir, it has been a help, I can assure you," Julie said.

Julie got up, and left his office, and made her way to the park. She walked around it, and then checked around the bench. She knew she would not find anything after the downpour, any evidence would be either washed away or destroyed anyway, but she still looked.

She sat down on the bench in the afternoon sun, watching as the sun dried up the flags, the steam rising in a slow-moving mist. It had been forecast that it would rain, and then sunshine.

She watched as a mother, and her two children came out of the pub, and into the playground, she wondered if that was one of the women who had been there when he was shot, and dismissed it.

An elderly man approached her, and sat beside her.

"This is the dead man's seat, you know, shot here in broad day light he was, and no-body noticed. They are all too busy making money to see anything apart from the bank balance. It's sad, I am old enough to remember when people cared about their neighbour, and today they don't even know who their neighbour is, it's sad. You don't mind me talking to you, do you?" He asked Julie.

"No, not in the least, I am not old enough, but I do remember my dad telling me that they never

99

locked the front door, excuse me, but his terminology, 'You never shit on your own doorstep.' All it meant was that your neighbour may be a thief, but they would not steal from you. Then again that was when people had principles, not today, nowadays it is, well I won't say it, but you know what I mean," Julie said thinking.

"Yes, my dear, those were the days, it is all money, the root of all evil," he said in a sad tone, "Speaking of money,"

"When did you last have a decent meal?" Julie asked him looking at his bedraggled state.

"Now let me see was it last, no, the, perhaps, no, erm, I forget Miss, it seems so long ago now, perhaps as long as when I was in the SAS," he said sullenly.

"Was that when it was a Territorial Army unit? I ask because of your age, what are you eighties. It was formed in nineteen forty-one, then disbanded and reformed in nineteen fifty, as a Territorial Army unit, and later became part of the British Army as a regiment. Don't lie to me mister, I was in the SAS, and now I am a police Inspector, and I am not stupid, I will buy you a fish and chip meal, but I will not give you money to piss up the wall. Do we understand each other?" Julie asked him smiling at him.

"We do, Inspector Ma'am, but I assure you I did fight in the Falklands war, as a private, does that let me off your bad side," he asked giving Julie a bright smile.

"Come on, I need to eat as well," Julie said, and got up, he followed her, "And by the way, it is the love of money, not money itself that is the root of all evil," Julie corrected him.

"You said you were a police Inspector, are you investigating the dead man, erm, killing him, his murder?" He asked.

"Yes I am; did you see anything?" Julie asked him.

"Yes, but the police don't want to know what I saw, because I am a fool," he said sullenly.

"They may not, but I do, tell me what did, you see?" Julie asked him.

"She was odd, didn't fit, a wig," he said.

Julie stopped and looked at him, "You definitely saw, a wig?" Julie asked.

"N-no, but her hair moved, hair, does not move," he said.

"Just a minute how did her hair move, what do you mean?" Julie asked eagerly, it was her first break, if he could be believed.

"Well, she was very pretty, all dressed to kill as they say, but her coat caught in a strand of hair, and it moved, a slight tug, not a bit, all of it, it was a wig, it had to be," he said looking down, fearing she would not believe him.

"OK, I have to ask you this, how much had you had to drink, and where were you when you saw this?" Julie asked, eager for him to be believable.

"I swear Inspector Ma'am, I had not had a drink, it was too slow, not much money coming my way, you see. I was enjoying the sun by the tree to the left of the bench. I was going to sit down there, but he beat me to it, and I gave him my nasty stare, people usually get up when I do that, but he didn't, so I stayed watching them. She sort of moved a half inch turning like so, her hand moved, and then a pop. She kissed him and left. When she turned that was when I saw her head move, and that is how I know it wasn't her hair, it was a wig," he told her.

"And you had not had a drink, you swear on your oath as a British soldier?" Julie asked him.

"I do Inspector Ma'am, not a drop passed my lips," he said nodding his head towards her.

"Hum," Julie said pondering if he was telling the truth, and looking at him hard.

"Can I have fish and chips twice, please, and peas?" Julie asked.

She was served, as the other customers, and the service staff looked at her with the tramp. She was not asked if she wanted to eat in or not, her food was wrapped, and handed to her.

"Thank you," Julie said, wishing she could tell him just how vital the tramps information was, in her investigation, but thought better of it, and left. They went back to the park, and sat on the bench eating their lunch.

"Hey, these are good, almost as good as the ones where I come from. Tell me, was there anything else, was her walk odd say, and if so in what way?" Julie asked him, her newfound friend.

"Now you mention it yes, she had an odd gait, too long for such a refined woman, they float, she was heavy footed, a long stride," he told her.

"Interesting, what about her breasts? Someone commented that they seemed odd, did you notice anything/" Julie asked him.

"She had two, and they were full, big, looked big, narrow back, all up front, and on display, but not naked you know, just erm, exposed, erm," he said.

Julie interrupted him, "Tantalising, rather than showing them, giving you the come on, yet you knew she would not fulfil the offer," Julie said.

"Yeah, what we called a prick teaser, all show and no action," he said between bites, scoffing his meal as if he had not eaten in ages.

"Her hair was false, were they also, false?" Julie asked.

He stopped and thought about it for a moment, "Naw, they was real I think, silicone doesn't show, and I wasn't able to grab a handful," he said thoughtfully and laughed.

"No it doesn't," Julie said smiling at him, "Interesting," she added with a smile, a penny had dropped.

"Inspector Ma'am, thank you; will I see you again, they were good?" he asked.

"I don't work around here, my station is North London. I only came because of the shooting, my case is very similar. My card, if anything else comes to mind, go to the station, and ask them to contact me, will you do that, for me? Just a minute," Julie said, and left him coming back with a bag for him, "There pudding, and a pie for your evening meal, you have been very helpful," Julie said handing him the bag.

As she walked away, she glanced back to see him tucking into the cake she had bought for him, and smiled.

Julie made her way back to the station, and went into the chief's office, where she told him about her day.

"Chief, what else is false about her? We are not looking at the person, but what she wants us to look at. It is a constructed person by her; false hair, what colour is she? False breasts, are her breasts smaller or larger, her buttocks, has she had implants put in them, plastic surgery, just how much, has she changed her looks?" Julie asked him excited at the supposition.

"You do realise Inspector that not only have you said that everything we know about her is wrong, but that we are not even at the starting gate? Is she even, female?" The Chief asked her.

Julie got up, and walked up and down his office thinking.

"Not everything Sir, her gait as my informant, not the most reliable I agree, but it has been commented on before, her gait. She has a long stride; she is heavy footed, more of a marching gait, so ex-army, a guess, but a start. Assuming that sixty to seventy per cent of armed forces are still male, we may be hunting a trans-gender. How far he has taken his transformation we don't know, but he has the breasts," Julie said slowly, thinking as she paced up and down his office, looking at the floor in deep thought.

"Inspector, at best it is a theory, one we cannot overlook, but even so, just a theory," the Chief said.

Chapter 10
New Approach

Julie rushed to the Chief's office clutching a paper, and burst in.

"Oh, sorry Sir, I-I didn't know you had company," Julie said and began to back out.

"Inspector Ashton, come in. Sir, if I take this on; I want Inspector Ashton as my second. She knows more about this case than any other officer, and is a dam good officer, if a little over enthusiastic," the Chief said, making the point about her entering without knocking.

"Inspector, what was so important that you burst into the Chief Inspector's office?" the man sitting in the Chief's office asked.

"Well Inspector?" the chief asked, raising his eyebrows.

"Sir, look at this," Julie said, slapping a photo on his desk.

"You have broken one desk already, please, I'd like to keep mine," the Chief said.

"Sorry Sir, but please, just look?" Julie asked.

"Yes, it is a photo of a very pretty young lady, so?" the Chief asked.

"It isn't a lady Sir, it is the photo of a lady boy, very popular in the Far East, they have breast augmentation and learn how to apply make-up, and buy expensive dresses to look the part, but below the dress they have male genitalia, they Sir, are male. Now how silly is my guess that the killer is ex-army, and male. Look at it, male or female, you could not tell. My gut is telling me that our killer is male, and ex-army," Julie said as a fait accompli.

"OK, I will consider your suggestion, but as you can see, and rudely interrupted my meeting with the Chief Superintendent of the Met. I will discuss this suggestion later, once this meeting is over, you may go," he said hinting very strongly that she leave his office.

Julie left, and they continued their meeting.

"Rather brash isn't she, does she have the decorum required for a case like this? Senior political figures may have to be questioned, even if only at council level. A prospective Member of Parliament has been killed, and I feel that she may thump them, and then ask her question's, which is not done, is it, Chief Inspector?" The Chief Superintendent asked him.

"Sir, if I may, Inspector Ashton does have what we call a vicious streak, six men attacked an officer in my force, she put four of them in hospital, and as you said, then asked them questions. She also sat down with a suspect, and talked to them calmly, and collected. She is a woman of many traits, and as yet I have not seen her mix them up.

When she needs to be hard she is very hard, but when she needs to be soft, she is so gentle. Her information came from a tramp the local officers ignored, and refused to talk to. She fed him, and got more out of him than anyone else.

The killer wears a wig, they have a gait, a marching gait, they show enough to tantalise, mesmerise. It was Inspector Ashton who came up with every detail we have of the killer, so far, by her calm intuition leading to the right questions, and the best information. Ten quid on a fish and chip lunch, and she got more information than we have had so far. She will talk to the Prime Minister, and then the lowliest tramp if they have relevant information. My case, my team, and she, is my second, Sir," the Chief said, with emphasis.

"Hum," the Chief Super said, and thought for a moment, "Your case, your neck, so, your second. I have organised for some offices to be set aside for you at the Met, and a team of sixty officers. We need a quick result. I do not want to have to report no progress to the PM, do you understand?" He asked.

"Yes Sir, I presume that means that I have all the support I may need," He asked.

"Within limits, there are other crimes to be solved, and their requirements must be given the priority they need. You do not have carte blanche, but your case is, a priority," the Chief Super told him.

"Thank you Sir, I will meet the team at Oh, nine hundred hours tomorrow morning," the Chief said.

"Good luck, I have a feeling you are going to need it," the Chief Super said, holding out his hand.

"Indeed Sir," the Chief said taking the hand outstretched, and shaking it.

The Chief Super left his office, and the Chief sat down and shook his head, '*A great opportunity, or a noose to hang myself with? I wish I knew?*" he thought.

He got up, and went to the door, and leaned out, "Ashton, my office, now," he shouted, and went back in.

His actions were not normal; he was still mulling over what he had agreed to, and was angry at himself for not thinking about it for a moment before jumping in with both feet.

In the Inspector's office Williams looked at her, and smiled.

"Whose arm have you broken this time, Julie?" he asked her.

"No-one's, honest Indian, I am as baffled as you are, apart from well that doesn't really matter, does it? Bursting in when he was in a meeting with the Chief Super, I did knock," she justified her actions with.

"You didn't wait to be told to enter; you just knocked, and walked in?" Williams asked her.

"Well erm, yes, sort of, as I knocked, erm, hit the door it opened and I entered," Julie said humbly.

"Breaking someone's arm, is a lesser offence, I'll start clearing your desk, Inspector," Williams said, and laughed.

Julie got up, and made her way to the Chief's office, she wasn't contrite, but she knew what she had done was rude, and inappropriate, so was ready to apologise.

"Come in and sit down, Julie, the case has been made official now, and is classed as a serious crime. I knew it would be, it just takes the powers that be, a little bit of time, before they accept it as such, because of the costs involved in mounting an operation of this nature. We all have to bow down to the god money, to some degree. I have been asked to lead the investigation, and I have accepted the appointment, it is a career maker, or breaker. I want you as my second in command.

You know more about this case than anybody, I have agreed to meet the team at Nine o'clock tomorrow morning at the Met. The Chief Super has agreed that you can be my second, but I don't know if I am asking you to be my second, or ordering you?" he said.

"You know you do not need to order me, this is my case, and I want the bastard. This is great news Sir; I will gladly be your second. I ask that Williams is my partner. I have got used to him, and he is beginning to think like me, I do not want to waste another six months training a new partner," Julie said.

"I am not sure that is possible, but you do make a good team, I will try," he said smiling at her.

Chapter 11
The Met

The sun was shining when Julie pulled up in the car park of the Met; she decided it was a good omen, and her step was brisk as she was shown to the offices set aside for them.

"OK everybody, calm down, and if possible find a seat, allow me to introduce Chief Inspector Adam Taylor, he will be leading this investigation.

We have an assassin roaming our streets, and for a price they will kill their target, no remorse, no feelings, just a mark to be killed, if the price is right. This makes our task, a lot harder. There is no system, no selection process, or characteristic similarities we can use to locate or track down, the killer; it is random. I will also introduce Inspector Julie Ashton, who has had a keen interest in the case ever since a man was murdered in their area, and she is currently, our expert, Chief Inspector," the Chief Superintendent said by way of introduction.

"Good morning, I can add very little to what the Chief Super has said, I know several of you, and I will soon get to know the rest. I operate an open-door policy, but there will be times, when that is not possible. It would be pointless, and a waste of time for me to brief you, so I am going to ask Julie, to do the honours, Inspector Ashton," he said.

"Hello everyone, the first murder took place in Humberside," Julie said writing 'Humberside on the board, and drawing a line down beside it, "Motive unknown, but they were involved in the by election

110

as a front runner, so possibly the motive was to reduce the odds, a political kill, with a question mark, I am not happy with that reason.

The second was in my patch, and as yet we do not have a motive, purely random, apparently.

The third one was again political, a secretary to a minister in Hamburg. The forth was again political, an aide to a minister in Paris. What they gained by these murders we don't know, no-one is talking. The most recent one was in Seven Oaks, and again political, we are assuming, because he was a clerk to the council.

Previously, I had to ask, beg, and sometimes just ignore protocol, and burst in, I am not very popular, in Humberside, and I told the chief he was an idiot. I am outspoken, and if you don't like it, I do not apologise, I am more likely to smack you one.

We are looking for a female, question mark, she is elegant, tall with six-inch heels on, question mark, attractive, question mark, walks oddly, has a long stride, more of a marching step than walking, and has blonde hair, question mark.

Almost every fact has a question mark, because I believe she is male, not blonde, with breasts, and ex-army. Reduce her height by removing her heels, and she is not over six feet, but more like five feet six inches. Remove the blonde hair, and she could be any colour. Look," Julie said pausing, "Tramps may be alcoholics and losers, but they do have eyes. Take what they say with a pinch of salt, but note it, delve, talk to them. I did, and he told me that her hair moved, not a strand, but all of it, useless, definitely not; that made me accept that, she was wearing a wig, as a disguise. We ignore nothing, we document everything, until we have a picture, we can recognise.

Names I don't know, so sorry, you, you, you and you, I want details of every Trans sexual, every Transgender re-alignment on the books, get court orders if you have to, but get me the details. I am interested in breast augmentation; not for me, you understand?" Julie asked lifting her breasts with her hands, to laughter, "Forget below the waist; that does not show. I want a team of pen pushers, good you, you, and you, again court orders if necessary. I want to know what the victims were working on, or their bosses, apart from Humberside, no find out what he was standing on, what was his platform.

We tried forensics, but she does not leave a trace, so a new tack let's try why, why were their deaths necessary, better still who wanted them dead, and that involves reading, asking questions, and more reading, scrutinising every document to find out, the why. The rest scrutinise, and re-interview every witness to every murder, in the UK, OK?' Julie informed them, and asked.

"Ma'am, Can I ask, if we have any CCTV footage?" one of the officers asked.

"First of all let me say; you do not need to ask if you can ask, just ask the bloody question. Secondly a good idea, we know that for my case there is none, the pub had as yet not had any installed, but wait, you could try any locally, it's a long shot, but maybe we can get a shot of her going to the scene. An excellent idea, get all the footage you can of all of the cameras close to the scene of every murder, and analyse it with six other officers, and ask all the operators to hold footage from cameras further afield for future scrutiny," Julie said.

The meeting broke up, and Julie followed the Chief into his office.

"Why the cameras, Julie; that will involve a lot of man hours?" The Chief asked her.

"It is a long shot, but she must have passed a camera on the way to each murder, somewhere? If we can isolate one car that passes every camera at the time of the murder, we have a suspect vehicle," Julie informed him.

"She used a yellow Range Rover, which she left behind so she does not use the same vehicle, or had you forgotten that?" The Chief asked her.

"Thank you for reminding me, about that. You mean the Range Rover that was stolen the night before, and the plates changed, which she left at the scene or close by, and escaped in a different vehicle. We traced the owner by the VIN, and he had reported it the night before. Sorry Sir, I got up awake, this morning. You do have a point, Sir, there is no reason to presuppose that she uses the same vehicle, but there is also no reason to presuppose she does not. It may be a waste of time, and lead nowhere, except it will close one avenue of supposition. Sir, we do not have any facts to work from, all we have is, supposition," Julie argued.

"Although I hate to admit it, you are right. We have never had as little to go on in any case I can remember, and there has been a lot. I think the idea of looking into the shootings has legs, far more than the cameras. If we can find out why, we can find out, who; and from that the killer," he said.

"I hope you are right, I believe she is too careful to deal with the person directly. Even if we find out who ordered the murder; I very much doubt they will know who the murderer was. E-Mails are anonymous, and banks send money so easily. What chance is there of tracing the money, when it can be moved at the press of a button. She can open an account to receive the money, and send it immediately to a different account, in a different country, which is why I don't think following the money will help us, Sir," Julie said.

Julie left his office, and went into the hubbub of the main office; she looked at her white board, and thought about how little they had, every item contradicted itself.

As the day wore on the team seemed to settle in, and begin their work, but made no progress, they seemed to spend most of their time organising the workload. They shouted good night, as they left.

Frustrated, she went to the window, and looked out over the night sky across the top of the houses, and lights. It had started to rain again and she watched two rivers of rain flow down the glass, joining the puddle forming at the base of the window. She mused it was different, but as she watched she became aware that two into one, will go, when it is two identities into one person.

She smiled, it wasn't much use at the moment, but worth remembering, and noting, Steve and Sandra, but which was which, Peter and Petra schizophrenic; two totally different identities, the money was a total waste of time, even if they found Peter, they would not find Petra, or visa verse, until they caught one of them.

114

Julie went over to the white board and wrote in bold letters, '**SCHIZOPHRENIA!**' Julie added an exclamation mark to it, being a revelation.

"Good night everyone, bright and early tomorrow," The Chief shouted as he left the office, not realising everyone had gone, apart from Julie and Williams.

There was not the general hubbub of a good night. Just Julie, and Williams who replied and smiled, it had been a long day, as they organised court orders, and collected all the information she wanted.

She knew it was to all intents and purposes, a wasted day. They would be no further forward at the end of it than they were at the beginning, but tomorrow was another day; when they would begin analysing the information, and scrutinising the footage from the cameras.

The team had worked well together, which she was pleased about, but tomorrow when the drudgery of reading endless reams of paper, and watching miles upon miles of film footage would begin, was different. They would need gallons of coffee, and eye drops would also be needed to soothe tired eyes, and to keep them focused.

It was a daunting task, but one that had to be followed, diligently, missing nothing.

Chapter 12
Analysis

"Morning, please, gather around for this morning's meeting. Never think yesterday was wasted. We may not have found anything, but we are now set to make big strides. Trivia is of no use, I heard someone say a few years ago. I disagree, just before I left, I watched as two raindrops slid down the window. They met up, and ran into a puddle at the base of the window. Trivia, watching raindrops, but it led me to thinking, schizophrenic, just how, or to what degree, can it affect people? I arrested someone suffering from it; she was a senior bank teller, and her manager spoke up for her, as being the most honest person he knew. She was arrested for shoplifting, and when we searched her flat it became obvious that she was a kleptomaniac.

Two personalities in one brain, what if the brain took over; not just in personalities, but the person, one a good, honest male, the other, a female killer? From my research, this has never been proven to exist, but does that mean that it does not? I began to wonder if taken to extremes could this be possible, and it turns out that although unlikely, it is possible. Instead of seeking help, the person nurtures the condition, and actively enjoys even, being two people.

I agree that there is a lot of supposition in my theory, but think about it, our killer could be here in this room right now, and we would not know it. The profile suggests that they are above average intelligence, in a middle to above middle management, articulate, well groomed, OK that excludes you lot then," Julie said, and they all laughed, "it also says that they are white, they get up Mister or Mrs average, and then go home, after work say, and become Mrs killer. Every murder has happened at the weekend, apart from Seven Oaks, was that a day off?

Rodney you have something for us?" Julie asked.

"Yes Ma'am, I stayed late last night, and as you know I come from Humberside, and knew a little about meetings at the council. I noticed a project to build, rather, extend the underground system. In the nineties a local village became the overspill for the city; an investment business owned by a councillor bought up land, there was a ripple about him being underhand, and forcing the sale of the property, to him, nothing was proven.

This is long term planning, the village grew and grew, and the roads became congested, so the proposal was to build a dual carriage way from the village, which had by now become a town, and into the city, except in name. A councillor, brought up that to avoid the nature preserve, it would have to go a long way around, but if the underground was extended, it could go right under the reserve, not disturbing it, and the cost although more expensive than building a road, because of the length of the proposed road, having to go around the preserve, it would cost only a fraction extra.

Nothing new about that, but the councillor that now owned the land stood to get say twelve million from the sale of the land to build the road. The objector to this proposal, and avid supporter of the underground was killed by a woman in a yellow Range Rover. Silencing the opposition to the road, very conveniently, in my humble opinion," Rodney said smiling.

"There is never a coincidence, which you have implied, Andrews, go with Rodney, what you have told us is circumstantial, bring back proof. Good work, very good work," Julie said smiling, "Everybody else, there are several pots of coffee, and boxes of eye drops, start reading and watching, apart from you six. You will go through all the notes for every case, check all the forensic evidence, and interview all witnesses, apart from the foreign cases; with those you will not be going to interview the witnesses, Williams, with me," Julie added.

"Ma'am," he said, and went to her by the window looking out on late summer sunshine.

"If you see me slipping into uncertainty, doubting myself, I give you permission to thump me. We began our case looking for a woman, a specific type of woman, after my revelation this morning that has gone out the window. There are fifty-five million people in the UK, assuming that say twenty million are below twenty years of age, and another fifteen million are over sixty-five, that leaves us with one in twenty million suspects, the haystack has just doubled, in size.

We have to find a way to reduce that pool of suspects," Julie said adding quickly, "That is not doubt, be careful, just an observation." Julie added with a smile.

"There are currently some six million non-white people in the UK, does that help?" Williams asked.

"Ha typical, so we have a one in fourteen million chance, yes it does, not much, but it helps, we have been told that the suspect is white by witnesses, something they all agree on, the one thing," Julie said laughing ironically.

Julie knew that Rodney had transferred from Humberside police to the met, which made him her ideal choice, and Andrews had been seconded from the Manchester police. Rodney knew the area and people, and Andrews knew his way around the council, having been a councillor, if anything was to be found, they would find it, they also had the court order to delve deeper, if they needed to.

Julie was not one to sit back, and order her team, she was one to take a pile of files, and get stuck in, whilst the Chief seemed to float in and out, ask some questions, and offer advice, where it was not needed.

"Williams, how do I tell the Chief to get lost, he is more of an irritant, than a help," Julie asked him, seeing the Chief giving advice.

"Julie, this is friendly advice, putting him in hospital is not a good career move. He is out of his depth, and he knows it, running a cop shop is about his level, this is above his pay grade, but he has to show willing," Williams said.

"So why take the job?" Julie asked.

"It is a career maker or breaker, if he runs it, it will break him, but with you here, you carry the can, and when we solve it, which we will, he gets the kudos, and he will not hog it. He is honourable; you and I will be more than mentioned in dispatches. He will use his political skills to get us both a promotion; that, he is good at. Why retire on a chief inspectors salary when you can retire on a superintendents pension?" Williams asked.

"I agree, he will allow us to take the fall, but he will also speak up for us. OK, that is my ten minutes self-pitying, considering what we have, the profiler did a good job from the information available to her, we can discount two elements, female and white," Julie said.

"Why white, I accept your idea about them being schizoid, but why not white?" Williams asked her.

"Very simple my dear Watson," she said smiling at him cheekily, "I saw a film last night, and the person wanted to be aged, so they made a mask, and I had an epiphany, with a mask and wig, we have no idea what the hell the killer looks like. Our killer is very clever, and has assets, skills, and wherewithal, we are just beginning, to learn about," Julie said.

"Yes Ma'am, but to save me having to thump you for being pessimistic, we are learning. As you said, chasing the money or E-Mails is as yet impractical, but Rodney will bring something back, even a morsel can be built upon," Williams said smiling at her.

Julie looked at him smiling, "As I said, my ten minutes of self-pity or uncertainty is over, we will crack the case, or I will die, trying," Julie said brightening up.

"Ma'am, Ma'am, I have this BMW on the Seven Oaks, Humberside, and your case," Johnson said excitedly.

"Good work, show me," Julie said.

She followed Johnson to the viewing room, and watched as he ran the tape. A dark coloured BMW with just the driver passed by the cameras, going and coming from the general area.

"Good, where exactly is this in relation to the scene?" Julie asked.

"That is the bad news; it is too far away to be positive that it was involved, but I felt close enough to inform you, Ma'am," Johnson said.

"You did right, it is a possible, rather than a probable, can you clean it up so that we can see the driver?" Julie asked.

"Unfortunately Ma'am, that is the best shot, and it is from a camera on a chemist shop. The one shot by our camera has a fly just where the face is, and the other shot is again not one of our cameras, and it is poor quality. I have however managed to clean up the plate, and the owner is a Mohammed Khan, and I have his address," Johnson said smiling.

Julie leaned in, and pouted her lips, "Johnson, I could kiss you, hum, as one avenue closes, another opens, hey Williams, get the car, I'll meet you at the front," Julie said smiling, "Good work Johnson."

Julie met Williams at the front, and they drove to the address. It was a pre-war semi-detached house with a small front garden. They pulled up a few doors down in the first parking space, and walked back.

"Not a bad area, Mister Khan must be doing alright for himself, married, two children, and he is a geologist, recently employed by a building firm. Why would a building firm employ a geologist?" Julie asked reading her file.

"It must be a large firm to employ a geologist; they are usually employed for a specific job. Doing ground surveys to see if, or what is needed for the structure, rock formations, and the like, but that is usually on tower blocks, tall buildings where serious foundations are needed," Williams said.

"I am impressed Sergeant, I didn't know you knew so much about construction," Julie said.

"I don't, I am just guessing, I do know you cannot build a thirteen-story building on a beach, so I just used that," he said giving her a smile.

"The Arabs seem to be able to; Arabia is just one big bloody beach," Julie offered and laughed.

"You have a point, Inspector," Williams said pressing the doorbell.

"Good afternoon is Mr Khan in please Inspector Ashton and Sergeant Williams, we would like to have a word with him?" Julie asked.

"He hasn't come home yet," the lady answering the door said.

"Isn't that his car?" Julie asked pointing to the BMW parked by the gate.

"Y-Yes, he took the train, he is working in the city today," she said.

"I see, when are you expecting him back, it is very important that we speak to him?" Julie asked.

"Erm, later to-night, what is the problem?" she asked.

122

"It's to do with our enquiries, my phone number, please get him to ring me as soon as he comes home," Julie said calmly, handing the woman her card.

"What is it? I mean, has he done anything wrong, why do you want to question him? He is a good man," she said, as they turned to leave.

"I really need to speak to him, about it. So please, ask him to ring me, thank you." Julie said, ending the conversation.

At the gate she turned, and smiled at the woman stood on the doorstep,

"Just one thing, do you ever drive his car?" Julie asked.

"Me, no, I can't drive," she said smiling, but her voice was hesitant, something both Julie and Williams picked up on.

"Do you agree, she is lying?" Williams asked.

"Yes, but about what? All of it or just that she can't drive?" Julie asked.

"My gut is telling me that not one truthful word, passed her lips," Williams said.

"That is why I like working with you; we have the same gut feelings. He's in the house, isn't he?" Julie asked.

"Well unless they have live curtains that twitch by themselves, yes," Williams said.

"You saw them as well. Ignore it, or make a scene," Julie said.

"We ignored it, so what about watching the house, and following him?" Williams offered.

"That works for me as well, get a car over, we will stay until they arrive. We may just have, need I

123

say more, we have, he is on the move, we have spooked him," Julie said.

"Why is it that on the tele, the police car is facing the right way, when in my experience, it never is?" Williams asked as he moved off.

"What are you doing, he went that way?" Julie asked.

"Yes, but he has to go around the block, we don't. We will meet up with him as he exits the estate. See, like so, Ma'am," Williams said, parking, and waiting for a few moments,

"How did you know that?" Julie asked.

"This estate is where I grew up, and unless they demolish it they can't alter it, with the railway on two sides, and the canal on the other, and the entrance on the main road, it is boxed in," Williams said.

"What is this, Sergeant; you were conceited, but are now perfect?" Julie asked him, being cryptic.

"Why thank you Ma'am," he said being cryptic back, and they laughed.

They followed him for a good half hour to an old industrial estate, and to a rundown factory.

"Sergeant, I do not like this one bit," Julie said, and picked up the microphone, "Inspector Ashton, send back up to Walter street industrial estate, re one Mohammed Khan, silent approach," Julie said cautiously.

"Ma'am there will only be about six of them, we can manage that, can't we?" Williams asked.

"Yes we can, we have in the past, but I have been warned off breaking too many arms and legs. The other thing is if you will look down there, there is a car, it is an unmarked police car, something is going on here, and I do not want to mess up a sting operation, or any other, for that matter," Julie said.

They waited for a few minutes watching, there was an uneasy tension in the car, they wanted to make a move to see what the hell was going on, but Julie wanted to wait for a bit longer, and just watch.

Their radio burst into life, "Where are you?" the radio asked.

"Facing you, equidistant from the entrance, we are interested in Mohammed Khan, the person, not this activity," Julie said in reply.

"Back off, we have been working this for twelve months," the radio said.

"He is of interest to us in a murder enquiry. What is your interest?" Julie asked.

"That is none of your concern," the radio said.

"I am making it my concern; now we work together, or I go in there and drag him out," Julie said forcefully.

"Wait, there is a wagon approaching, and that is what we have been waiting for, on my command we rush the place all units in position?" he asked.

The wagon pulled up, and then reversed into the warehouse; Julie and Williams sat pensively waiting.

"Drugs?" Julie asked.

"No, that was Trevor Hastings, a sergeant with serious crimes; we worked together before he moved into serious crimes. I had heard that they were interested in a human trafficking ring, but that was like he said, some twelve months ago. I lost touch with him, after hearing that," Williams told her.

125

"We wait then, only because the truck has arrived, and once khan is arrested we can have a chat with him. My gut is telling me that he is not our man, human trafficking doesn't usually mix with assassination, then again nothing is impossible, is it, Sergeant?" Julie asked him.

"No Ma'am, I think something is wrong, it will soon be dark, but to arrive in daylight, means to me, something is wrong," Williams said uneasily, a worried frown creased his brow.

"What like Sergeant; the wagon is full of clothes. Your friend has been played?" Julie asked him.

"Yes, these people don't usually move about in daylight. It isn't right Ma'am, if Trevor makes his move now, he will lose twelve months work. He may be on to them, but they are also, on to him," Williams said.

"Sergeant Hastings, this is Inspector Ashton, hold your position, and that is an order, something is wrong; hold your position. Come on Sergeant, we can have a look in line with our investigation, without letting on as to the presence of the other officers. Hastings stay put, if we see anything we will alert you," Julie said, and got out of the car with Williams.

They walked down to the door, and knocked on it, nothing happened so Williams put his foot to it, and they burst in.

"I want to speak to a Mister Khan, in connection with my investigation, I have a search warrant, so step to one side," Julie said.

"We are just working here, and I don't know a Mister Khan, I am the manager, as you can see we are unloading a shipment of clothes ready for delivery to the shops, we supply," the man who seemed to be in charge said.

"Innocent are you, why didn't you open the door to our knock, and I saw Mister Khan entering these premises, so I know he is here. What you know him as is of no concern to me. He drives the black BMW parked outside. You have two seconds to decide if you want to be arrested for obstruction, or not," Julie said forcefully.

"I am Mohammed Khan, what can I do for you, officer," a man said from behind the wagon, and coming into view.

I am Inspector Ashton, and I would like to ask you a few questions, can we go to your office for a private chat? With me is Sergeant Williams," Julie said introducing him.

"On June the sixteenth, your BMW was seen passing this camera on the High Street near Watford, on August the twenty seventh, it was again seen by a traffic light camera in Humberside, on the ninth of September it was seen passing a chemist shop in Seven Oaks, can you account for these sightings, and what you were doing at these particular locations?" Julie asked him, once they were in his office.

"Wow, erm, six months ago, wow, and you expect me to remember? I have been to a lot of places since then. I import clothes and sell them, so I presume I was out and about, selling the clothes," he said, not very convincingly.

"You don't keep a diary of your appointments?" Julie asked, "How do you know where you are supposed to be?" Julie asked.

"Oh, yes, I do, but it is at home in my briefcase," he said adding a smile.

"What time did you arrive here?" Julie asked.

"I didn't look at my watch so erm, late afternoon, say four o'clock?" he said, questioning his answer.

"Four o'clock, strange, when we called at your house we were told you were not at home. Yet your BMW was parked outside, which is now parked in the road here. Mister Khan, don't waste my time, you have lied, why, what are you hiding? We can go down to the police station if you prefer, but if we do, you will be charged with obstruction. Do I make myself clear, Mister Khan?" Julie said in no uncertain terms, what was to happen to him if he didn't stop, prevaricating.

"OK, OK, this delivery is very important, and I needed to be here to receive it. If I had delayed talking to you, I would have lost it, and that would have been very expensive for me. So I told my wife to say that I was not at home. I was going to come down to the station tomorrow, saying that you had called. I have nothing to hide, but I had to be here," he said pleading with her.

"Why did you have to be here?" Julie asked him.

"These are next season's fashions, and the supplier wanted cash on delivery. This is a very competitive marketplace, to have next season's fashions in my shops first, gives me a big lead in sales, and the designs are top secret," he said.

"I am not happy Mister Khan, how much does the supplier want?" Julie asked.

"One hundred thousand pounds," he said.

"That is a lot of money, how did you bring it here if you didn't bring your briefcase?" Julie asked.

"I brought it in this case, leaving my brief case at home," he said.

"Isn't it a bit unusual to pay a delivery man so much money, in cash?" Julie pressed him.

"I am waiting for the supplier, we check the invoice first, and then he will come to be paid," he said.

"So everything is above board, which means that you have no objection to us having a look around, is that correct?" Julie asked him.

"No, no indeed not, please, have a look around," he said waving his arm around.

"May I use your bathroom first," Julie asked.

He showed her to the ladies, and she entered, and radioed Hastings, telling him that she was going to have a look around, with Khan's consent, indicating that Williams was right, they knew they were about to be raided.

Julie and Williams wandered around, noticing things, yet not letting on, they walked around the warehouse part, and then opened several doors leading off the area, into smaller storerooms, or offices.

"Where does this door go Mister Khan, it is locked?" Julie asked.

"That, oh yes that is to a store where we keep expensive jewellery for our accessories collection. There is about one million pounds worth of diamonds in there in necklaces and the like. So it is kept locked, and I don't have the key with me," he said amiably.

"Then you won't mind if I open it, will you?" Julie asked.

"Yes, yes I do, I object very strongly to you breaking into rooms, damaging doors when there is no need," he said.

"I will not break the lock or door, so is it alright if I take a look?" Julie asked.

"Erm, well, erm, yes, I suppose so," he said uncertain if he could object, which he wanted to.

"Thank you, these locks are so easy to unlock with a hair grip; there see no damage, and I can lock it afterwards. Really Mister Khan, so much value in here, and such a pathetic lock, you really do need to change it for a five-lever dead lock, a child could pick this lock," Julie said, as she opened the door, and looked inside.

Julie already knew what the other officers were looking for, and she was well aware that the obvious is not that interesting. She had noted with interest his reluctance to open the door, and his uneasiness when she opened it. It was not that it had opened easily to her actions, and how insecure the room was, it was his apprehension.

There was indeed a safe in there, and show cases with some jewellery on display, which she noted, taking a closer look she smiled as she accepted that there wasn't a diamond on display. Not that she had expected there to be.

"Can you open the safe, or would you like me, to open it?" Julie asked him.

He accepted that she was a woman of many talents, and could open it so he pulled out a set of keys, and opened it.

"Tell me Mister Khan, why have one hundred thousand pounds in an easily stolen briefcase, when you have a perfectly good safe, on site?" Julie asked him.

"The money was in there, and I removed it in readiness, so that he doesn't know what is in the safe, or that I have one. You can never be too careful, these days," he said.

"True, very true; Mister Khan, you told me that you brought the money from home in that briefcase, leaving your other one with your diary in, at home. Have you told me the truth about, anything?" Julie asked him, pointedly.

"Y-Yes, I brought the brief case with me, but it was empty, and then I put the money in it, once I arrived here. What have I allegedly done, I am co-operating with you, I have answered all your questions, and you do not have a warrant, so I am asking you, to leave?" He asked her.

"Indeed you have answered all the questions, but each time with a lie, which upon closer examination you came up with a plausible, if doubtful, reason. Which leads me to think you have something to hide, and by the unease you stand there fidgeting, I am getting close to whatever it is, you are hiding. You know slight nuances make me nervous; it is not what is said, but how, or with what clarity. You have as yet not answered one question fully, or honestly. What do you have to hide, Mister Khan?" Julie pressed him.

"Nothing, now if you don't mind I want you to leave," he said.

"Sweating, are you, just how close to finding out your secret am I, and I am very close, am I

131

not?" Julie asked him, now drilling him with her stare; it made Williams, feel uncomfortable, it was so intense.

"As soon as I leave, I will be back with a search warrant, quicker than you can hide whatever it is you are hiding. Perhaps it is behind this wall. It originally had a door in it, didn't it? This room is considerably smaller than the other side of the wall. A room you do not use anymore perhaps, this show case is wrong, it would make more sense if it was on that wall, easier to get to, and then you could open the door to it fully.

Here it is not as easily accessible, and the door only opens halfway making it hard to get the goods off the shelf. Little things make me wonder, like. Why has the floor been swept apart from this area? Is it to hide the scratches made by swinging the cabinet open, to reveal the door? Come on Mister Khan, tell me why, I like fairy stories?" Julie asked him, staring into his eyes deeper, if it was possible.

"I have asked you to leave my premises, now go," he said formally.

"Sergeant Williams, will you go and collect the search warrant, and some help please?" Julie asked him.

"Ma'am," was all he said, as he left them.

Outside he waved to Sergeant Hastings, and he came over.

"My Inspector wants your search warrant, and now is the time for you to enter; she has him on the run. She has told him that I am getting the warrant and help, but she is still with him, smiling no doubt, so bring it on," Williams told him, and the area seemed to erupt with male, and female officers, all walking towards them on Hastings's signal.

Williams led them to where he had left Julie.

"Sergeant Hastings will you show Mister Khan the warrant please, and then pull that cabinet away, it will swivel this way onto a door behind which, you will find what you are looking for," Julie said, pleased with herself.

She turned to Mister Khan added a smile, "Well Mister Khan, what do you think we will find behind this door, it will be I suspect, the toilets. There is quite a strong odour just here, of urine," Julie said.

Hastings pulled the cabinet out, and looked at the door, "An electronic lock Ma'am, we need the code to open the door," he told her.

"Well Mister Khan, if you do not open the door, we will break it down, legally, because of the search warrant, it covers all the premises, and I want to see what one million in diamonds, looks like?" Julie asked him.

Julie looked at him smiling, his face was a picture; shock and awe were both etched on it. He turned to try and get away, Williams was the nearest and quickest grabbing him, and holding on to him.

"Tell me Mister Khan, what year were you born?" Julie asked him.

"Nineteen fifty four," he said.

"Ma'am, you don't think it is as easy as that, do you?" Hastings asked her.

"Good grief no, on his desk there was a diary, with yesterday's date ringed, and BD in bold in the circle. Very few people forget their own birthdays, but their secretary might, or he might forget his wife's birthday. Try eleven fifty four," Julie said.

"No good Ma'am, I guess your idea isn't working," Hastings said cheekily.

"Try five, four, one, two," Julie suggested.

"How did you work that out?" Hastings asked.

"That is a Perkins sequence lock, the first code was a basic guess, his birthday the eleventh, actually of the eleventh, but you can't have six digits so I stuck to the day, and year. That type of sequence lock advances one day at a time, so I again guessed that it was today's date, the twelfth, and his year of birth, to give almost four different numbers and not in sequence," Julie said, giving Khan a special smile.

"Mister Khan you are under arrest for human trafficking, anything you say will be taken down, and used in evidence against you. Do not say anything that you will later rely on, in court," Hastings told him.

The female officers entered the room, and led the young females out one at a time. They were frightened and crying, as they were led out. Outside in the warehouse, the workers were being rounded up, and taken away in police vans to be charged, and put in prison.

"Some bloody use that was to us, but he is off the street, so it wasn't a total waste of time. Why were they going to take him, today?" Julie asked Williams.

"Hastings, why attack him today, what was so special about today?" Williams asked him.

"We had information that he was expecting a delivery of more women today, and we wanted to get his supplier as well, which you messed up, thank you," he said angrily.

Julie went over to the women, and spoke to them in Arabic, then returned.

"All is not lost, they took a bit of convincing, but in the end, they told me that this was the same wagon they came in, and that the men were the same men that brought them here. Just because they can't speak English, does not mean that they don't have eyes and ears, try asking them. Hastings, you have a mole, they knew you were going to charge in today, even the women did. Clean your team up," Julie told him, and they made their way to their car, "Williams it is obvious to me that he sells the women at the three places we had murders. Pass any information we have on to the local police stations, perhaps they can collect some more of these bastards. If not, put it on my desk for when we have solved this case," Julie said angrily.

Williams, drove them back to the office, they were quiet it had not been a very successful day, but not wasted as Julie liked to believe. He was not the killer so they didn't have to waste any more time on that avenue of investigation, even if it was the only avenue open at the moment.

Julie went into the offices, the night crew were on duty, and there was the general hubbub of them working. Julie turned around, and left no-one was rushing to tell her of a break, so she left disheartened.

Chapter 13
A New Break

Julie was one of those people who were optimistic, even after the down hearted end to the day before; she woke up enthusiastic, and expecting a lead, her motto if she had one would be, 'As one door closes another opens, immediately,' it was with this optimism that she entered the offices.

"How did it go yesterday, Inspector?" The Chief asked.

"That depends, on how you look at it, we got a result a good one, but not for us, serious crime broke a human trafficking gang, with our help, so it wasn't a failure, it just closed an avenue we had been following. Today's another day Sir, and some tiny morsel will turn up that will ultimately break the case open. Where it will come from, and how; I have yet to find out, but it will," Julie said perhaps being more enthusiastic than she felt.

"Ma'am, we have spent a couple of hundred hours viewing the tapes, and cross referencing the vehicles with other tapes. Don't you think we have done enough watching?" An officer asked her.

"Have you found a vehicle that passes every camera at the time relevant?" Julie asked him.

"No Ma'am, that is my point, it is a wild goose chase," he said respectfully.

"What do you suggest?" Julie asked him.

"There must be something that we can do, which is more productive?" he asked.

"I agree, I am sure there is, and when you think of it, tell me. Until then, keep watching," Julie told him.

"Gather around for an update," Julie said, and walked up and down as she thought about, how she was going to report yesterday and what could be done to break the case.

They all gathered around expectantly, listening to the general chatter.

"OK, yesterday we had a lead from watching the cameras. It proved of no use to us, but it did lead to a bust for serious crime squad, and it closed down a human trafficking ring, so it was not a waste of time," Julie said emphasising the word, 'not.'

There was a general cheering as they applauded the work done.

"Settle down, we just did our jobs, your job is to catch this murderer, and we are no nearer to finding them. Is Rodney back yet?" Julie asked.

"No, Ma'am, he said he needs an extra day, he is on to something, but didn't say what," an officer informed her.

"OK, for today it is boring and tedious, I realise that, but keep on doing what we are doing. I don't see our killer using public transport, and I don't see them being ostentatious, don't ignore anything, but look at the middle range cars, two, three years old. I think he, or she, will try to blend in on the approach. They make a show of themselves immediately before, and during the action. What car she was in entering the car park of the pub, we have no idea, but she made herself visible, walking to the table. That is why I think we should be looking for a middle range car, and not a new one," Julie told

137

them, and the officers broke up going back to their jobs.

"Ma'am, Ma'am," An officer almost shouted, and again almost ran to her as she was looking at the display board.

"This must be good Evans, what's with all the yelling?" Julie asked him, smiling at him for encouragement.

"Ma'am, I have her," he said eagerly.

"You do where, show me," Julie said just as eagerly.

"I was watching with Mayberry, when I have to admit Mayberry, spotted it. There Ma'am, the long blonde hair, her nose in the air, so aloof, and isn't that a camel coat around her shoulders?" He asked.

"You know I do believe you are correct, interesting. Where is this?" Julie asked excited.

"Morning Ma'am," officer Mayberry said as she joined them, "That is the car that tripped the camera when it ran a red light. It is not near a scene, so it was discarded, but on closer look, we noticed the driver of this car, and we believe it is her car, or we think, may be her car," Mayberry told her.

"Good work, this is really excellent work, both of you, I am sure we now have a picture of the female, and their car, what is it?" Julie asked.

"It's a white Mondeo, I have tried to get a clearer picture, but she is too far forward to get the number plate, because the camera was taking the other car that ran the light," Mayberry said.

"Good work, now we can look for a white Mondeo, are there any distinguishing marks?" Julie asked.

"No, it looks as though it has just come out of the showroom," Mayberry said.

"Go back, and isolate all white Mondeos, and then take a closer look, especially on the cameras closer to the scene of the crimes," Julie said.

Mayberry and Evans gave each other a disappointed look, they had not reduced their workload; they had increased it, as they now had to go back to the beginning, looking for a specific car model.

They started work with the first tape, and took a still of every white Mondeo passing the camera; clarity of picture was not their concern; that could be attended to later, enhancing the picture if one looked suspect.

The process was quicker because they could fast forward until a white car came into view, and then slow to check if it was a Mondeo, if not fast forward again; if it was, they would slow the tape until the best photo was visible, and then click the print button taking a picture of the still.

Julie went back to her office, and stood by the window gazing out at the roof tops, she appeared to be in a daze, Williams saw her, and smiled, this was her classic pose, for thought.

"They are probably not worth it, but I will give you a penny for them," he said entering her office.

"You are right, they are not. London to Humberside and back is not exactly a trip you would complete in a day. It is possible, but what time would you have to leave to be sure you were where you wanted to be when you wanted to be? These days with road works, accidents, rush hour traffic, I would not risk driving all that way when my pay check depended on it, would you?" Julie asked him.

"No, it makes sense to arrive the day before, and stay overnight, but I would return the same day I had killed my target," Williams said.

"Hum, interesting, what about asking the hotels about their guests the night before, to see if any booked in with a white Mondeo, or at least arrived in one? We could also ask if they remember seeing one in the car park. Do they remember one being parked in the car park, overnight?" Julie asked thinking as she spoke, and not moving from her position gazing out of the window, deep in thought.

"The yellow Range Rover would be more, erm noticeable?" Williams asked.

"Indeed it would be, but would you have the murder vehicle delivered to your accommodation, no. She collected that at the car park. Sergeant this is complicated, she would need three vehicles, to avoid discovery. The one she arrived in, the yellow Range Rover, and one at that car park for her get away, so where did she collect the Range Rover?" Julie asked brightening up, and turning to look at Williams.

"Her timing had to be perfect as well, so it needed to be close by the hotel he had lunch at, which means her car had to be parked there whilst she murdered him. She drove to the car park in her car, picked up the Range Rover, killed her mark, and then picked up a different car to go and collect her car, and drive home. Ma'am, she would not want to wait too long so the mark left the hotel at thirteen thirty hours, she would know this, not to the minute, but close enough, so we want a white

140

Mondeo entering the car park between twelve thirty hours, and leaving around fourteen hundred hours to fourteen thirty hours. I will tell Mayberry and Evans, it will cheer them up, Ma'am," Williams said smiling at her.

"Unless, she took a taxi, try the hotels first, and then taxi firms for a drop off at the nearest car park to the hotel he had lunch at, let's not put all our eggs in one basket?" Julie asked.

"Wouldn't a taxi leave a paper trail, for us to follow?" Williams asked.

"Yes, but from what we know; she is not averse to being noticed, she just hides her actions. I have been puzzling over where she hides her gun. Her handbag is over the shoulder, she puts up against the victim we presumed to hide the gun while she shoots them. The gun is not in the front of her clothes, it would be seen, yet she does not put her hand behind her back to pull it from her waist band, according to my tramp friend, so where is it?" Julie asked.

"Just a thought Ma'am could it be a holster, inside her coat perhaps; like a shoulder holster?" Williams offered off hand.

"Possible, but unlikely, she shot one on her right-hand side the other on her left-hand side, so she would need two holsters, one on each side, and believe it or not, you can tell when someone is wearing one. My tramp friend would have known; if she was wearing one. He may be blinded by alcohol, but he is very observant," Julie said.

"I'll put Mayberry on the car park, Evans will not be happy, but it will only take a short time for her to view the tapes," Williams suggested.

"Yes, she is observant, and try and get supporting views from traffic cameras on the route," Julie said thoughtfully.

"I will be back; I have yet to get my penny's worth, something, is troubling you. I've known you long enough to know when you are worried, thoughtful," Williams said.

Julie smiled at him, "We will have lunch together, twelve thirty," Julie said smiling, he was concerned about her, and she knew it.

Julie made her way to the main office, and joined Williams taking him out to lunch, across the road from the offices they were using, was a cafe bar, a bit further down the road there was a pub that served food, Williams made for the cafe, and Julie redirected him to the pub. They sat at a table, and Julie went to the bar to order their drinks and meal; then came back and sat facing him.

She looked down at her place mat, and grimaced, and took a deep breath.

"Dan, this must never be repeated to anyone; I know I can trust you, which is why I am telling you this. My job is to catch criminals, as is your job, my actual job is to lead a team of dedicated officers, give them direction from my experience, and analyse their findings, sorting them into useful, and useless pieces of information. In the main, I have some idea of what to look for; we have witness statements, and corroborating CCTV footage say.

This is the first time we have none of these things, because the person is an illusionist, I have used the term many times, it fits.

Last week I was at home watching the late film, when there was a knock at the door, and a distraught woman was standing there.

I said, "Hello," and asked what the problem was.

She told me that she needed my help, being a police officer, so I asked what the crime was, and she blushed, a very deep shade of red.

"There hasn't been one, I-I am sorry to trouble you, but I, it is very embarrassing, erm," she said, I thought she was about to start crying so I invited her in, and she refused, asking me to go with her, begging me.

You know me, I was intrigued to say the least, she lived two doors down from me, and I followed her in.

"Please don't tell anyone it will be our secret, it isn't illegal, honest," she begged me.

So I agreed, even more intrigued, and followed her upstairs to her bedroom, and there on the bed was a woman handcuffed to it spread eagle. Then I noticed the chest hairs, shaved, but stubble, the unusual bulge in her panties, and that was when the pin dropped, and her need became apparent.

"He has swallowed the key," she told me.

I knew it would be wrong to laugh, and fought every nerve in my body to suppress the desire, but it also showed me that our suspect is human. We do not know if it is even male or female, we know nothing at all about our suspect. So how can I lead a team of dedicated officers, when I don't know where to lead them?" Julie asked him.

"I see, so finish one story first please, what was wrong?" Williams asked wanting to laugh.

"She told me he was a bit of a Houdini, and he could escape from the handcuffs, it was play. She handcuffed him to the bed, and gave him the key in his mouth, she would then have oral sex with him, to arouse him, and leave him high and dry; telling him that she would be waiting downstairs. He had half an hour to get free, or his time would be up, so if he wanted to have sex with her, he had to get free in half an hour. Normally, according to her, he managed it, but this time she landed heavily on his stomach, he gasped and swallowed the key.

The point is that at first the casual glance to all intents and purposes, it was female, the bust created by balloons in the bra, the corset, panties, stockings, and an excellent job with make-up, and the wig of course, long and blonde. It was the wig that made me realise we did not have a sex for our perpetrator. There are signs, but as witnesses said at the pub murder, there was something odd, about her.

I was looking at a man in drag, and didn't recognise it immediately, which I thought I would do, that is the point to this, the circumstances are what happened, but that realisation was like a kick in the gut, a hard kick.

I picked the lock and left, listening to their laughter and thanks. I don't know if he got his evil way with her or not, I didn't care, I was doubled up in the pain of what I had discovered. We know nothing; we do not have one single clue as to their identity, sex, hair colour, vehicle, age, race, or where they come from, where they live, is it even England? Williams we have nothing," Julie said, intently looking into his eyes deeply.

"Julie, Ma'am, you worry me, I have never seen you so pre-occupied with what we don't have, and judging by this beautiful steak I am eating, it is really getting to you. I must admit we do not have any idea of what our perpetrator looks like, just the face they put on; their facade. Then again we now have their car, don't we?" Williams asked her.

"Do we, the person driving that car looks somewhat like the killer, but you have heard of car hire, I suppose?" Julie asked him.

"I have, and speaking openly, respectfully," Williams said.

"Williams this is you and me, no bullshit, talk to me openly," Julie said.

"Right, then you have heard of a thing they call the telephone, and computers? It took me one hour to go around the local hire firms and find out that a White Mondeo has not been hired in the last ten days, Corsa, Fiesta, Peugeot two, oh, five, they all have, but not one Mondeo, any colour.

Rodney and Hastings will come back with something, they always do. Now let me see, I seem to have heard that somewhere before, does that count as plagiarism?" Williams asked Julie.

"Not if you include who the quote was from," Julie said smiling at him.

"We may not have an accurate description, but we do have a suspected car type, and whatever Rodney and Hastings bring back, and to stay an extra day means they are following up on, a lead. The next time you wish to voice your doubts tell me, and I will pick the place, and it will not be a rather nice steak and chips in a pub, more like

Tornados Rossini at the Ritz. I have expensive tastes," he said, and laughed with Julie.

It had worked, Julie was less pessimistic when they got back, and again scanned the photos of white Mondeos, looking for that small clue as to the killer's identity, from the vehicle registration number.

Chapter 14
Thin Ice

"Inspector, your office please," the rather officious man ordered her.

"Sir," Julie replied, recognising him as the superintendent overseeing the case.

"Close the door, now Inspector, I must say I am disappointed at the lack of clues, leads, and or evidence collected in this case. I and my superiors are of the opinion that you do not have a clue as to what you are doing. Hundreds of thousands of pounds have been spent, and we are no further forward than we were this time last year. What do you have to say for yourself, Inspector?" he demanded.

Julie walked over to the window, and looked out, she raised her head high, and clasped her hands behind her back, and then turned to face her accuser.

"A very elegant woman characterised as almost aristocratic, walks into a very busy pub garden in broad daylight, sits next to a male, and shoots him. She then gets up and walks out, seen by several people, who describe her as I have said aristocratic in her demeanour, very pretty and odd. We have exactly the same description at the Seven Oaks scene, yet not one complete description; we cannot build even an identikit picture to resemble what she looks like. From my own enquiries, I have established that the perpetrator wears a wig, so hair colour is not established. I have here a photo, tell me, is it male, or female?" Julie asked him.

"I am not here to play games, is this, what you have been doing, playing games?" He demanded.

"One, it is not a game," Julie shouted, losing her control and banging her fist on the desk, "And two, you will be wrong if you had answered the person in the photo is not female, take a good look at it. Everything about this case is a contradiction. How can a person male or female walk into a crowded pub beer garden shoot a man, and walk out without a single person being able to construct a picture of the person. How can a bright Yellow Range Rover drive down a main street seen by all, but not the driver, who shoots a man, and drives away without anyone seeing where they went?

Sir, we have a white Mondeo on CCTV close by the scene, is it her car? We decided to follow it up, but without a number plate, a photo of the driver, or any distinguishing marks it is just a guess, she is female, it is just a guess, she is blonde, it is just a guess, because we cannot find anything at all to confirm anything. It could be a Negro, obese, with black curly hair for all we know.

My team have put more than average effort into this, and I will not have them decried, or criticised. They have worked very hard, dammed hard. You have given me the nails and the hammer, but without the wood I cannot build you a table. They have watched miles upon miles of CCTV footage, interviewed and read statements over and over, looking for that little something.

This team will catch the person responsible, but it will not be tomorrow or the day after. This case will snowball, some little thing will lead to another, and another, and our case will grow and grow, but finding that little something takes painstaking work, and hours of it. My team is dedicated enough to find that little something, is the next team?" Julie asked him.

"Inspector you are very close to insubordination, be warned; I will not tolerate it. The Chief Inspector has had a heart attack, and that is the other thing I needed to tell you. I do not want him to return to the case, sort it before he is well enough, to come back," the Superintendent said.

"Six months is the average time for him to be able to return to active duty. Unreasonable it may be, but I will assure you we will do our utmost to achieve the goal," Julie said accepting she had no other choice.

"I will from now on be visiting you at regular intervals for an update and I want results, we have as yet not got anything, and that will just not do. I want evidence, facts that lead us to the murderer at every visit, or I will change the team, starting at the top. You were chosen because your chief demanded that he pick his own team, and why on earth he selected an insubordinate dreamer like you I will never know but he did. We accepted it because of an excellent arrest record and ability, if unorthodox.

Do not rest on your laurels, they are too fragile, results are what count, and as yet, you have none, and I do not like insubordination. I also do not like cavalier officers, who do not follow the rules. The Chief may have known your father, and you, since you were a child, but I did not, and you have now lost, his protection," he told her, turned and left.

Julie swept her hand across her desk in a fit of temper; how dare he speak to her like that? The team had not rested on anything, neither had she; they had all put one hundred per cent into the case.

"Are you alright Ma'am?" Williams asked her.

"He told me not to rest on my laurels, and to work harder, he wants facts and evidence. As if it turns up just like that, the team have worked so hard, and he dismisses them so casually, the ingrate," Julie said angrily.

"The joys of being a superintendent I suppose. He sits in his office and looks at reports, graphs and costs, no longer involved in the day to day effort every officer puts in. So long ago now since he was last walking the beat, he has forgotten what the demands are, and how hard it is, to get a result.

Julie, there isn't a better or more dedicated team out there, than the one we have," Williams said.

"Leave the mess in here, and gather the troops," Julie said despondently.

She walked into the main area where they have the briefings, and looked at the board, she wiped it off, and put the duster back then turned to the gathered officers, she walked back and forth, her head down in thought and her hands clasped behind her back.

"OK, almost twelve months ago a murder was committed in a beer garden, following that, a politician was murdered in Humberside, and subsequent to that a politician was murdered in Seven Oaks. Prior to all of these, two other politicians were murdered, one in Hamburg the other Paris.

We have a description of the murderer as being female, elegant, pretty, and almost aristocratic. She uses a point two five calibre gun, and commits the murders in full view of all around, yet we do not have an accurate description.

The entry wound is that of a point two five bullet, but there are no striations. I have heard of a bullet being sleeved so the gun used is of a larger bore than the bullet.

It has been proposed that she wears a wig, so the hair colour may be wrong. In essence we have nothing, and that situation will not continue.

I have wiped the board clean, everything on it is supposition, and from now on I want facts. Eye colour green, supposition, she could be wearing coloured lenses, poke her in the eye make sure that what you are seeing is fact, and cannot be countered, female; grab her genitals, make sure the person is female. OK, that is perhaps not recommended, but you get my gist, facts, irrefutable facts go on the board, if I can question the evidence or suggestion, in any way; it does not go on the board.

By tomorrow, I want the first fact on the board, once we get one then another will appear, and so on, it will snowball, but to begin with we need one fact, find it," Julie said, and marched off.

"Ma'am if I may, we do have one fact, the killer uses a point two five bullet, unfortunately we don't know the gun, but we do know what bullet is used," Evans said.

Julie looked at him as if considering his fact, and smiled, "You are correct, we do have that fact, and it is, indisputable. Well done Evans, nice to see someone is awake. Look people, I know you have all worked very hard, and hit brick wall after brick wall, so what do we do, retire with a headache, or keep banging that brick wall until it cracks and breaks?

From what I have heard Rodney is bringing back something useful, and will be here after lunch. Now are we going to allow two good officers show us up, when we have fifty officers? No we are not, so go back, look again, find me something to stop those two from lording it, over us," Julie said smiling at them.

"Yes, Ma'am," they all seemed to say, and broke up, rejuvenated by her talk.

"You know Ma'am, they can't find something that isn't there," Williams said.

Julie gave him withering look, "Thank you Sergeant, I will remember that when I need depressing. I believe I am perfect, yet I know I make mistakes, our killer is not unlike me, they are also perfect, but have made a mistake, all we have to do, is find it.

The Super is on my back, I am sure he knows the Chief is cruising into retirement, as we all do. Solve this case, and he can retire on a high, and it will not do us any harm either. Fail and fifty officers will feel the effects of failure, a negativity they will find very hard to shake off. For their sakes as much as anything, we cannot afford to fail. So Sergeant, get rid of any negativity, and find me something.

Here's an idea, our murder, it does not fit the criteria of the case, yet we know it was the same killer. What made the killer suddenly change from political assassination, to plain murder? That has had me confused all the time. Get the file, and go over it with a fine-tooth comb. Was that their mistake? Why kill, a nobody, what was their reasoning?" Julie asked thoughtfully.

"It definitely does not fit the profile, maybe you have something Ma'am, and I will get to it right away. Perhaps the reason, erm motive, may be the break we are looking for?" Williams asked smiling.

Julie went back to her office, and to the window gazing out over the roof tops; she found a peace and tranquillity that helped her think. The Thames meandering relentlessly yet casually around the artistically carved bends, sculptured into the landscape. Below the hustle and bustle of London's busy streets, silenced by the double-glazed windows, seemed a distant reality. Julie took a deep breath, and turned around she looked around her office at the paper strewn desk, and piles of files in the cupboard to one side.

'I think, therefore I am, and therefore everything around me is my creation. Really, Einstein, is that what you meant? Who but an idiot, would create this mess, and does your theory mean that I am responsible for these deaths, I don't think so, but I am going to find out who is,' Julie thought, bolstering her own spirits and began to read the file uppermost on her desk.

Chapter 15
Pressures

"Ma'am," the officer said entering her office after knocking, "Rodney is back, and he has some news," the officer said.

"Great, send him in please, with Hastings," Julie said smiling, 'Was this; the break she had been waiting for?' she wondered.

"Ma'am, I am sorry to say it isn't good news. We followed up on the lead, that the assassination was politically motivated, and asked the question, who would benefit from the murder. We interviewed his opponent, over the road versus rail link, and it was a dead end.

We interviewed him, but he has covered his tracks very well, and we didn't have any evidence, so could not put pressure on him. We tried for court orders, but again without evidence, they were refused, insufficient grounds. The only thing we did get, was what was not said, his refusal to confirm or deny involvement.

His shifty look at his solicitor when questioned, and that told me that he knows who did, organise it, and it was to remove the competition. Ma'am, if he did not personally organise the hit, one of his supporters did, or office staff, which means that it had to be a senior member of his team.

We left the Chief Inspector in no doubts about our concerns, and he is a good man, he will follow it up, he will not bury it under the carpet, Ma'am," Rodney told her.

"I have the Super on my back to get results, or he will cut my team, and you increase my team by using another force. That will not be well received, when he hears about it. Was the trip a total waste of time? What is your opinion?" Julie asked him.

"No, we gave the local force a tentative lead, which they can build on. We will get something out of it, but later on, when they have been able to get some evidence.

Ma'am, our hands are tied, and now the courts make it impossible to do our job. The team supporting the politician for the road; organised the death of the politician for the underground, it is as plain as the nose on your face, but the judicial system is stopping us from bringing the criminals to justice. How the fuck can we fight the criminals when the judicial system is on their fucking side? Sorry Ma'am, but it is true, the system supposed to support us is not, it is supporting them," Rodney said frustrated.

"I will ignore the outburst, this time, Rodney. There is no need to use that kind of language, I sense your frustration without swearing, and the depth of the frustration, and I agree, but that is the cross we have to bear.

It is local council members and should, quite rightly, be dealt with at a local level. Having said that, it will not do any harm to do a background check on all his staff, will it? Have it on my desk by tomorrow morning.

It was not a waste of time, you have brought back a crack, delve into it, dig deeper, open the hair line crack up into a breach in the wall. I know, and you know, you can do it, so go on, delve," Julie said adding a smile for encouragement.

Julie sat back in her chair after they had gone, and felt the shroud of depression covering her like a dark veil; every avenue was a dead end. What could she show the Super as a positive step, when the judicial system was against her, there had to be a way. If she must, she would fight the judicial system, but that was fraught with danger, she had to be careful, yet forceful, and resourceful. It was time to call in some debts.

The day ended as it had begun with just one fact on the board, Julie looked at it wistfully, as she made her way out of the office.

She looked at her desk the next morning, at the increased pile of files she opened the top one, and it was the background check she had asked for. As she had expected knowing that the criminal records office does not respond in minutes to a request, it was not complete, she smiled; Rodney had taken her at her word, and delivered what he had on the staff at the politician's office. Julie picked up the phone, and dialled a number.

"Sergeant Waters, this is in case you have not guessed, Lieutenant Ashton. How the devil, are you?" Julie asked, bright and cheerful.

"Lieutenant, a very formal greeting for you, you want something," he replied.

"Me? When have I ever wanted something that was not needed, in the line of duty?" Julie asked.

"Oh now let me see, what was the mission when you required transport to Iraq, for a weekend?" he asked her.

"That is not fair, I only wanted a seat on a transport plane that was going there, so that I could ensure my Sergeant was doing his duty," Julie said.

"By whom, he was not on official duty that weekend, the army had given him a weekend pass. As I found out, transport of an officer on a private trip to see their boyfriend, aboard a transport plane filled with ammunition, and supplies, is frowned upon. Then there was the," Julie cut him off.

"Don't tell me you hold that against me? What about the time I covered for you, when you were absent without leave; shacked up with that local girl. Wait; just wait a minute, what about when I helped you account for the four cases of ammunition, you lost?" Julie said.

"I did not lose them; I just couldn't remember where I had put them," he argued back.

"You are right, I need your ballistics expertise, how can I fire a point two five bullet at close range, and not leave gunshot residue?" Julie asked him.

"Simple, don't; fire it from a distance, there solved that problem for you, now if you don't mind I am just about to test fire a flint lock I have rebuilt," he told her.

"I presume on the army range, and whilst on duty, I was thinking that I should ask the Colonel about my problem, does he know you are not at your post?" Julie asked him.

"I used to like you, that is, below the belt, even for you," he said as if shocked.

"Jim, I have a major problem, and I can't get to test it myself. I will be honest, I am working on a case, and we know that the killer puts the gun up against the victim's chest, they use a point two five bullet, and there is no sign of a close contact shot. It is impossible, yet that is what happens. Dinner on me, the next time you are in London," Julie offered her friend.

"Some offer that is. You know I avoid that place like the plague. If Manchester is uncivilised then London is barbaric," he said with a laugh.

"OK, at enormous expense, because you are such a nice guy, I will come to you, where is it you are based?" Julie asked him.

"Shall we say this Saturday I am off for the weekend?" He suggested.

"Jim, Jim I am not a fool, I will not commit before I know where you are. I am ashamed of you trying to trick an old and valued friend like that," Julie said smiling she knew he was not in England by his suggestion.

"Try Calcutta, I am here as an adviser on munitions with a small delegation, we are trying to sell our weapons to the Indian army, but I am wondering if it is an excuse to give me typhoid, so that I have to retire?" Jim asked being glib.

"You can't have that long left before you have to retire, and they could not send a better munitions expert," Julie said.

"Blackmail didn't work so now try flattery, what about bribery, oh that didn't work either. You are no-where near here to honour your offer.

A point two five pressed up against the person, and no gunshot residue? Hum, it is intriguing, OK, I will conduct some tests, and it has my interest. What about tearing and burn?" He asked.

"Minimal tearing, no burning, well some trace, but not as much as I would expect to see," Julie told him.

"Hum, a barrier, but what, there has to be something stopping the residue," Jim said thinking.

"Jim, you are a dear, why the hell did I not think about that, you are right, there has to be some form of barrier to stop the residue, oh one more thing, the bullet must be fired with a reduced charge, it enters the chest between the third and fourth rib, and stops in the heart," Julie informed him.

"Is a silencer involved?" Jim asked.

"No, he is sat in a beer garden full of people, and is shot, what do you think, of course there is," Julie said.

"Wow Julie, calm down, that is not like you; do not let this get to you, there is an answer, and I will find it," Jim said feeling her frustration.

"Sorry Jim, it is getting to me; twelve months I have been on this case, and all I can tell you is that the victims were shot with a point two, five bullet," Julie told him.

"What about the gun, anything there?" Jim, asked her.

"No, the bullets are clean, no striations," Julie told him.

"Interesting, I have heard about something, let me try it before I make a fool of myself. No gunshot residue and no striations, interesting, yes, and limited wound depth, hum very interesting," Jim said.

"Jim, before I lose you totally in thought, you have my E-Mail address, time is of the essence, please, and thank you for the ideas you have given me, there is a light at the end of the tunnel. I have heard about sleeves and you just confirmed it for me," Julie said now smiling at the ideas their conversation had triggered, and she hung up.

Julie picked up the background checks again, and looked at them carefully, analysing each one carefully.

She read the files, and then decided to have some lunch, her head bent down her hand to her chin, and her eyes fixed; she made her way to the door oblivious of everyone. Williams came around a corner to join her, and saw a member of the team coming as if to say something.

Williams shook his head at them, "Not when she is like this, she will not hear you, she is lost in thought patterns, something has clicked," Williams told the officer quietly.

Julie stopped half turned, her hands moved as it organising something, and then she half turned again, and made for the door.

Williams followed her out, and into the cafe across the street, she didn't look, yet stopped to allow traffic past before moving off when it was clear. He could only put it down to a sixth sense of special awareness. She sat at a table, and Williams went to the counter ordering pie and chips for them, and a cup of tea, and then joined her at the table.

Julie raised her head, and smiled.

"Ma'am you worry me when you are like this. How did you know it was safe to cross the road?" Williams asked her.

"In a trance like state I may be, and am to a large degree, but I am not out of it. Thank you for

160

stopping Graves, see I saw him, and heard you, but I didn't want to lose the train of thought.

It is possible to shoot a point two, five bullet from a gun with a larger bore, by packing something around the bullet to make it bigger. The bullet is still spinning, created by the wadding touching the sides, but the bullet is clean, no striations because it does not touch the sides.

Usually the packing, can we say, drops off as the bullet flies through the air, it is lighter, and does not have the inertia the bullet has and so falls away. I discounted this, because of it being close contact, where is the wadding? It is not in the wound track, and if as we assume the barrel is in contact with the skin, then it cannot fall to the floor, so where is it?" Julie asked.

"A very good question Ma'am, forensics didn't search the grass, they did look, and try to find any evidence, but she could have pushed the wadding into the ground say, with her foot, and they would not have looked to that degree. Is it worth them going back specifically to look for anything that could be, wadding?" Williams asked her.

"It is, but I think we would have a better chance at Humberside, the same bullet, but now not pressed against the victim, so the wadding could still be in the car. Yet I doubt them missing something like that, but it is worth another look, just to be sure. When loading the gun she would not need to wear gloves if the outer casing was going to fall away. Find that, and we may just get a fingerprint; am I clutching at straws, Sergeant?" Julie asked.

"If you'd asked me that this morning, I would have asked you, what straws?" Williams asked her smiling.

"Very true Sergeant, we don't have much, but a lot more than we had this morning," Julie said with irony in her voice, "And yet we still have nothing, we are no closer to catching them than we were twelve months ago. It won't surprise me if they close the investigation, and it is clocked up as the one that got away," Julie added ruefully.

"Ma'am, perhaps the Super may reduce the team, we do have a lot of foot soldiers, and they have scanned miles of CCTV footage, and reams of reports and statements, which has yielded little, or nothing. May I suggest you accept the reduction, but keep the erm, more experienced, erm, officers? I don't mean to be disrespectful of the bulk of our team; they have all worked very hard, and diligently, but say a small unit, erm twelve of us, each dedicated to one aspect, may prove more effective. I have wondered if we are being too diverse, looking at every angle in hope, a more focused approach, may work," Williams suggested.

"Interesting, you and me here collating the evidence, clues, Rodney and Hastings working on the Humberside investigation, Jones and Evans, no, you and me working the ballistics, Jones and Evans are more adept at collating. Mayberry and Adams working the CCTV, without distractions, and four others, would work," Julie said deep in thought about the idea.

"Yes Ma'am and I would suggest Andrews and erm, let me see, of course obviously Cusack, his mastery of languages for the international aspect.

What about Cuthbert, he is in with the judges for warrants. He wanted to be a solicitor, you know Ma'am, but failed to get in a University, and chose the police as an alternative, he is very astute, and set to be a highflyer, but who to partner him? Susan Ashburn, yes, she is also well up in the legalities, her dad is a judge. Nepotism has its uses," Williams said and smiled.

"You are not suggesting that she go to her dad, and ask for a warrant, without just cause, are you Sergeant?" Julie asked him in a light-hearted way.

"Ma'am, would I do something like that?" Williams responded shocked.

"I know you too well Sergeant, yes you would do," Julie said and laughed with him, "I think I can argue my case tomorrow, when the Super will come to close us down. He wanted results, and we have none to show him, but to avoid failure, I can suggest reducing the task force as we have just agreed, thank you Sergeant. I knew there was a reason to keep you on the team," Julie said mocking him, and laughing with him, then she added more solemnly, "I think, well it is stronger than think, he wants rid of me.

My dad was an inspector with Manchester police, and our old Chief was his Sergeant. I have known him since I was a child. He would never and I did not want him to, help me. I am an independent sod, but recently he has covered for me like the fight we were in, when I broke all those bones," Julie added.

"Ma'am, I would argue they were justified, six against two, you did as you needed to, and I would argue that all day long. Just another thought Ma'am,

163

can I suggest, you suggest to him, the reduction, before he closes us down, beat him to the base line. I believe it will throw him off guard as it were, and catch him unawares, erm, taking the wind out of his sails?" Williams asked.

"You stopped, have you run out of metaphors?" Julie asked light heartedly.

"Yes Ma'am," Williams said smiling at her.

"Come on, let's go back to the office, we have some organising to do," Julie said getting up, and putting her coat on.

They went back to the office, and Julie called each member of her chosen team into her office, and spoke to them. She told them not to say a word till it was out in the open, and that she was reducing the team not because the others were not capable, but to give the team more time, rather than close the investigation down.

She also told them that they were in danger of being transferred from the case.

Julie ran some figures, and case scenarios to enhance her case for the reduced team, rather than closing the team down, ready for her meeting the next day. She left her office, and met up with Williams in the corridor.

"Come on let's go home, we have done everything we can today, and we have a problematic day tomorrow," Julie said.

As usual Williams drove Julie home, and then went home for a well-earned rest, or so he thought.

"To whom are you married, Dan, me or the police force? I see you late at night, and then before I get up you have left for work, and that is seven days a week. Isn't it about time you threw in the towel on this case, before I throw it in with you? I love you very much, but I am a police widow. I have a daughter who now asks who that big man is that comes at night, she sees so little of you," his wife berated him.

Dan approached his wife his arms outstretched to wrap her in them.

"Don't come near me, you know I just melt when you wrap those warm, strong arms around me. I am angry, and I want to stay angry. How much longer will you spend more time with that Julie person, than me?" she demanded.

"Alex, you know there is no-one else, and you also know I am not a quitter. Julie is a very warm and good partner, she saved my life as you know, but she is my boss, and we will catch this killer, but how long it will take, I don't know. Don't be angry, tell you what how about if I put in for a week's leave, and we go away, the four of us, on holiday? Samantha, and Tom have half term coming up, book a holiday for that week, and we will spend all week together," Dan pleaded.

"So you will not ask for a transfer, then there is a blanket and pillows on the settee. Until you are free to spend time with me, and your children, let's face it, it is only six hours every day that I get to see you and then you are asleep," Alex shouted angrily.

Dan stripped to his underwear, and covered himself with the blanket, and lay down. He had to admit that this case had taken over his life, but he was not about to quit. Then again he had never seen his wife so angry. It was a very troubled night, and sleep evaded him for the most part.

Chapter 16
Decisions

Williams picked Julie up as usual at eight o'clock, his eyes sunken and dark from lack of sleep.

"Morning Sergeant, what is troubling you?" Julie asked him.

"Nothing Ma'am, I just didn't sleep too well last night," he said.

"I see; I am astute as you know all too well, and have a sixth sense which tells me all, is not well, at home. We have been working long hours to get a result, but we cannot neglect our home life.

I do not have one, being single, but you have to attend to your wife and children. I will have you transferred out of my team if I see you after four o'clock this afternoon, and or on Saturday and Sunday. The alternative is that I kick you up the backside all the way from the station to your house, and that will be painful. Do not try and hide from me, I am too in tune with your feelings. Dan do not go the way of many, and lose the love of your life, I have seen it too many times.

The criminals will still be there tomorrow, your wife may not be. There is a florist's shop on the way, get her some flowers, and take them home with you, that is an order," Julie said staring straight ahead as they drove to the station.

"Yes Ma'am, I should have known better than to try and hide something from you," Williams said.

They parked the car, and Julie got out as did Williams.

"Where do you think you are going? I gave you an order, now go, and I will require you this afternoon, be in my office at sixteen hundred hours," Julie said officiously.

"Yes, Ma'am," Williams said.

"Morning everyone, gather around for the briefing," Julie said entering their offices, "Right, the situation is that I have a strong feeling we are going to be closed down. I will not allow all your efforts to go to waste, but it will mean changes.

I am going to suggest to the Super who I am sure will turn up today that we have a reduced team, so that we can continue, and not waste your efforts. This will mean that most of you will be returned to your stations, and previous jobs.

If we crack the case, and make an arrest, it will not be because of a dozen or so brilliant officers. It will be because of the work fifty officers have put into this case, and the hours spent starring at screens, and delving into reports and statements, without whose help, we would not succeed. It is with a heavy heart that I have had to make this decision.

I hate to lose so many hard working, and diligent officers, and it is for them that we will crack the case, in their honour.

I am proud to have known you all, and worked with you, I could not have asked for a better team, thank you.

I have a list of the officers I want to keep, they have specific skills I will need, but until it has been agreed with the Super, I cannot tell you all, but I am sure that by tonight it will be good bye to most, if not all of you, and thank you for the work you have done," Julie said, and walked to her office.

Some said it was with a tear in her eye, but she refutes it adamantly.

Julie was right; it was as the clock struck ten o'clock that the Super made his appearance. He made straight for her office, and some said stormed in.

"Morning Sir, I have been thinking hard about the situation, and feel that as a leader it is my duty to suggest that we reduce the team. All of the groundwork, the scrutinising of CCTV footage, and documents, checking the statements and reports, has been done diligently, and with extreme care. I believe everything we could learn from these elements has been learned, and I believe it is the right time to select a team to work on a specific task, to be focused, on one particular element of the case, and rip it apart, dissect it microscopically. I am therefore going to ask for twelve officers to be my new team, just twelve dedicated and effective officers. I feel sure you will see the sense of this adjustment to my team, and the financial savings of working with a reduced team can bring," Julie said before he managed to comment.

"Have you been up all night practicing that speech Inspector, in an effort to dissuade me from my reason, to catch me off guard? Inspector you do not get to be a Superintendent, by being easily put off from your task. That said, there is still an element of the chief super, and his aides that want you to continue, and you have offered a very nice compromise, but I want you off the case for the same reason they, want you to stay, your cavalier attitude, and disrespect for your superiors. They feel that bending the rules is the way to crack this case; I am a stickler for the rules. This inevitably puts me in an awkward position, a dilemma. I have my own compromise, you have six months with a reduced team to make an arrest, or you resign," he told her.

"Six months, OK Sir, but I want to select my own team. I want twelve specific officers to work with me, including me. I also want access to extra officers, if and when needed," Julie said.

"Don't push it Inspector, a request for extra officers every week will not be tolerated," he said bluntly.

"I do not anticipate that happening, but with a strong lead I will need perhaps surveillance officers, forensic officers, which I could do with right now.

It has come to my attention that the bullet was fired from a gun of a larger calibre, which is why there are no striations, a point two, five bullet fired from a forty five gun seems impossible, but padded out it is possible, and the padding will fall away leaving a bullet without striations. I need to test my theory, and prove it. We have questions, and the more I can answer the better our chances are of finding the killer," Julie said.

"That is ridiculous Inspector; you cannot fire a bullet from a gun it was not designed to be fired from, a point two five bullet fired from a forty-five, impossible. Now I know why you have failed with such ludicrous ideas," he said in temper.

"May I suggest that you check my army record with regard to ballistics, as a lieutenant with ballistic expertise? You won't like my other idea either; it isn't a female we are looking for, but a male. At this point I suggest you leave, or sack me, I have a lot of work to do. I do not wish to disrespect you, but I am going to find this killer, and of that point, I have never been more sure, and when I do, I will ram it right," Julie said, and thought better of it.

"You tread dangerously close to insubordination Inspector. Six months, and then I will have the pleasure of accepting your warrant card," he almost shouted in temper and walked out slamming the door behind him.

Julie smiled, she didn't like him, this did not change the fact that she had made a challenge, and it had been accepted, putting her on the spot. She now was committed to arresting the killer within six months, or hand in her resignation. She banged her fist on the desk aggravated by her silly actions, but he rubbed her up the wrong way, with his arrogant attitude.

Julie walked out of her office, and called the people together.

"Everyone is to report to their stations tomorrow for duty, apart from, Rodney, Hastings, Mayberry, Jones, Evans, Williams, Cusack, Adams, Cuthbert, Andrews and Ashburn, I will lead the team, with Williams.

I again want to thank you all for your valiant efforts, and ask that you put your work in order, tidy up, and then go home, ready to begin back at your stations tomorrow morning, thank you.

My new team, my office please, and bring chairs with you" Julie said and went to her office, listening to their unhappy chatter at being disbanded.

They gathered in her office, and sat in a semicircle around her, she couldn't decide if they were angry faces or aggrieved faces that looked at her.

"We have worked together now for twelve months, and got to know each other, you know me as being unorthodox, and a bit of a cavalier, I make no excuses; that is me.

To achieve our goal we must be focused, which is why I chose you, Rodney and Hastings you will focus on the Humberside killing. I want every scrap of evidence that comes out of that office. I am not seconding you to Humberside, but I want you so involved, you may feel that I have.

Adams and Mayberry, you are to take charge of the CCTV footage and statements, don't get bogged down in the volume, be selective.

Cuthbert and Ashburn, you are to be my legal team, you get any warrants we need, sleep with the judge if you have to, no I don't mean that, but you know what I do mean. I want the warrants on my desk before I ask for them, and help Evans and Jones, collating.

Cusack and Andrews, keep me abreast of the international scene, I want any reports, evidence translated, and on my desk as they come in.

Williams and I will orchestrate, interview, deal with ballistics, and brew the tea, we are a solid team, if you are clear of work, find someone who is not, and help them.

I do not think we will be left here, I am sure they will find some dark recess to hide us in, ignore it, focus, and find the killer," Julie told them.

"Ma'am, is it true that you have put your job on the line?" Jones asked.

"When I took this case, I knew then it was, so that has not changed," Julie told them.

"Sorry Ma'am, but I have to ask; the Super does have a rather loud voice. I believe we have just six months to find them, and make an arrest, is it possible?" Evans asked.

Julie smiled at them, "Really, did you, or were you, naive enough to think, it was open ended? There is always a time limit; it is down to the powers that be to decide what it is, not us. Now are we going to mope around, or catch a killer?" Julie asked them.

They all stood up, and went to their respective workstations, and began the job of sorting out what they thought was relevant, and of use to them, and putting it to one side for assessment.

Julie knew that her outspoken approach would land her in trouble someday, and that even though her chief inspector had told her in the past to speak her mind, perhaps it was not the best idea to take him at his word, especially with the super. She knew the super had opposed her appointment as Inspector, and that was because of her outspoken approach, and past incidents.

It happened in Iraq initially, when she told her lieutenant, his son, that he was mad, and out to get the patrol killed. A captain was also close by in charge of the whole operation, and he heard the rather loud disagreement, and approached them.

172

Julie had her say after the lieutenant, and the Captain sided with her opinion. Perhaps when she said that he was a college kid without experience, albeit true, was not the right thing to say, and cost him the promotion he wanted. Recently she had again been outspoken.

'*If only I could learn to keep my council, my mouth closed, I may have been a chief Inspector by now,*' she thought and giggled, '*as if.*'

Chapter 17
Fresh Start

Williams arrived as she had said, and now he was smiling, only to find the place in a mess, mayhem seemed to have descended.

"Don't you dare touch those; they have been set in order, take those boxes," Jones was shouting, "Dan, a little help please? We have spent the last hour organising the boxes and papers, and these removal men are just dumping files into any box. We have to be out by this evening, but I do not want to spend a week having to check the files all over again, just because they want us out."

"What is in these boxes?" Dan asked.

"Nothing, we don't need them," Jones replied.

"You," Dan said pointing to a removal man, "These boxes are ready to go, do not hamper my detectives work, they will tell you which boxes to take, and where," Williams told him.

"They are all to go with us, but I have put a big red cross on the boxes I need, the current ones, relevant to the case. I just hope the dark recess they are putting us in, isn't too small," Jones joked, looking at all the boxes stacked up.

"Good afternoon Ma'am," Williams said.

Julie looked at him through half closed eyes, "It is not; the Super has gone out of his way to find the most unhelpful, ignorant, louts he could do, to move us, of that I am sure," Julie said angrily.

"Would you like me to go and come back, my wife sends her thanks to you, she knew it was you who sent me home, with the flowers, and now you regret it, understandably," Williams said.

"Do not move, I need a barrier between me and these monsters, I am liable to hit one or more of them," Julie said.

"You know, moving, is the third most stressful thing there is, even moving office. Julie, as a friend; take a break, let me handle the move. Do you know where we are going?" Williams asked her.

"The basement, he seems to think I spend all my time starring out of the window," Julie told him angrily.

"I have noticed," Williams began, until he saw the wide eyed stare she was giving him, "That your best ideas come, after standing by the window, as if it gives you inspiration, Ma'am," he said quickly, and smiled at her.

"OK, thank you, I needed that," Julie said, and took a deep breath, "I have been warned often enough that my attitude will get me into trouble, and it has. Sorry about the situation we find ourselves in, blame me," Julie said relaxing a bit.

"It occurs to me that the team are very busy ensuring they have the files they need separated. What I wonder is if they will be, when down in the basement?" Williams asked with a smile.

"Oh my god, what am I thinking? Jones, Atherton, Mayberry, Cuthbert; get down into the basement now, and watch these morons," Julie shouted running into the main office.

"It would appear luck is on your side, there isn't a moron in sight," Williams said, smiling at her expression.

"For now, like I said, stand by my side to protect them from me. I am ready to burst, and that is not good," Julie said laughing with him, at the escape.

"Ma'am, I have cleared all my boxes and papers would you like me to go down, and begin organising?" Jones asked her.

"We will, I have yet to see this cubby hole we have been given. I envisage sitting on boxes, and using boxes for a desk," Julie said sullenly.

"I will lodge a complaint, if that is the case, Ma'am," Williams said.

"Don't that is my trait, you are chief inspector material if ever I saw it, don't bugger things up like I have, and you Jones, early days yet, but you have it in you, learn how to be diplomatic, I never did," Julie said making light of her situation.

The basement was better than Julie had expected, there were four rooms, a main room where the eleven detectives worked, and an office for her, with two storerooms for all the boxes. It was well lit, and warm, but lacked windows. Julie stood stock still, and just gazed at the growing pile of boxes in the centre of the room.

"It isn't as bad as it looks Ma'am, we are sorting the ones with the red crosses on, and putting the others in the storeroom, after noting on the box what is inside, generally," Evans said cheerfully enough.

"By generally, you mean?" Julie asked.

"Statements, evidence, CCTV footage, sorry it is just a generalisation. We are keen to get to work, and catch the killer, rather than sort boxes out," Evans told her.

"OK, that will have to do, Sergeant, see if you can acquire a white board, for me? Who you steal it from, or how you get it, I do not care, but I need one?" Julie asked him.

It was eight o'clock at night before they were settled in, and ready to begin work.

"Gather round please, it is late, so nine o'clock tomorrow morning, we have had the briefing, and nothing new will turn up before then, so, let us see what we can find out tomorrow.

The white board will be up, and as the clues come in they can go on the board. Watch it carefully for anything you can follow up on. Anyone's ideas or clues can be enhanced by a different person. We are one, one unit dedicated to finding this killer, work as a unit, not individually. I have faith in you; have faith in yourself, and your colleagues. We can do this," Julie said encouraging them.

Williams took Julie home, and she said a weary goodnight and went inside, she flopped on the settee and fell fast asleep.

The banging on her door wakened her; she got up and answered it.

"Ma'am, I am sorry to disturb you, but I thought you would want to know immediately that there has been another shooting. I couldn't sleep so I went back to the office, and because of us asking about any murders with this M O, Manchester made contact," Jones said heatedly.

"I am half asleep, but you did right. What time is it?" Julie asked.

"Three in the morning, Ma'am," he told her.

"You mean there are two, three o'clocks in every day; what will they think of next?" Julie asked laughing.

"I afraid there are, Ma'am," Jones said laughing with her.

"Come in, I need a shower, put the kettle on, in there, and make a brew for us, to waken me up fully. We won't call the others in just yet, and whilst we are drinking your excellent brew, you can tell me all about this new case," Julie said, and went upstairs to shower.

Julie came back down showered and changed, and went into the kitchen to join Jones, and she smiled at the cup of steaming tea on the side.

"Jones, point one you are in trouble. We have been given the shitty end of the stick, with regard to the lack of facilities, we can make up for that with skill and expertise, but for it to be at its peak, we need sleep, and I am very annoyed at you for not realising this. You cannot work a twenty-four-hour shift, and be at your peak, having said that. I want to thank you, for being there to receive the information, and for your dedication to the case. You are right; I do need to be informed as soon as possible, so that I can act quickly. How do you feel about a trip to Manchester, like now?" Julie asked him.

"It will not cause me any problems at all, Ma'am," Jones said eagerly.

"Good, drink your tea, and I will drive, you can sleep, leaving now we should arrive by eight o'clock, the roads will be clear," Julie said.

Julie's estimate was not far off, they arrived in the middle of the rush hour, and she parked in the car park at the main police station in Manchester.

"Morning Sergeant," Julie said cheerfully.

"Jules," he replied with a certain amount of shock in his voice.

"Jules, really Sergeant, don't you have any respect for an Inspector?" Julie asked light heartedly.

"I had heard they were desperate for inspectors in London," he replied and laughed.

"Robert, it is good to see you again. They are missing a good Inspector here, what is holding them back from offering you the job?" Julie asked.

"They are afraid I would show them up, that is my excuse," he replied.

"Jones, Sergeant Robert Manns, I would hate to say he taught me all I know, but I learned a lot, working with him," Julie introduced them, "Robert, I am here about the murder, it has a lot of similarities to the case I am leading a team on. An Inspector Roberts I believe is in charge, is he in yet?" Julie asked.

"He wasn't, but that is Inspector Roberts just entering now. Can I ask why you are interested?" he asked.

"Robert really, you just did. OK, I have an unsolved case, and your case is identical. I wish to compare notes, and yes it is worth the drive from London to here. What about lunch, can I buy you lunch, to catch up on old times?" Julie asked.

"I see you are prone to the same slip you just did, and yes, as long as you are buying, it is your turn, if you remember?" Robert asked.

"You call a bacon sandwich, lunch?" Julie asked.

"On a sergeants salary, it is," he said and laughed, "Inspector may I introduce Inspector Ashton, she has driven up from London, just to speak with you, Sir," Robert said by way of introduction.

"Inspector Ashton, pleased to meet you, believe it or not I have heard quite a bit about you, all good, I must say," he said holding out his hand to her.

"Morning, with me is my colleague PC Jones; I am here because I believe your murder is linked to my murder. Can we discuss it in your office please?" Julie asked.

"Indeed yes, this way," he said and led them to his office, and offered them a chair each.

"I didn't want to say too much in reception for obvious reasons. I have been tasked with finding a killer with exceptional abilities. My team consists of twelve officers, and we have been hunting the killer for twelve months, without a decent lead. All we know is they use a point two, five bullet, with no striations, and the same M, O, was used in Humberside, Seven Oaks, Hamburg, and Paris. That is not strictly correct Hamburg was a sniper shot as was Paris, but in every case a point two five bullet was used and a blonde female was seen, and she was elegant, but looked odd.

Please tell me you have something to help me?" Julie asked him.

"Ha, I wish; last night, at eight pm the local Labour council member was shot dead. I do not have the autopsy report as yet, but I was called to the scene, and it was a long range shot with a point two, five bullet from my experience at the size of the hole, the autopsy report is, also not in yet.

The only person close by the councillor was an elegant, female, who was sat next to him just prior to the murder, some say she was next to him at the time of the murder; others say she had moved away. He was sat on a park bench, his security were feet away, and saw nothing.

An eye witness saw her sit down, put her arm around him, give him a kiss on the cheek, she, the witness presumed, it was because the woman liked his policies, she got up and walked away, ten minutes later he was due to speak, and they found him dead, shot in the side," he explained.

"Don't tell me, let me guess; the bullet was lodged in his heart either the right or left ventricle, there was minimal tearing and no gunshot residue or burning. Your case is the same as mine, she shot him. Jones, move in close. Watch this, see, she pulls them in close like so, her arm over their shoulders and holds onto them, then she shoots them like so, hidden by her handbag and kisses them, then she gets up and walks away leaving them upright. Ten minutes in a crowded rally is plenty of time to escape, a camel coat, blonde hair, very pretty.

I need to get back to London, but I want to take with me as much evidence as possible, and to be kept informed. From my experience, the more you delve into this case the less you know. As I said twelve months work, and all we know for certain is that the killer uses a point two, five bullet. Yes, I do not know that it is female even, a witness to the Seven Oaks shooting said her hair moved, and he was convinced it was a wig." Julie told him.

"Inspector," he began.

"Julie, please?" Julie asked him.

"Thank you, Julie, I was pleased to see you, but it has been short lived. I thought I had a killer, probably male from a nearby building with a rifle. Little, but I had high hopes that as the investigation progressed I would learn more. Now you tell me everything I know, and am about to find out, will be false?" he asked.

"Unfortunately, yes, which is why, I want to be involved in your initial enquiries. I am building a picture of an illusionist, what we see is not what happens. First of all, my ex Sergeant in the SAS, a bomb disposal and ballistics expert is looking into how you can shoot a person leaving a barrel impression, but no gunshot residue. He is also looking into how to shoot a bullet, a specific distance.

The basic idea is that we reduce the charge, but to be so specific as to stop the bullet in the left or right ventricle, he is working on. Secondly the gun being used may not be a point two, five, but a larger barrel, probably a forty-five, only the bullet is a point two five. This brings me back to the fact that everything we know is wrong, it is just, an illusion.

Imagine it; a middle-aged man walks up to a political figure, what will happen?" Julie asked.

"He will in all probability be stopped," Roberts said.

"Carrying a handbag?" Julie asked.

"Definitely stopped," Robert said.

"Now imagine a middle-aged woman, who is well dressed, elegant and demure, walking up to him?" Julie asked.

"Looked at, but I agree she would in all probability get through unless there was some kind, of alert," he agreed.

"Carrying a handbag?" Julie asked.

"My answer would be the same," He said.

"My theory is that it is a man dressed in drag, with small, but not too small breasts, easily hidden under his male clothes. He is ex-army, probably a sniper, and has got used to killing so much so; that he enjoys it. He likes the power it gives him over life and death; it is the ultimate power, life and death. I have as yet not voiced my opinions, because my Super doesn't like me, and will laugh, I am hoping that you can see it for what it is, a theory, but plausible," Julie said.

"Hum, I must say, I do not like it, but as you say as a theory, it is plausible. Just how big would his breasts have to be, to be able to hide them, and then make a display of them?" He asked.

"It isn't that easy, but with the right bra, you can assist them to look bigger than they really are, by uplifting them, and perhaps some filling, padding. You only need the illusion, so show enough flesh, and allow padding to do the rest. Then as a male you strap them down. I can think of two famous actresses that gave the right impression, one with a suitable bra, the other with strapping, for a film, or films.

The rifling or striations can be removed, rather not made, by using a smaller calibre bullet in a sleeve, the sleeve fits the barrel and does have striations, the bullet is heavier, and therefore has more energy, leaving the sleeve behind, and no striations on the bullet. What has me baffled is the way the killer stops the bullet in a virtually exact place, the charge has to be measured to the gram, and they have to know what it must penetrate, but how?" Julie asked.

"Ma'am a shirt is usually of about the same density say, the difference between silk, cotton and nylon is minimal, in this context, so we can perhaps discount that piece of clothing, in every case the victim was wearing a sports jacket these can vary in thickness, erm, density, but as luck would have it, they all had expensive jackets on, and were of a very similar density.

Could our killer watch her target, to assess what they wore, somewhat like casing a job?" Jones asked.

"A good observation Jones, and probably, correct. The killer will not get the job, and go out and kill the victim, they will make plans, and learn about the habits of their victim, to pick the correct time, and place," Julie said.

"I am off to interview the security team, would you like to come?" Roberts asked them.

They said that they would, and followed him out of his office, and into his car. He drove them to the security firm's offices, and after the introductions they were shown into an empty office, but were quickly joined by a member of the security team on duty at the rally.

"Mister Griffiths, you were on duty at the rally, tell me what you saw prior to the shooting," Roberts asked him.

"Not much really," he began.

"Do they pay you to sleep on the job, just resting your eyes were you, come on man? Did you

184

see that there was a crowd, or did that pass by you, as well?" Julie asked angrily.

"Whoa there, Mrs, I was employed to watch the rally for troublemakers, not some stuck up councillor. He was the one that went behind us," he replied just as angrily.

"How many personnel were on duty that evening, and how many were close by you?" Roberts asked calmly.

"I don't know how many, but where we were there were just the four of us. Jimmy next to me said look at that, and I turned around. She was one fit bitch, I can tell you that. She was tall and so elegant, I couldn't see her face in the semi dark properly, but she had two watermelons, and long, long legs," he said dreaming about her appearance.

"So she did have a face, but these what, one handful or two handfuls were what you noted," Julie asked.

"You just could not miss them, two and a half, if not three handfuls," he replied.

"Just as I thought, put them on display, and males see nothing else. I don't suppose you noticed what shoulder she had her handbag over, did you," Julie asked.

"No, it was red," he said.

"Sorry you didn't see which shoulder it was over, but it was red. How do you know that?" Julie asked.

"It caressed her breast," he drooled.

"So I am facing you, was it caressing this breast?" Julie asked pointing to her left breast.

"No, the other one," he said.

"Interesting, the victim was sat on her right-hand side, so the handbag would be on the wrong side. Did she change the side?" Julie asked.

"I don't know, a squabble erupted, and my attention was drawn to that, but Billy might know, he was coming to relieve Alan, who was due a break," he said.

"So you didn't see her sit down, just approaching the councillor?" Roberts asked.

"Yeah that's right, she looked so wow, I couldn't take my eyes off her," he said.

"Yet you cannot describe her, apart from her breasts, can you?" Julie asked.

"Thank you sir, if you think of anything else get in touch with us, please, no matter how small you may think it is, it may be important to us, to catch this killer," Roberts said.

"There was one thing insignificant really she was like I said wow, but she was also odd, I don't know if that helps, and I can't say how it was just her overall, erm walk, stance, attitude I can't say, but it struck me," he said.

"Actually that is a big help, thank you," Julie said.

He was shown out by Jones, and Julie smiled, and looked at Roberts.

"There we have it again, odd, it is an instinct, they use not sight, and not female. I am convinced that is the reason, a thicker neck, fatter hands, minor details they notice, but do not see, because of her overall appearance, being so elegant, and pretty," Julie said eagerly.

"Or just the fact that she has big boobs," Roberts said ironically.

"No, even the women say the same, with them the focus is not on the size of her breasts, but he creates the illusion by the expensive clothes and aloof approach, distracting them from the flaws, but sixth sense, instinct, notes the flaws, as odd. I also find it interesting that they all say she was pretty, yet they have not seen her face. Elegant, demure come from the stance, but pretty, is usually linked to the face, which they have not seen clearly; that I do find odd," Julie said.

"I was going to say a working theory, but it is more than that, isn't it?" Roberts asked.

"To me yes, I am confident I am right, but I accept that to you and others, it is a working theory," Julie said.

"I accept it as far more than probable, even after that interview, but if you don't mind, can I sit on the fence, for now?" Roberts asked with a smile.

"I don't mind as long as you have no objection to those nasty, sharp spikes sticking up your bum. It will be very uncomfortable, until you side with me. We are hunting a male, who dons a female persona when out killing, it is his camouflage," Julie said factually.

"I must admit I have seen photos of 'Lady Boys," and they are very feminine, in appearance. I would be hard pressed to tell the difference," Roberts said.

"That is a photo, a still; the walk, and the attitude, are the things our witnesses find off, or odd, but cannot put a name to it. One said the gait was more of a marching gait, traits one cannot hide, a long stride, heavy footed. An elegant well educated and trained female, as they pretend to be

187

will put her toe down first, it is less forceful, and roll onto her heel. A man marching tends to put their heel down first, heavily, and roll onto their toes. As a girl, I was eight at the time; my mother decided that ballet was what I needed. She was worried that my climbing trees, and playing rugby, was not what a young girl should be doing.

So Saturday morning I attended Ballet lessons, and Saturday afternoon I would sneak out, and join the lads in a game of rugby. All my dolls are in pristine condition, I never played with them," Julie said, and laughed.

Alan the next person they were about to interview was helping clear up after the rally, and Julie said that she wanted to see the scene of the crime. Because Roberts had only seen it in the dark, he suggested that they do that, and interview Alan at the scene.

Roberts drove them to the park, it was on the outskirts of Manchester, he parked the car, and they walked into the park, Julie as usual noted various things like the entrances, and any other means of exiting the park, like broken fences, and gaps in the bushes lining the sides of the park.

They entered through a tree covered area, and into the open area where the rally was to take place. It was still littered with discarded papers, and several workers were picking up the discarded papers, others were dismantling the stage.

"Excuse me where can I find Alan Baxter or the person in charge?" Roberts asked a man picking up papers with a grab.

"Erm, I don't know an Alan Baxter, but," he said scanning the area looking for the person in charge, "Him, the tall guy with the suit on by the stage, he is in charge of the clean-up," he told them.

"You don't happen to know his name do you?" Julie asked.

"No, I am a volunteer here," he said.

"Did you see the ankle bracelet, community service, I bet," Julie said as they made their way to the man pointed out.

"No wonder he isn't interested in what is going on," Roberts said.

"Hello, I am Inspector Roberts, this is Inspector Ashton and PC Jones, are you in charge here? We need to speak to Alan Baxter; can you point him out, to us?" Robert asked.

"What do you want miracles? I have over one hundred people here from technicians, volunteers, and employees and you expect me to know everyone's name?" he asked short tempered.

"That's OK," Julie said, and mounted the stage, "Don't unplug that microphone," she said to a technician and picked it up.

"Would everyone stop what you are doing and gather around the stage please, come on that's it. Great, now I am Inspector Julie Ashton and I believe one of the security personnel from last night may have some very important information for us, so would Mr Alan Baxter, please make himself known, to us?" Julie asked them.

"Hey, stop that, you can't do that, we have to have this place cleaned up by this evening, and there is a lot of work to do," The man in charge said.

"If you don't know who it is, then I will find him anyway, I have to. So I suggest that you find

189

him, and fast. I seem to have everyone's attention at the moment, and work has stopped, it can begin again once I am talking to Mr Baxter. A councillor was killed last night, not by Mr Baxter, but we believe he may have information leading to an arrest, and I will do whatever it takes, to catch the killer," Julie told him in no uncertain terms.

"Excuse me, I am Alan Baxter," a man said coming up on stage.

"Thank you Mr Baxter, will you show us where you were when the murder took place; I believe you were coming back from a break?" Julie asked him.

Mr Baxter led Julie, Roberts and Jones to the area he was in last night. It was covered by trees to the side and rear of the stage, about fifty feet from the stage there was a bench, shaded by trees.

I was coming up the path; we had a burger van over there, where we could get a coffee and a burger for our evening meal. I came on duty at nine in the morning, and helped the police search the area to make sure there wasn't any bombs, and the like, and then made sure no-one left one after the search. Some of the lads went for a break at seven O'clock; I was in the second lot at seven thirty, for half an hour.

The councillor was due to speak at eight thirty, and we were all to be on duty at that point in time, it had been rumoured that there was to be trouble. He was proposing something that would alienate a lot of people, prominent people, so there was a heavy security net around him, and the stage.

Jim and Tommy were close by him, about ten feet away, maybe fifteen, and I walked up the path towards them. I saw the woman, she was tall about six feet, long blonde hair, and had expensive looking clothes on, a camel coat, it was chilly and red shoes, stiletto heels, very nice. She was average build, nothing special," Alan was saying.

"Nothing special, that is not what we hear, she had a rather large bosom," Julie said.

"Erm, yes, Ma'am, I didn't want to erm, well you are a lady," he said embarrassed.

"Your considerations have been noted, and I thank you, but even that is important, and I do not embarrass easily. They have been described as watermelons," Julie said.

"Ha, I bet that was Graham, he is obsessed with breasts, sorry, well I would not go that far, but they were big enough to be noticeable, rather put on display. She had a floral dress on, and it was fitted, with a leather belt in red to match her shoes, and handbag," he told them.

"Thank you that is the best description we have been given, you have a good eye," Julie said.

"Tell us what happened, what did you see?" Roberts asked him.

"She was quite a long way ahead of me, and I saw her approach the bench, and bend down to speak to him. Then she sat down next to him a moment later; she had her arm around his shoulders, which I thought odd, and then her hand moved, and she kissed him on the cheek, stood up, and walked away.

I joined the lads, and they told me everything was quiet, so being in charge of this area I sent them to the places I wanted covered, and then went to the councillor to tell him that he was due on stage, and he was dead, shot in the chest. I raised the alarm, and sent Jimmy to go after the woman, but she had disappeared, poof like in a magic trick, it couldn't have been more than five minutes later, but she had gone," he said shocked.

"You didn't happen to notice the colour of her eyes, did you?" Roberts asked.

"Yes, a bright green, like cats eyes, that yellow green, and bright," he said.

"What about her walk, did you notice anything about that?" Roberts asked.

"A long stride and quite quick, like a soldier marching, I put it down to her aloofness, if there is such a word, she was arrogant, determined, erm, self-confident," he told them.

"What about scent?" Julie asked.

"I didn't smell any, but she wasn't that close to me," he replied.

"Thank you, you have been very helpful," Julie told him with a smile.

"Yes, very helpful, if we need to ask you any more questions will you please give PC Jones your address and contact, and here my card, if you think of anything, please don't hesitate to contact me," Roberts said.

Julie looked around generally, and then walked away from the scene, and came back looking all about her. She bent down, and looked under the bench, and then made her way to the stage, and returned.

"Forensics, didn't find anything," Roberts told her.

"I didn't think they would do, nor did I think I would do, but it is habit. I like to get a feel of the scene, and this was perhaps his most audacious murder, so far. Security all around and he walked up to a councillor, and shot him in cold blood, and walked away," Julie said frustrated.

A mobile phone rang, "Yes," Roberts said, "Thank you we are finished here, and on our way back," he said and hung up, "The background check on the victim is in. I asked them to let me know as soon as it was," Roberts said.

"Yes, good, perhaps we can find out why he had to die, and then who orchestrated it, and get the killer that way?" Julie questioned.

They went back to the office, and began to read the report.

Chapter 18
Pictures

"Ma'am, this is very interesting, if I may?" Jones asked.

"Please, give me something; this is just his personal history, but first let me read it, it may help me understand what you have to say.

He was born in Manchester as we knew, and educated here, and went to Oxford University where he joined the Communist party. Realising that he would never become an MP standing as a Communist, he change sides, and joined the Labour party, but was considered by many as a radical," Julie said, and nodded to Jones.

"Thank you Ma'am, it says here that he was proposing, erm, radical changes to the traffic in Greater Manchester, there it is again radical. He was proposing to charge the owners of any vehicle over two thousand CCs' or two litre engines one thousand pounds a year in duty, and to use the money generated to reduce the Council Tax on terraced houses, he accepted that there would be a shortfall, and that would be covered by an increase in the top end Council Tax. He was also going to charge more for the more powerful engines, at a rate of fifty pounds per CC. Taking the most powerful engines, Rolls Royce and Bentley, the owners of these cars would be charged three and a half thousand pounds a year, and that was just to own one.

In my opinion, if I may, that would make a lot of powerful and wealthy people very angry, angry enough to have him killed.

The kicker is that he owns a Rolls Royce, but does not live in the Greater Manchester area; he moved out nine months ago, so it would not affect him, and there is a question mark over his financial dealings. It appears he was being investigated for lining his own packets, shall we say?" Jones asked.

"I knew there was a reason to bring you along, I think you have just found our motive, as you said," Julie said.

"Ma'am, it is the reverse, but isn't it very similar to Humberside? If I remember correctly, the councillor killed there was supporting an underground rail link, but the other councillor, we suspected, wanted a road link, to enhance his bank balance, by twelve million?" Jones asked.

"Circumstantial and supposition, as the judge we asked for a warrant said, but it is all we have, and I am in favour of it. The only problem is that here we have several thousand wealthy suspects; there we had just the one," Julie said ruefully.

"I now understand why after twelve months of investigation you have nothing, female, no, green eyes, no, big bust, no, blonde, no, all false, a close range shot made to look like a long range shot, all of it, every detail, everything is contradictory, all false," Roberts said uneasily.

"Try ballistics, we both know that she was sat next to him, and for a long range shot to kill him it would have had to pass through her, so it wasn't long range, it was close range and she did it, we know this, she had to have killed him. We know it was a gun, a bullet that killed him, but how was it fired?" Julie asked, "Do you mind if I knock a hole in this wall with my head that is what I feel like?" Julie asked.

"Be my guest, I am beginning to feel the same way," Roberts, said.

"Ma'am, can I ask," he began.

"Jones, what have I told you about wasting time asking if you can ask, just ask," Julie said with force, "Sorry, please, ask away," Julie apologised she had been too sharp, unintentionally.

"What are the component parts of a gun?" he asked.

"Pardon, why are you thinking of making one?" Julie asked.

"No, but from what we know it isn't a normal gun, it can't be, so I was thinking, what if he/she just made what they needed, I mean a barrel a trigger, and a bullet what else is needed?" Jones asked.

"By the power vested in me I make you a Sergeant, apart from the fact that I can't, but I will make a report to that effect. Jones is right, we have been bogged down by impossibilities, what if as I have heard, who said it I don't know, but if everything is checked, and does not fit, then it has to be the impossible, no matter how ridiculous, or words to that effect?" Julie asked in a joking way, "What do we need well, as you said a barrel with groves to make the bullet spin, a chamber strong enough to contain the explosion, but that can be part of the barrel, again as you said a trigger mechanism, sights, no, she puts the gun barrel against his chest, she will not need sights, erm, a firing pin. Breaking it down to the most basic parts of a gun that is all that is needed," Julie said going into a trance as she thought about what a means of firing a bullet consisted of.

"How can we find out if it will work?" Jones asked.

"Simple," Julie said and picked up her phone, "Sergeant, my good and dear friend, I need you to make me something," Julie said, "That was not bullshit, and you know it, and yes I need a favour. How is the weather in India, hot and sweaty I bet? Do you fancy a spell in good old England, the weather here is beautiful?" she asked, and waited for his comments, "No, no, no, it isn't cold, it is above zero, which is warm for this time of year. OK, I will be honest, any luck with the gunshot residue test, only you see the killer has a handbag, and they would be seen putting their hand inside, and pulling the trigger. I originally thought that they had it behind the handbag, in their waist band say, and pulled it up to shoot their victim, but my very clever PC, suggested that it was the most basic gun, with silencer. Can you make me one?" Julie asked.

"Well?" Roberts asked when she hung up.

"He is stuck there unable to leave, but did suggest a friend. The only problem is that he is shall we say not, erm, registered, and will not speak to the police, in case it lands him in trouble. So I am going to have to find a roundabout way, to get what I want," Julie said thoughtfully.

"Ma'am, aren't the rifling just to make it fly straight, with close contact, are they necessary?" Jones asked.

"Yet another good point I am slipping, obviously the old flint lock didn't have rifling, they had a smooth bore barrel, good at close range, but useless over any sort of distance. To be accurate you would need to be within twenty yards of the person you were about to kill. This person is resting the barrel against the victim, so a tube capable of containing the explosion is all that is needed, and a means to fire the bullet," Julie said thoughtfully at first, and then excitedly.

"Ma'am, what have I just done or said, to make you so excited?" Jones asked.

"We have motive now, they are to get something, money, either to save it or make it, so money, is the motive, or power. We have opportunity, created, in most cases, but even so it is there, and now Jones, we have the means, all three requirements. I need an engineering workshop, is there one close by?" Julie asked Roberts.

"I can find one, do you need anything else?" Roberts asked.

"Yes, bullets," Julie said.

"They might be a bit difficult; do you have firearms training for the police?" Roberts asked.

"No, but I was a sniper with the SAS for two months, so I am more than qualified," Julie said.

"You need to be qualified with the police, before I can get you any bullets, I am not, so I can't help you there," Roberts said.

"Isn't there a gun club near here, they will have some," Julie said raising her eyebrows, and smiling at him.

Roberts arranged for her to go to an engineering workshop with a local officer, whilst he made noises at a higher level, and arranged for her to visit the gun club, his Chief Inspector was a member of, and Jones had a break.

Julie knew what she needed, she was shown to the General Manager of the engineering firm, and began to explain what it was she wanted, much to his surprise.

"You want, let me get this straight, you want a short length of metal tubing, a rod of iron, and a nail, oh I almost forget a spring. Can I ask what it is you are making?" he asked.

"A gun, of course," Julie said, as if were a normal request.

"My dear, far be it from me to question your erm, abilities and reasons, but you can't make a gun from those items, apart from it being illegal," he said patronising her.

"My dear, I am an Inspector with London Met, and I am fully aware of the legalities with regard to weapons, and not just guns. I am also an ex-member of the British Army, and an expert shot, having trained as a sniper, for the SAS.

A gun is a very simple piece of machinery; it is a barrel which fires a projectile an unspecified distance. The refinements dictate the distance, and effectiveness of the projectile, which is not a requirement. I am about to make the most basic gun there is, a barrel, a firing pin, and a means to make the pin strike the bullet. Now my dear, are you going to assist the police in their endeavours to catch a murderer, or not?" Julie asked him making sure he knew she did not like being patronised.

"Erm, oh, sorry, of course, this way," he said, and led her down into the work area.

"Collins, help the Inspector with whatever she needs. Collins is our works foreman, he will help you Inspector," he said and walked away.

"OK love, what do you want?" Collins asked cheerfully.

"Ee, it's a long time since I heard that expression, by heck," Julie said and laughed, "Sorry, call it my sense of humour, I have been in politically correct London for far too long, call me Julie or love, I don't care.

I am going to make a gun, but a very basic gun; it is part of my enquiry into the murder of the councillor, whether you agree with him or not does not matter. Killing him is illegal, and it is my job is to find out who did it. He was shot, but she didn't use a gun, yet she must have, so I want to make one, one that could have been used," Julie told him.

"I see not a normal sort of request, but let me see what I can offer you. How thick do you want the tube to be?" he asked.

"It needs to be thick enough to contain the explosion, the size of which I do not know yet, I do have someone working on that. Oh, I almost forgot I need something to stop blow back," Julie said adding a smile.

"Look love, you want a tube the thickness you don't know, the length you don't know, and it is for a gun. I have had some odd requests in my time, but nothing as misleading as this, I need your help if I am going to help you," he said.

"Yes, you are, so shall we have a look around the yard, it needs to be steel so that it doesn't shatter, but the thickness, can I say thick, rather than thin, weight isn't a problem," Julie said, and he led her to a pile of steel tubing.

"This is for steam piping, it can take up to one hundred and fifty pounds of steam pressure, is that the sort of thing you need?" he asked.

"I will only know when I put a bullet in, and fire it, but I think it will be strong enough. Can you cut me say five inches off the end," she asked him.

"Five inches off the length, the boss won't be happy when one tube is five inches short, but he said anything you wanted," he said giving her a smile.

"Nice one, now I need a bolt, that needs to slide into the tube, and a spring to hold it back, until it is fired," Julie said.

"How are you going to stop the bullet from falling out, and what will the spring rest on to be a spring?" Collins asked.

"I am losing it; this case has made me stupid, of course, no change it. I want two inches of tubing that fits over that one, and very tight, and then the rod to fit into the larger tube, and spring. No, can you make the larger tube screw onto the smaller one," Julie asked.

"Can I suggest we go to the drawing room, and begin again, perhaps with a drawing of what it is you need? It will make my life a lot easier, and it will get you what you want, a lot quicker," Collins asked her.

"Yes, yes, of course we can, I am sorry, what must you think of me? I am not usually as muddled as this. I know what I want, and it will work, but I need to prove it, if not to myself, but the powers that be," Julie said, and followed him into the drawing room, and to a draftsman.

He drew the item as Julie described it, and made a couple of minor adjustments, and handed her the drawing, which she took to Collins, and he smiled.

"There now that is a lot easier, Andy, cut five inches off this, and one and a half inches off this, Bert put a screw thread on the outside of the five inch piece, and on the inside of the one inch piece, no more than half an inch. Andy, I also want half an inch off this length of rod, and bring them to the canteen. Right love, come on they will cut the pieces whilst I get you a rubber cup, and then whilst we have a coffee I will assemble it for you," Collins told her, and smiled at her.

Julie bent down, and picked up a screw, and looked at it.

"Can you cut it off here say, and weld it onto the rod in the centre," Julie asked him.

"You are having a bad effect on me I missed that, the firings pin, sorry. Alf, take this, and cut the end off say, an eight to a quarter of an inch, no longer, and weld it to the centre of the rod, Andy, has?" he asked.

Quarter of an hour later they were all stood around Julie, and Collins, who were drinking their coffees, eager to know what the hell they were making. Julie took the parts, and assembled them then removed the wider tube, and smiled at them.

"Great the bullet fits into there, and then I screw this part on like so and now when I want to fire it, I bang this hard like so, and bang. That is the theory, it may not work, but I have the means to adjust it, to make it work. I must tell you doing this is dangerous, it may explode, and if it does the person firing it will be badly injured, or killed, but I will do that safely, by remote, until I have what I want. Thank you lads, you have been a great help," Julie said.

"One thing Miss, won't the barrel get hot with the exhaust gasses? How are you going to hold it?" he asked.

"Like I said I have a model, the firing pin may be too short or long, the bullet may not lodge properly there are several things that may go wrong, but at least I have the start. If you want to see the test give me a phone number, and I will let you know where and when I will be testing it," Julie told them.

Julie gave them a smile, and thank you, and left with the officer back to the police station. She had no sooner entered than Jones, came up to her with a sullen look on his face.

"It can't be that bad Jones, we are making progress, slowly I admit, but progress none the less," Julie said upbeat.

"They have found another body Ma'am, this time it is a dump site. The coroner has the body, and is doing the autopsy as we speak; forensics, are at the scene," Jones told her.

"A dump site, our killer does not do that, so why the interest?" Julie asked Jones.

"Close range point two, five bullet, no gunshot residue. The Chief thought it too close to our investigation for us not, to be told," Jones told her.

"Hum, interesting, what about time of death, do we have any idea?" Julie asked.

"No Ma'am, about twelve months ago, the body is badly decomposed," he told her.

"Twelve months ago, where, was it found?" Julie asked.

"In a shed in the park, the council were pulling it down, it hasn't been used in years, and they decided to replace it, or clean up the site," Jones said.

Julie rushed to Robert's office and entered, "Sorry about this, but please keep me informed, I have to go back, they have found another body, with very similar details, but not the same, it confuses me, so I need to see for myself. They were shot around the time of my first victim. Will you cancel my appointment with the gun club? I will have to make other arrangements for testing the gun, it is made," Julie asked him.

"Yes, that isn't a problem, will you keep me informed?" He asked.

"Sure, the body is badly decomposed; we will have a problem identifying the remains. I'm sorry, as I said it confuses me. Why change the MO, or did they? Was this the first one, and they decided to, erm, no. What if they decided that moving the body exposed their actions, and changed that part?" Julie said from the door way thinking hard, and saying little, as she considered the probabilities and possibilities, but courtesy required her to thank him, and say good bye, "Erm, thank you, I am deep in thought, please excuse me, good bye," Julie said, and closed the door she was holding open.

"It does seem to be a case with more questions than answers, good luck Julie, nice to have met you," he said, not expecting a reply as Julie closed the door, and he smiled at her focused attention.

Jones and Julie drove back to the station they were based at, it again took several hours for them to arrive, Jones drove whilst Julie sat back deep in thought. Jones didn't say anything, he focused on the road allowing Julie to consider and concentrate on the crime.

"What are we doing here? Jones, take me to the scene, and then the mortuary, and then we can come here," Julie said abruptly.

"Yes Ma'am, sorry Ma'am," Jones said, as if he should have known where she wanted to be.

They arrived at the scene, it was still cordoned off, and Julie without speaking entered the area whilst Jones showed his card, and introduced Julie, who was already inside the area, concentrating.

"Jones, why dump the body, and why in here? You said it wasn't used. For how long, and did they know it wasn't being used, and why didn't someone notice the smell of a decomposing body?" Julie asked, her eyes looking all around.

There was still a damp patch where the body had lain, as the soft tissue turned to liquid decomposing.

"From the position of the body there was no attempt to hide it, apart from being inside the shed," Julie observed.

"No Ma'am, it was just inside the door, and when the workmen opened the door they found it, just lying there," Jones said.

Julie went outside the shed, and looked around.

"This park is well off the beaten track, there isn't a main road; close by; just the road leading

205

down to it. Hum, I know this area; we have been here before, why?" Julie asked scanning the area for clues.

"Yes Ma'am, twelve months ago, to interview the wife of the first victim, you came with Sergeant Williams. I know this because that is the file I was reading before we left at the Manchester station, his street is down that road and turn left, about a hundred yards and six doors down," Jones informed her.

"You are right Jones, I thought I recognised the houses as we drove in, but couldn't just place it. When we get back I want you to search missing persons for that time, let's hope the coroner can narrow down the possibilities with the sex of the victim, age and hair colour. I do not want to wait for DNA results, I need to know, now," Julie said.

Julie turned, and began to walk back to the car her head moving from side to side as she walked getting every little detail of the area.

"The Mortuary, Ma'am?" Jones asked just to be sure.

"No, the first victims house," Julie said as she got into the car.

"Hello Mrs. Johnson, my apologies for disturbing you, but can you tell me if your husband ever went for a walk and if so, where did he go?" Julie asked.

"Inspector, come in," she invited Julie.

"No, I only want to know the answer to those two questions. Did your husband go for a walk after work, say?" Julie asked.

"Yes, he went down to the park, it is just down there. A mile a day the doctor told him, and it is just

206

a mile from here down to the end of the park and back. I dare say he stopped for a pint at the pub at the far end of the park, by the canal," she told Julie.

"Did he go at the same time every night, or did it vary?" Julie asked.

"It varied, it depended on when he got home, and if he had a new team out at night," she said.

"Thank you, thank you very much that helps me quite a bit, and I am sorry to have disturbed you," Julie said, and turned on her heel back to the car and Jones, who she had told to wait for her.

Chapter 19
Clues and Evidence

"Ma'am was that helpful, I am confused?" Jones asked her in the car.

"Yes, it was, Confucius say, confusion is enemies ally, never admit to being confused, even if you are, pretend you are not.

Why was our first victim killed, confused, there was no motive, so why?" Julie asked him.

"Again I would have to say that I am confused, as to why," Jones said.

"As we all were, there was no motive. Now we use logic, and guess work, what if he went for his walk as usual, he saw nothing, but the killer didn't know this. They made some enquiries found out that he worked with sales teams door to door, they make arrangements for an interview as we know they did, and killed him because they thought he had seen something. Now, we have motive," Julie said excited.

"So Ma'am, they thought he may have seen something, so arranged a meeting, and changed their method erm, yes method, because they thought he saw them moving the body, and changed things so that they didn't have to move the body. A good working theory, Ma'am," Jones said.

"I have to agree, it is just a working theory, but a good one. If only we knew what time he went for a walk on that particular night, we would have a date and time," Julie said pleased with the new clue.

"Jones have you seen an autopsy before?" Julie asked.

"No Ma'am," Jones said.

"Then I suggest you stand by the sink leaning against it. One of three things will happen, you will be sick, hence by the sink, pass out hence leaning against it, or accept that it is a lump of meat, the person, no longer exists. That is how I cope with it, just a lump of meat, beef, pork, chicken, it does not matter, as long as you view it as meat, and not, a person," Julie said with compassion.

"I may become vegetarian after that, Ma'am," Jones said with irony.

Julie giggled and looked at him, "Have compassion for the victim, but don't allow your compassion to cloud the job you have to do. We need to know how the victim died, and when, who they were, helps us, but isn't critical. I have solved murders of Jane and John Does' no name just the evidence of when, and how they were killed, and where also is a big help. We build a mental jigsaw, the pieces come to us in a steady stream, and all we have to do is put them in order. What confused me about this case; was that I did not have all the pieces. One main piece was missing, the motive. Now that I have that, I have three quarters say of the puzzle; all I need now is the, who. By arranging and rearranging the pieces, the picture will become clearer. Even with a full picture I need to frame it, the evidence, before I can present it. A judge will not convict unless we have the picture framed, ah here we are, remember by the sink," Julie told him.

Jones was apprehensive, but followed Julie down the corridor into the autopsy room, where he was violently sick, having rushed to the sink just in time. The smell was nauseating, and that was enough for him to be sick, before he had even accepted the piece of meat on the slab.

"Ah Inspector, good evening I understand you needed the autopsy doing in a hurry?" He asked Julie.

"Yes Doctor, although we didn't know it at the time, we have been hunting the killer of this person for the last twelve months. Please, excuse my friend, he will get used to it," Julie said.

"Good to see you Julie, as usual you have warned a newbie; that is what I like about you. Now we have here a female from the pelvis, age I would be guessing at the moment, but about thirties from the full set of teeth, including the wisdom teeth, and all in good order. The bones have fused in the areas we expect of a person in their thirties. She was brunet I believe, but the lab will confirm that, eye colour no idea, sorry, but from the facial bone structure a well-balanced face," he said.

"You mean pretty, but without actual features you can't say?" Julie asked.

"I am not here to guess, but yes, I believe so. There are no broken bones, from childhood accidents, and because of the degree of decomposition, I cannot say if she was sexually assaulted or had given birth, but there are two rings on her finger, indicating that she was married," he said.

"All good doc, but what killed her?" Julie asked impatiently.

"I thought you had been told that part, ah well, she was shot between the third and fourth rib. The bullet clipped the third rib, and from the position of the bullet, and without the heart tissue to be precise. I would have to guess at it stopping in the heart. That is between you and me. I do not guess, I deal in facts, only," he said smiling at her.

"Your secret is safe, I will not tell anyone, and I think Jones is too far gone to hear anything. What about, I was going to say time of death, perhaps a date may be more appropriate?" Julie asked.

"Yes, it would be, and again I am guessing, over nine months," He said.

"I have a murder some twelve months ago, and I believe she died before that, is that possible?" Julie asked, "And what, or where is that smell coming from, she does not have any flesh on her?" Julie asked.

"I have a female who has just been found, and from the state of decomposition I would say she died a week ago, rather a nasty smell, but I need to find the cause of death, and I will cut her open tomorrow," he told Julie, "And yes it is possible, I will run some tests to see if I can give you a better time line," he added.

"Jones, come on, let's leave the doctor to his smelly mortuary," Julie said.

"A night in the fridge will help, she has just been brought in," the Doctor said with a smile.

Julie and Jones went to their office, although it was by now into the night, she was surprised to see Williams and Evans still there.

"Evening Ma'am, we decided to stay until you arrived so that we could brief you," Williams said with a smile.

"Fool hardy, I could have decided to go straight home, and catch up in the morning," Julie said smiling back, pleased to see them.

"I have worked with you for too long; that is, the last place you are thinking about, right now," Williams said.

"Yes, you are right as usual, you know me far too well Williams, so tell me?" Julie asked entering her office with Williams, Jones and Evans in tow.

"Jones, you go home, it has been a long day, thank you." Julie said feeling for her companion.

"I'd rather stay if I can Ma'am, I am not that tired, and will mean that you don't have to waste time telling me tomorrow, what has happened," he said.

Julie smiled at him, his eyes half closed, and perched herself on the edge of her desk.

"OK, but no earlier than ten o'clock tomorrow morning. First you Sergeant what have you been up to, apart from spending time in the pub and sunbathing in the snow?" Julie asked, adding a smile.

"I am hurt Ma'am, we would not do that," Williams said as if hurt and laughed, "Our killer has been very busy whilst we have been hunting them, here they have been to America, Mexico, South Africa and the Philippines. All with the same MO, it is unmistakable and all political personages, nobody too senior, like a prime minister, but all with monetary erm, and connections. They all either stood to gain or opposed someone who stood to gain substantial sums from government works.

We did get the list of passengers from the airlines looking for a recurring name, but no name was duplicated. We concentrated on flights the week prior to the murders, and it took some time to go through every flight. Then we decided that being direct was perhaps not what he or she would do, so we reversed the search, and got the lists of every flight entering each country again during the week before the shooting. We didn't find a name recurring on any flight. So I am sorry to say we might just as well have spent the time in the pub, Ma'am, for what good it did us," Williams said dejected.

"Not in the least, it tells me that we are looking at this from the wrong angle. Williams, I want you to commit a murder, take tomorrow morning off, and bring me how you are going to do it at one o'clock, and get away with it. We have to start thinking like the murderer.

Evans I want you to get a list of every missing person over the last twelve months, who have as yet, not been found, and compare it to the list of passengers arriving.

Jones, I will tell you in the morning, you are too far gone to remember," Julie said and laughed with Evans and Williams waking him up.

"Oh sorry Ma'am, you were saying?" He asked.

"It is time for the rest of us to go home; I will drive, and drop you off, do not enter this building before ten o'clock tomorrow, do you understand me, or I will boot you all the way back to your bed," Julie said and smiled at his sleep ridden face.

"Yes Ma'am," he said wearily.

"Ma'am what did you find out?" Williams asked.

"I will tell you all tomorrow at ten thirty, to give sleeping beauty time to get here," Julie said laughing.

Again she flopped onto the settee, but did remember to set her phone alarm this time, and fell fast asleep.

Her alarm woke her, and she showered and dressed and had breakfast before setting out for the office, she entered to a sea of eager faces for news from her trip.

"Morning everybody, I will hold a briefing at ten thirty, there isn't a lot to advance our investigation, but we have brought back some good leads we can follow up, and I believe you also have some good leads. Then again you may not know that you have, as yet," Julie said, and went into her office.

She sat at her desk, and shuffled some papers selecting the one she wanted as the phone rang.

"Morning Inspector I won't waste my valuable time coming down to hear that your expenses paid trip was a waste of time, you can tell me that over the phone," The Chief said making a point.

"Good Morning Sir, may I say Manchester hasn't changed one bit since I left. I presume you do not wish to know that, I have found out how he shoots his victims. I just have to test my theory, which is important, because it clears some of the mud clouding the case. At all points we were left with questions, which only led to more uncertainty and questions. As I bring clarity to these uncertainties, we can see more clearly the way to go.

I now know the motive for our first victim's death; I know exactly how the gun is used, what type of gun, which means I can begin to build a better picture of our criminal. I have five months left, and with each month I am getting closer and closer, to catching the murderer. At ten thirty I will be briefing my team. Perhaps you would like to, join us?" Julie asked him, upset by his offhand attitude.

At ten twenty five Julie saw the Chief going past her office into the main area, where she was to brief her team, she got up and followed him in.

"We have on the loose, a killer; they are very clever, and we have accepted for a long time that they are, an illusionist. Illusions are tricks, and with every trick there is a plausible explanation. Our time has not been wasted, we have been deciphering, the trick.

In Manchester I had a brain wave, from what someone told me, and then Jones added to it, and it became clearer. This team is a gun; it does not look anything like a gun, but trust me, it is, see. A barrel, a firing pin, and a trigger mechanism, and that is all a gun is, in its most basic sense.

We were clouded by the idea of a sophisticated weapon, it is not. You put the bullet in here, and bang the gun down, pushing the pin onto the bullet and firing it, it will fit very snugly in the bottom of a handbag and by leaning in close to the victim you can fire it by squeezing the gun between you and the victim, like so," Julie said holding up the gun and pushing the two ends together.

"Does it work Ma'am?" Evans asked.

"This may not, it is just my first attempt, but the idea and drawings are sound, so once I have the strength of the barrel sorted, and the size of bullet, it will work. Remember it is close contact, our killer does not need sights, and they kill with one bullet, it does not need a magazine.

The shoulder bag has had me confused for some time, as to why she needed it, now it becomes clear. Once I have ensured the gun is safe, I will pull a ballistics dummy into me, and shoot it to prove my point.

Last night when we arrived, we went straight to the scene, and then to the mortuary. At the scene I discovered why our first victim had been shot, our killer thought our victim saw the shooting, or the body being disposed of, and could not take any chances, the motive at long last, which again has had me confused.

The mortuary confirmed that they were killed by our killer, so first job a name, here are the victims details as far as we can tell. Search all missing persons from the week or two weeks prior to our first victim, for a female, five feet six inches, brunet, and married, about thirty something, and giving what we already know, political association.

The easiest way to get a false passport is to use one that is legal, so I have asked Williams to search missing persons, and the arrival of them, at the airports of the countries where an assassination has taken place. It is easy to fly to Paris, and then the destination, so don't bother with flights leaving here; check the countries' arrivals, instead.

Finally the killer is male, and is made to look female, we got a very good description from a security person at the rally, where the Manchester victim was shot, including eyes like a cats, green with yellow, contact lenses, a wig, a long stride, marching; all add up to a military person, and male.

The net is currently so wide we could only catch a whale, we need to close the net so that we can catch a mackerel.

Good work people, a clue lost or avenue closed down, is not lost, it brings our focus closer and closer to where we need to be. Do not think that just because a line to follow goes nowhere, and we have wasted time, we have not. We have just exhausted that line of enquiry, leaving fewer lines to follow, and one will lead us to our killer, rest assured, it will," Julie told them, boosting their egos and confidence.

Julie left them on a high, and starting the lengthy job of getting a list of every missing person over the last twelve months that had as yet not been found. She knew it would be a mammoth task, cross checking them with the arrivals at the airports in each country a killing took place.

"Winston Churchill would have been proud of that speech Inspector, but it does not help. Perhaps you are more suited to politics than policing. I came down here to hear about the evidence and clues you brought back from your trip, not some pontificating speech about clues lost, but not wasted, of course they are, and the time, and your time, is running out, Inspector," the Chief Super said.

"Permission to speak freely, Sir?" Julie asked.

"Yes," he said slowly unsure if he was about to be abused.

"Then please take your negative attitude out of my area, we have work to do, and I need my team positive. They have a lot of tedious work to do, boring, mind-bendingly boring, and your attitude is not helping, please, go," Julie said bluntly.

"Are you audacious enough to attempt to throw me out of your office, Inspector?" He asked shocked.

"No Sir, I merely suggested that a negative attitude will not help, and seeing as you quite rightly said, 'I am running out of time,' I need my team focused on their job, and not negative about the possible outcomes of their work. It is far from me to even consider throwing a chief Superintendent out of my office; I merely asked that you leave. I am sure you have far more important work to do, than waste your time down here," Julie said.

His look was enough to tell her she had again rubbed salt in old wounds, and her time was limited. He would dearly love to take her warrant card; her mouth again had opened, to help sink her boat.

As he walked out in a temper, Jones knocked on her door, and she told him to come in.

"May I speak with you Ma'am?" Jones asked tentatively seeing the angry look on her face.

"Jones, do not waste my time, just bloody well ask," Julie said abruptly, "Sorry you got me at a bad point, what can I do for you?" she asked him.

"You said you would tell me today how I can help?" He asked.

"Yes, yes, indeed I now need a gun club to test my gun. I want you to find me one. I have to prove, even to myself, it works, it's an odd feeling, and I know it will work, but I have to prove it. I can't explain it any better so do that for me, and thank you for yesterday, it was one hell of a long day," Julie said smiling at him.

Julie went to the outer office, and asked Williams to join her.

"Sergeant, come in and sit down," Julie said pacing up and down behind her desk, "Dan, you know about the animosity between the super and me. I am convinced that I will be leaving; he will find a way to have me moved, unless I make the move.

I want to go, if I have to, on my terms that will be by me selecting my next station, once I have solved this case. We have become friends over the last couple of years, which is why I am telling you this, but what is said in this room, stays in this room.

I am building a good picture of our killer, but it is in my mind, to share it with the others, it is just supposition. I am lacking the proof to put it on the board. Our team will still operate the same, and they will follow the leads, and we will crack the case, but I am going to operate shall we say, independently, using what they find to support my own investigation and to follow up on my ideas.

I will need a wing man, and it is not an order, just a request that you be that person, it will mean working out of the office, and office hours. You need to make sure Alex is OK, with it. So what do you think?" Julie asked him.

"Alex, will agree, she also knows you, and that there will be no improper actions, but I will ask her. Secondly I am surprised that you needed to ask. I do know the problems you have with the Chief Super, and there isn't one member of the team that would not pack up right now and follow you. Pack up here and move the investigation to Manchester and every member of the team would come with you," Williams said.

"That is very loyal of them, and I appreciate their commitment, but the powers that be would not allow it. So it is down to you and me, with their help. Will you help me set up in my house tonight?" Julie asked.

"I can't, Alex has her weekly meeting with the amateur dramatic club, and we would need a babysitter, but we could leave early, and set up," Williams offered.

Julie carried on pacing up and down as they talked; she stopped and banged her fist on the table, and looked Williams in the eye.

"Amateur Dramatics, of course, Widow Twankie, Peter Pan, and all that. Don't you see Dan, males dressed as females, and females dressed as males, who better to advise us on how it is done? I am losing it," Julie said as if the idea was obvious.

"You are not losing it Julie, just under tremendous pressure. I suggest I leave at say two o'clock, and go and buy the items we will need. The chief would object if we took things from here, and he would suspect that we were up to something. Can I also suggest that you include Jones, he is loyal, and you worked well together, in Manchester? He is bright, and thinks outside the box," Williams suggested.

"Yes, a good idea, take him with you this afternoon, and ask him in the car," Julie said, her hand to her chin in thought.

By lunch time Jones had found an arms manufacturer that would allow Julie, to use their test range, and it was only an hour's drive away. Julie took Evans with her, so that Williams and Jones could buy the things they needed, and deliver them to her house.

Julie and Evans entered the factory, and spoke to the receptionist who made a call on the internal phones, and they were shown to the Managing Director's office.

"Afternoon, I am Inspector Julie Ashton, and this is Detective Evans, thank you for allowing us to use your facilities. As I am sure you are aware, this is an ongoing investigation, so I am not allowed to explain fully what we are doing, and why.

There have been several, can we say, murders, and the weapon used is unusual. It isn't a serial killer, but a contract killer, so the murders are not restricted to just this country. I have here what I believe to be the type of weapon used, and I need to test my theory," Julie said placing the barrel on his desk.

"This is very unusual, but may I?" he asked picking it up, and looking at it.

"Please do, I need expert advice, the bullet only travels say six inches, so a full charge of powder is not required, and rifling also is not needed, because of the short distance," Julie said.

"I see, hum, is the barrel length a pre-requisite feature?" he asked.

221

"I believe it is. The barrel is pressed up against the victim like so," Julie said, taking the gun and placing it against her chest, "And then sharp pressure is applied to the other end, causing the firing pin to make contact, and fire the bullet. It is at this point very amateurish and crude, which is why I came to you. It was never intended to be sophisticated, just functional," Julie said.

"Hum, OK, yes we have something to work with. The barrel would be the explosion chamber as well, so the whole of the barrel would need to be tempered steel. This part needs to be tight, to avoid back blast from the explosion, reducing the power of the explosion, and injury to the killer. Hum, very clever, yet as you said, crude. What size of bullet do you want to use?" He asked her.

"A point two, five, with reduced charge say, and I am guessing here, thirty per cent of a normal charge," Julie said.

"Copper jacket for penetration, hum," he said.

"Penetration is not that necessary, as I said six inches is all that is needed, and no mention of a copper jacket is in any report," Julie said.

"May I test this, just to see what happens to make any adjustments needed?" He asked.

"That is what we are here for. I am not sure the barrel will take the charge, it was just a guesstimate, it may blow apart," Julie said.

"Probably not, it is a heavy gauge metal, and with a reduced charge it may hold, but only for one shot. For this to slide there is a small gap that can allow a back blast hot exhaust fumes to come out at the back reducing the power of the explosion, and therefore the distance the bullet will fly. But the

222

main problem is that it could injure the shooter a second degree or third-degree burn, nasty," he said considering what he now held, "Have you considered how it is to be held, this explosion chamber will get very hot?" He asked.

"I have, and that is not a problem the, I am overstepping the mark here, the gun I believe is held in a handbag," Julie said reluctantly.

"A female killer that is interesting, but not unusual, I understand they tend to use poison, rather than a close contact weapon," he said.

"Not all of them, when premeditated it is their most common method, but as we know in a frenzied attack, in rage say, then a knife can be the weapon of choice. Assassins' are usually male, but not all of them," Julie said, trying not to give too much away.

He leaned over to his intercom, and pressed a button, "Tea or coffee?" he asked.

Julie said, "Coffee, please," and Evans also chose coffee.

"Three coffees to the test range please, Angela," he said into the intercom and got up.

Julie and Evans followed him down to the test range, where he asked the tester to set up a test firing position, they stood to one side whilst he fixed the barrel Julie had provided in a clamp, put a three sided screen around it, and fixed a toffee hammer in a spring loaded clamp.

He then clipped a bullet into the barrel and screwed the end on and set the hammer. Once it was all set he walked away a safe distance and pulled a length of string releasing the hammer and bang.

Julie and the others moved forward to see the result.

"OK, Inspector, we have here the back blast," he said indicating the blackened area on the screen, "Someone close to the gun would have got third degree burns from that. The barrel is too weak in structure and as you can see is blown apart allowing most of the power of the shot to escape. But the bullet managed a reasonable three inches from the barrel, and not your kill shot, I am afraid," he told her showing her the result.

"I had half expected that, the barrel was not tempered, and as I said it was more of a design, than the actual gun, but it proved my point all I need to do now is, make it work," Julie said happy that she had proven her point, but as expected it needed refinement.

"Charlie, you saw what it was, can we make it work from that design?" he asked the tester.

"I have shot many ideas to ribbons, literally," he said indicating the barrel ripped apart from the blast, "but this is one idea that can be made to work. Would you like me to make it work?" He asked.

"Yes please, but it has to be as simple a design as that is. Is that possible?" Julie asked.

"You mean just literally, a barrel?" He asked.

"Yes, you see I have proven the principle, but now need to make it actually work, so a tempered barrel to stop it being ripped open, and something to stop the back blast, it does not need to be pretty or a show piece, just effective," Julie said.

"Give me a day, does it have to work by pushing the pin onto the bullet or, wait I have an idea, what if we pushed the bullet onto the pin?" He asked, "My dear this is a challenge I will enjoy, yes, a slide.

The bullet captive and the barrel slides back pushing the bullet onto the pin that way the explosion is contained inside the barrel increasing the power of the explosion," he said excitedly without taking a breath.

"Ha, I have never seen him so excited about a project, it will work, and I can assure you. His brilliance is only surpassed by his conceit; expect to be told several times how brilliant his idea is, tomorrow. He will build it and test fire it, and then show you how it works, and unfortunately why your idea failed, he is not the best diplomat here, but he is the best expert we employ," He said leading them back to his office.

"Thank you very much for your help, I do not care whether it is my idea or his, if it works, as I am sure it will, it is actually our killer's idea, and not mine," Julie said laughing.

"Very true, can we say two o'clock tomorrow afternoon?" he asked, and they said their goodbyes.

Chapter 20
Fact or Fiction

Evans drove them back, and as they passed through a town, Julie told him to stop by a dress shop. She got out, and Evans drove away to park the car.

Julie entered the shop having seen what she hoped was what they needed, a short shoulder bag. Julie went into the shop, and asked to look at it, she hung it over her shoulder, and checked it for height, and then she turned it from say a north south attitude, to an east west one. The shop assistant looked surprised as she turned it, using her left and right shoulder.

"Is the bag to go with an outfit, Madam," she asked.

"No, to kill someone; do you have it in red?" Julie asked, and laughed she had found the ideal bag.

"Yes Madam," she said not appreciating Julie's little joke, 'I'm sorry we don't have it in red that is the last one, it has been very popular," she added.

"I'll take it, thank you," Julie said, and paid for the bag, rang Evans who drove back to the store, and she got in.

"That was quick Ma'am; my wife takes hours choosing the right thing. I was with her once, and she had the shoe assistant pull out a dozen boxes of shoes. She tried them on, and then walked out, none of them were just right, and there's me stood like a prune to one side," Evans told her.

"I have met your wife, she has good taste, last Christmas at the party at Dan's," Julie said.

"Oh yes, you won't tell her, will you, Ma'am?" Evans asked.

Julie smiled at him. "Oh well, you know what we women are like for sticking together," Julie said, and laughed, "No I won't tell her just be grateful it wasn't an underwear shop," Julie said, and laughed.

"Yes, Ma'am," he agreed, and laughed with her.

When they got back Williams walked up to her, and asked if he could have a word, she invited him into her office.

"We have bought all the items, and set them up in your lounge, we had to make space pushing your furniture to the back of the room, I hope you don't mind," he asked.

"Not in the least. You take me home as you usually do at four o'clock, and tell Jones to leave at four thirty. My gun has possibilities, the main tester at the factory said he would have a working gun by tomorrow; we have an appointment at two o'clock. Where are the receipts?" Julie asked, Williams gave them to her, and she paid him back for the items.

Williams was getting up to leave, when Evans burst in excitedly.

"It is usual to knock, Evans," Julie said.

"Yes, sorry Ma'am, I have just heard from Humberside, and they have arrested the councillor, for the murder of the other councillor, arms were twisted, and debts called in, and they got the warrant to seize his laptop, and phone. Sorry for bursting in, but this is a massive lead. May I go with Hastings to inspect his computer? There has to be some sort of lead in his computer or phone, for them to arrest him, and a strong one," Evans said eagerly.

"I will have to ask the Chief Super, for your expenses. Can Humberside send the details?' Julie asked.

"Ma'am with respect, they are not as conversant with the case as we are, and Hastings and I are more efficient than they are with encryption and passwords. We are your IT experts, not them, Ma'am; it's the break we have been looking for. This could lead us right to the killer, you can't say no," he pleaded with her.

Julie knew he was right; Evans and Hastings were very good at computer work. She thought that they may be the best people in the force, where computers were concerned, but her trip, and the earlier one to Humberside. She knew would be used against her by the Chief Super, when push came to shove.

"Evans, it is good news, and as you say probably the break we needed, but they have excellent people up there to work on the computer, and can advise us of its contents. I will ask, but I believe the Chief Super will decline your request, as another wasted trip, thank you Evans, go back, and analyse what they have sent," Julie said formally, ending the interview, but hated herself for accepting the loss of a great opportunity.

"Yes, Ma'am," Evans said disappointed.

Williams stayed behind after he had closed the door, and came back to her desk looking at her, as she screwed her face up hating the position she was in.

"Julie," he said softly, "I have an idea, you may not like it, but it could get Evans and Hastings up to Humberside?" He asked her.

"Sorry Dan, I want to explode, but I am in control. What is your idea?" Julie asked him.

"I know the Chief Constable up there; he is a friend from when I was in the army. My idea is to reverse the request. What if he asked for our help, it would give the Chief Super a chance to hinder us, by taking two of our team off us, but in reality it would put Evans and Hastings right where we want them, and I do not think he will see it that way," Williams suggested.

"If you can pull this off, the beer is on me, for a week. Well what are you standing there for, sort it, Sergeant," Julie said brightening up.

"Yes Ma'am," he replied smiling back at her, "Just one thing it is perhaps better if I don't do this, with you in there," he suggested.

"I see, yes, you are correct, I will check up on things whilst you make the call," Julie said, and got up leaving her office.

It took just quarter of an hour for Williams to leave Julie's office, and join them in the main area, he wasn't smiling, and he had his poker face on. Julie looked at him, but he gave nothing away, so she returned to her office, and began to read the files. An hour passed before the Chief Super entered her office.

"Inspector, I have received a request from Humberside, for two officers specifically Evans and Hastings, apparently they are experts in computers and mobile phones, and Humberside need their expertise to unravel the messages from the suspect, to the alleged killer. You are not making much progress, so I agreed to loan them Evans and Hastings, they leave tomorrow morning, will you tell them?" the Chief Super asked her.

"Oh, I do need them, but if it is an order then, I don't have any choice, do I?" Julie asked him, wanting to smile.

"No, you do not," he replied, and left her.

Julie waited for a couple of minutes, and then said in a loud voice, "Yes," and left her office.

"Evans, Hastings, sorry about this, but I have just been told that Humberside have requested that you assist them in their enquiries. In particular with the computer and mobile phone they seized investigating the murder, up there. You will be on the ten hundred hours train from Kings Cross station, and you will be met at the station, and taken to the police station where the computer is being analysed. We will miss you, but hopefully you will not be away, too long," Julie said formally, for appearances sake, but she saw the grin on Evans face, he knew something had happened, which was not quite, above board.

At four o'clock Julie asked Williams to take her home, and told the others not to stay too long. They were now at a point where everything could wait till tomorrow, later there may be times when late nights are required, so she advised them to take advantage of the lull.

At home Williams and Julie looked at the set up, and decided it was just about right. Julie picked up the pen, and on the first white board she began to list what they believed was true, male in drag, gun in handbag, red accessories, wig blonde.

"Come on Williams, we know more than this, surely?" Julie asked.

"Not really, the rest are their traits, like, precise, detailed, nothing to chance, but physically that is all we know, oh and height about six feet," Williams said.

"In stiletto heels, so about five feet six, to eight," Julie said.

"Oh yes, and average build, with erm, large breasts," Williams added.

"OK, that is a start, now what do we know is true?" Julie asked.

"They use a special gun in their handbag," Williams said.

"Good yes, which also leads us to believe they are army trained, not necessarily an expert, but trained in ballistics," Julie said, and added. "Dan, whilst we are here I don't want rank to interfere with our work so please, call me Julie, and I will tell Jones the same. Now pulling rank on you, put the kettle on, Jones will be here in a few minutes, and I want him relaxed, I have a special job for him, and he will not like it," Julie said smiling at Dan.

Julie was right almost as soon as the kettle boiled there was a knock at the door, and Julie let Jones in.

"Perfect timing Jones the kettle has just boiled, now take a seat, as I have told Williams here we use Christian names and speak freely, I do not want rank interfering with thought processes, so call me Julie, OK, Tony?" Julie asked.

"Y-yes Ma'am, if you like?" he asked.

"I do, now take your shirt off, come on I want to see your chest," Julie told him.

231

Jones took his shirt off uneasily, and Julie admired it, "A fine figure of a male don't you think, Dan?" Julie asked.

"Erm, I am not into that sort of thing, but I will agree with you, Julie," He said.

"OK, put your shirt back on and sit down," Julie told him, and put two chairs side by side, and sat on one indicating for Tony to sit on the other chair.

"Now Tony, I have a special job for you, it is like going undercover, but you will not be in a gang, or anything like that, but you will have to pretend to be a different person. I have to prove two things to the Chief Super, one that the person is male, and that the method of killing the victim is how I say, and that is your, undercover job.

The gun is already being made, and it will work, the other part is for you to show him that the killer is male, simple," Julie said smiling at him in close contact, her arm around his shoulders, weakening his resistance, and bringing him into her.

"Y-yes, Ma'am, erm, Julie, b-but how?" He asked feeling it was not exactly as she was saying.

"Very easy, you will appear, as a female," Julie said happily.

"Erm, I am not queer Ma'am, erm, Julie," he said.

"I never thought you were, but you are about six feet, and a good-looking man, which will make the experiment far more convincing. Like any undercover mission, it will not be easy, but for you, an excellent experience. Dan and I are happy that you are capable of pulling it off. I realise that it is above and beyond the call of duty, but I have to

232

show the Chief Super exactly how it is done, and being female I can't do that, it has to be, a male," Julie said hugging him to her.

"For the team, and to solve the case I will do it, but I am not happy," he said.

"I am not suggesting for one minute that you are, anything other than a fully-fledged male, and I know I am asking a lot of you, but with this set, and the information from Humberside, we will crack the case wide open, in no time," Julie said, "The Chief Super believes that I have lost my edge and mind, I think, because of my ridiculous ideas. I have to prove him wrong about my mind. I have thought long and hard about this, once he sees that I am right, and then he will allow me to solve the case. A week on Saturday at the test range, we will show him that I am right. The factory closes for the weekend, so there will just be us three and the Chief Super there. You will walk up to a bench, sit down and shoot a ballistics dummy, and walk away, then come back and show him that you are male. Your time, undercover over," Julie said smiling at him.

Over the next ten days Julie spent a lot of time with Tony, teaching him how to walk in stiletto heeled shoes, and in particular the way she wanted him to walk more of a march.

"No, be careful Tony, too much heel and you are flat on your back, point the toe, better, don't worry about the hips, the Camel coat will hide that," she seemed to be saying most of the time.

His reply was invariably, "How the hell do you walk in these, all day?"

"See what we women have to put up with, just to please, you males," Julie would say, and laugh.

Dan was busy also, asking Alex if she knew a very capable theatrical make-up artist, and trying to get one without telling them exactly why, they wanted her.

Alex managed to get a friend to help, and she began by measuring Tony.

"How are they to be dressed?" She asked.

"An alluring, self-confident, wealthy female, with expensive jewellery, which I will organise," Julie told her.

When the day arrived, the fun and games began early on, the manager opened up the test range for them, and showed Julie, Alex, Dan, Tony, and Amanda, Alex's make-up artist, into a shed by the range. They were to get ready for the Chief Super's reluctant arrival at two in the afternoon, but as Amanda had said, there was a lot to do to get Tony ready.

"What is that?" Tony asked shocked.

"Tony, women have breasts, for it to work, you need a nice pair, now come on slip this over your head like so, and now your arms through here, there now, how does that feel?" Julie asked him as Alex helped her put the false bust on him.

"They are silicone the same as used in implants, and do have weight, but not as much as a real bust. I now need to hide the false bust, so I made this, it is a rubber covering, like the face masks it will be a tight fit," she said putting the rubber covering over his head and down to below the bust, "There now the glue is theatrical glue, and will come off easily. What do you think girls?" Amanda asked, Alex, "I like the small touches like the nipples, it makes it look real," Amanda said, appraising her work.

"Wow, it looks perfect, I would not be able to tell the difference," Alex said.

"The joint is now under the arms, and can't be seen," Amanda said.

"Beautiful, Amanda, here is this next," Alex asked.

"Yes," she replied.

"W-what is that, it looks like a torture thing, and I am not wearing panties, he will not be looking up my skirt," Tony said, feeling embarrassed.

"Awe, pity I had a nice thong for you to wear," Alex said, and laughed, "No Tony as you said there will be no need, but the bust and waist are very important, so breath in," Amanda said, and pulled on the cords with Alex.

They helped him put the tights on, and then sat him down on a chair, and Amanda pulled up a trolley.

"Blonde hair you said?" Amanda asked Julie who had just entered after setting the props up with the general manager and Dan.

"Yes, and it is shoulder length, some to come around the front to hide the Adam's apple," Julie said.

It took Amanda a good half hour to complete her task making him up after a couple of tries before being happy, with the result.

They now had lunch, and Dan was banned from the shed, to save, Tony's embarrassment, half dressed.

After lunch, they put the dress on him, heels and wig and assed their work.

"Well Tony, you most certainly look the part. The Chief Super will be here in a few moments, and when we are set, Alex will open the shed door, and you make your walk, the gun is loaded, and has been test fired so there is no danger," Julie said opening up the handbag for him to see it held in a wooden slot at the base of the handbag. "That is all he would put in his handbag. Feminine accoutrements we carry, he would not, he is not female, remember just turn the bag like so, easily and lean into the dummy, pull it into your side quite quickly, erm, forceful, to create the pressure to fire the gun. The mechanism will slide easily so a lot of pressure is not needed, but it needs to be sharp.

The dummy is naked, a Eunuch, it has no genitalia at all, but does have a heart, try and aim for it as you line the gun up with the heart, but quickly, then kiss the dummy as we know he does, and walk back to the shed, where Amanda will help you change, leave everything else, to me," Julie said.

"Hello Sir," Julie said as the Chief Super approached them, escorted by the General Manager.

"I was told that I needed to be here, what is this charade about, Inspector?" He asked abruptly.

"Well Sir, it is with the help of this arms firm that I have been able to create the gun I said is used in these killings, and on behalf of the metropolitan police I would like to thank the General Manager for his kind assistance.

What you are about to see is a reconstruction of the shooting in Manchester, which bears a very good resemblance to our shooting, but easier to set up," Julie said, and nodded to Alex.

Alex opened the door, and Tony came out, he walked with a confident stride Julie was proud of his actions, he was perfect, he sat down as she had told him, lifting the coat slightly as he sat, to stop it falling off his shoulders turned a fraction and lifted the handbag to the right position turned it and leaned into it. He held the dummy up and pulling it in close at the same time. There was a slight pop, and he let go, and walked back to the shed.

"Now Sir that was a reconstruction of how it is done, was the attacker male or female?" Julie asked.

"Don't act daft Inspector, it was a woman obviously, Ashton isn't in your team, so how did you get her?" He asked.

His comment took Julie by surprise, she hadn't made Tony look like a person, just female, but now as she sat there; she was struck by the resemblance to a female member of the original team.

"In fact Sir, this has been the whole problem all along. How could they have killed, it seemed impossible, until you realise that one, the perpetrator is male, and that two, the gun is the simplest form of gun, a barrel.

PC Jones, are you decent?" Julie asked, and he came out of the shed, now in his uniform. "You see Sir, our killer, is an illusionist, as I said all along, and to catch him we have to see beyond the illusion at how it is created.

He is ex-army, and has knowledge of firearms, probably from his army training. I now ask again for the records of all army personnel released, or who have left the army within the last ten years and in particular with any sort of ballistics training. Not how to fire a gun, but how to repair a gun. My trip to Manchester was not a waste of time; it cleared my thoughts, and clarified them as being correct.

This has been video recorded, and if I must I will go over your head, and show them this, as proof that I am not an idiot, but thinking with the clarity needed to close the case. I still believe that with a little help and tolerance I can close the case within the time limit you set, Sir," Julie said looking him in the eye, calling his bluff perhaps, but making sure he knew she was not bluffing.

"What help do you need?" He asked.

"I need those lists, and because of the time scale, and volume of names on the lists, another twelve officers to scrutinise the lists, and permission to visit Humberside and or Manchester, as I see fit," Julie told him.

"Don't push it Inspector, you can have the lists and officers, but visits are at my discretion," he said, turned on his heel and marched off.

"Right everybody clean up here, and by the way, where did the bullet end up?" Julie asked, and took out a knife cutting the dummy open and there it was exactly where she knew it was, in every case so far, in the opposite ventricle to where the bullet was fired from.

"Julie, did I do it right?" Jones asked.

Julie went up to him and gave him a kiss on the cheek, "Tony, you were perfect, and you make a really good-looking woman as well, very pretty," Julie said with a smile.

"I suppose I will have to accept that I will be a laughingstock after this," he said unhappily.

"Tony in the drains below here there is a parcel of cocaine that has been flushed away. What is the difference between being knee deep in shit, searching for a drug parcel, and what you did? They

238

both serve to find the criminal, to catch them, and put them where they belong. We proved my theory, which is all it was till now, when with your help, invaluable help I must say, it became fact. Tony you changed fiction into fact, a theory became a reality, because of your actions, and I am sure it was less, erm, smelly, as searching the drains, thank you," Julie said.

Chapter 21
Assessment

Monday morning came around, and Julie entered the offices, the Chief Super had kept his word, and there were boxes stacked up to one side, and before her were a dozen glum faces.

"What a miserable morning, it is set to rain all day, but in here there should be smiling faces," Julie said turning to the white board, "On Saturday we proved without doubt that out killer is male, and that the gun I have one like it here, is in the handbag he carries. It is very crude, but effective, as we proved, on Saturday.

There is a barrel which doubles as the explosion chamber, a slide. The bullet is placed in the slide, and then pressed up against the victim and the killer leans in quickly, compressing the barrel into the firing pin. The barrel will get very hot, several hundred degrees, and to avoid the handbag bursting into flames, crushed ice in a plastic bag is placed around the barrel. Any melted water escapes through the hole in the bag which also collects all, the gunshot residue.

We now realise that the killer is ex-army, with some degree of training in ballistics, hence all the boxes, which yes, we will have to go through searching for a needle in a hay stack, but I have another twelve officers on their way to help us search through, the files.

We are looking for a male, mid-thirties, five feet, six inches to five feet, eight inches in height, with as I said some ballistics training.

Cold and wet outside, but in here warm and lively, why because we now know the type of person we are looking for, the field has narrowed considerably. Evans and Hastings will also bring back more information, to help narrow the search, even more so.

Ladies and gentlemen we are at the half mile marker, I am not going to say it will be all downhill from here on, it won't be, we still have some hard slog to do, but there is a bright light at the end of the tunnel, and it is the brightest it has been since, we started," Julie said lifting their spirits.

Julie turned to the white board, and wrote down the things they were to look for male, mid-thirties, ex-army and ballistics training.

"Ma'am, if Evans and Hastings, are looking into his computer; could our guy also be, perhaps not an expert, but trained, in, computers?" Jones asked.

"It just gets better and better, good thinking Jones, add that to the list, computer training," Julie said with a bright smile, and added it to the list.

Julie knew the task before them was daunting, to say the least, she knew it would take days to read all the files to find compatible people with her requirements, but it was a task that needed to be done.

She consoled herself by thinking she had started the case with a fifty-five million suspect list, which as the early days progressed it went up to five billion. It had now been reduced naturally, down to about twenty million, and now it was down she hoped to no more than fifty-five thousand. Which would reduce quite quickly as the people below thirty, were discarded, females were discarded, and people above forty were also discarded, even so by the end of the week there were still boxes of names as potential suspects.

Computers now came into their own, as all the names left from the army lists were entered into the computer, and cross checked against the names of the passengers to fly into the cities where an assassination had taken place.

It was two weeks later when Williams entered Julie's office, and placed a thick folder on her desk, and smiled at her.

"Ma'am, in here there are twenty names of people who are ex-army, and fit the profile, and have visited one of the cities where an assassination took place. With photos from the passport check," Williams said smiling.

"Excellent work Sergeant, but I have been thinking, what if our killer is so wise that he flies into an airport close by, say a day's drive away, and hires a car, and leaves the same way, he will not be in that folder, will he?" Julie asked.

"A good point Ma'am, and no he will not be in the folder, and seeing as he has out thought us every step of the way, you have a good point. Ma'am, he has to start in the UK, so what if we cross reference the names with people getting connecting flights from the UK, to these destinations. Like the top one, they flew in from Paris, was it a connecting flight for a passenger from, the UK," Williams suggested.

"That is a good idea, yes; check to see if any of them started their trip in the UK. Just another thought, cross check the names against passengers on ferries to Europe, and Euro Star," Julie said, feeling the net closing in on her killer.

Julie was also apprehensive as well, there were so many unknowns, and to narrow it down to just twenty names, meant that most of them must be the same person, with different identities, which she thought unlikely. What were they missing? There had to be some clue, some piece of evidence that linked all the murders, what was it?

Julie got up, and thumped her desk in frustration she began to pace up and down, she could taste the sweet taste of success, she was so close, yet it eluded her. She had hoped to have heard from Evans and Hastings by now, but the computer messages were so heavily encrypted that they had brought in a specialist, a professor, to help them. They had followed the money, but even that was difficult, as it passed between countries, which meant that they needed court orders or warrants to access the details, which took time. It took so much time that by the time they had the warrants, the money was two or even three steps ahead.

Three weeks, and they had traced it to a bank in Hanoi, where it had been transferred to an account in a different name, and then transferred to a bank in India, the latest account. They were now trying to get court orders to access that account.

This was not the news Julie wanted, she was making a two-pronged attack, and neither action seemed to be making progress, as fast as she wanted. Her team were bogged down with reams and reams of paperwork, and the money trail was held up by court orders, it was frustrating. It was even more so, after her success at the gun factor y. She had known that was the key, but having opened that door there was now another locked door, and to find that key would be harder than the first one, or so it seemed, and all she could do was wait for something to break.

Another week passed, she had less than four weeks left before her six months were up. Evans rang her with the news she had been waiting for.

"Ma'am, we have the IP address, it has been bounced around the world so many times it has taken the computer two days, to isolate it," he said smiling at his success, "The address where he is operating from is number eleven Windsor Road, Watford, Ma'am," she knew he was excited at finding the address, and screwed her face up in dismay.

"Evans, thank you for that, but I can assure you that is not where he operates from," Julie said unhappily.

"Ma'am, we have checked and double checked, that is where he operates from," Evans said.

"OK, we will check it out, but I can assure you it isn't, his base. How do I know that? Because that is my address, and I can assure you, I have excellent alibis for every murder, you, are one of them. You need to think again, but we will go, and take a look, I suppose he could be living in my attic," Julie told him.

"No, sorry Ma'am, that is where we traced the signal to, I will ask the professor for his input," Evans said.

Julie looked glum, this was not the news she wanted, several things crossed her mind as she called for Williams and Jones to join her in her office, and told them what Evans, had found out.

"We are going to my house, and searching it from top to bottom, Williams you showed me the house, introducing me to the landlord, and he said something about the last tenant not staying too long, and leaving unexpectedly. After we have searched my house, I want to speak to my landlord, about him," Julie said thoughtfully.

"Ma'am, I hope you are not blaming me, you were desperate for somewhere to live, and at a reasonable price, under the circumstances it was ideal," Williams said.

"No, not in the least, it was an opportunity I could not afford to miss. I agreed to stay there; I was not forced or coerced in any way. I do not blame you, it is just circumstances and perhaps for the better, think of the grilling we would have given the occupant, had it not been me," Julie said, giving him a smile.

Julie, Williams and Jones were just about to leave the office when Evans joined them.

"Ma'am, not being funny, but you have no idea what you are looking for, or if you see it recognise it, wouldn't it be a good idea for me, to join you?" Evans asked.

"I was working on the principle that if it didn't belong, then I had found whatever it is, but you are right, someone who knows what they are looking for would be, an advantage," Julie said.

All four of them went to the car and drove to Julie's house, she let them in, and they divided up.

Julie and Jones went upstairs, and Williams and Evans began downstairs searching for something out of place or odd, yet none of them knew exactly what it was, they were looking for.

Julie came down to see Evans flat on the floor in the kitchen, the base boards of her kitchen units off, and he was using a torch to search the gap under the units.

"We didn't find anything upstairs either, and there is no cellar, so where can it be?" Julie asked.

"The highest point in the house, the attic," Evans said brightly, they got Julie's step ladders, and Evans climbed up into the attic. They could hear him scrambling about, carefully going from beam to beam.

"You," he said and paused, "You clever sod," was all he said, and scrambled back to the hatch.

"I am very good with codes cracking them, but Hastings is the technician, from what I can see, it looks like the messages come into a box, a receiver. They are then passed to a second unit, and sent on their way. The technicalities are that the IP address is here, but the originating IP address is not here. Erm, like a relay station, but because it hits the first computer that is the IP address, we traced it to. Then when it is sent on its way it goes via a new IP address, and because it is now hard wired, as we searched, it showed it ending here, we will have to start all over again, from this new signal, for the IP address.

I am not sure if I can unplug it, or if that would lose the signal, so I need to speak to Hastings and the professor. Sorry Ma'am, I wonder, no, yes, erm no, possibly, hum," Evans said.

"Evans, I always thought you were indecisive, now I know you are. What are all the yes and no's for?" Julie asked him.

"It is just a thought, but with this break in the links, if we could slip a Trojan horse in. If we could, then we can disrupt him, and find him quicker. But I am not sure, if I can link into his computer.

Sorry Ma'am, I will try and explain. Up there, he has put part of a computer, the part that receives messages, and it sends them to a second computer, which then sends them on their way. The break causes us to believe this is his IP address, when it isn't.

Now if I can attach a keyboard to the sending part, I can create a Trojan horse to disrupt him, and piggyback a search signal to locate him. I can create a Trojan horse, if Hastings can get me connected, and that is where my plan falls down, there are no ports to connect a keyboard to it," Evans said.

"Evans, come back with us, do not touch it just yet, take some photos, and ask the question first, if we cannot get inside then we will unplug it, but ask first," Julie said.

They returned to the office, and Evans took Hastings to a corner and they began to discuss what could be done. They also contacted the professor for his advice.

"Ma'am, the professor is intrigued and wants to know if he can come down to have a look?" Evans asked.

"Yes, book a hotel room for him and get a train ticket, it will be problematic if he wants to drive," Julie said.

"Williams, how are you doing, anything yet?" Julie asked him.

"Yes Ma'am, I have just received a message from Euro Star, they had a Mary Sullivan travelling from London to Paris, and I have a Mary Sullivan on a flight from Paris to Mexico. We have him Ma'am," Williams said brightly.

"Don't count your chickens Williams, get someone around to the address, I don't suppose we are lucky enough for it to be local, are we?" Julie asked.

"Sorry Ma'am, Manchester," Williams said ruefully.

"Leave that to me then, good work Williams," Julie said.

"Roberts, glad I caught you in. We have been given an address for the suspect on the passport; it is a Mary Sullivan, who took the Euro Star to Paris and then a plane to Mexico. Can you go around, and have a chat with her please. She may just be our man?" Julie asked him.

"Luckily, I know what you mean; she is our man, indeed! I can go now; I was just about to leave for home, what is the address?" He asked.

"Fifteen, Old Trafford Road, Manchester," Julie said.

"Not to put a damper on things, but there has been a lot of redevelopment around that area, it could be bogus, no very probably is, sorry, but I will go and make sure, I'll ring you later," Roberts said.

After the phone call, Julie looked out of her window into the outer office, to see the room empty now, except for Williams; he was always the last to leave.

"Time to go home Williams; Roberts is going to have a look at the address, and he will call me later, but it does not look hopeful. Apparently that area has been redeveloped, and not that recently. When was Mexico, twelve months ago now?" Julie asked, considering things.

"Yes, about that, may be fourteen months, about the time you moved into the house you're in now, I can get you the exact date," Williams offered.

"No, not now it will do in the morning, I was just wondering, if there ever was, a house at that address?" Julie asked no-one.

"You are the one from up there, and worked in Manchester," Williams said.

"Clever, yes, it is like London, sprawled out so much no-one knows everywhere. I worked the Salford area, Old Trafford was on the other side of the city, and now I come to think of it, industrialised, oh and that football team, what is their name now, not very good, but passable," Julie said, winding Williams up.

"Sorry Ma'am, it is home time, so you can't wind me up now. As you well know, the greatest team is Manchester United, and that is their home ground," Williams said high and mighty, and they laughed.

"What happened last night then, what was it, six nil, they lost by?" Julie asked him in the car.

"They allow minor clubs to win from time to time, and they lost by one goal, to Chelsea, their first defeat since Christmas. What were you doing watching football, you hate it?" Williams asked.

"Did you see what was on the television last night? The match was the best program, and that was dire," Julie said.

"Never mind Ma'am, the rugby season will be starting soon, and then you will be happy," Williams said.

Julie's phone rang, and she answered it.

"Well just another dead end, it is vacant, waiting to be built on, and from what Roberts saw, it has been empty for over twelve months, an ideal place to have a false address.

Tomorrow, I want you to search the obituaries for a Mary Sullivan, try the Manchester area first, and then nationwide, she will have died or gone missing say fifteen months ago, may be longer, go back twenty-four months. Get Cuthbert and Ashburn to help you. I will go and speak to my landlord with Jones. We will see what he knows about his last tenant, and if there is a forwarding address," Julie said, deep in thought as she organised things.

"Ma'am would you like me to carry you in?" Williams asked, being cheeky, because she had not moved after several minutes after arriving at her home

"Oh, sorry, I was miles away, the legs work, even if the brain isn't at the moment, thank you, see you at eight o'clock tomorrow morning," Julie said smiling at his joke, her hand to her chin as she walked to the door, and let herself in.

Chapter 22
Minor Details

The Professor was due to arrive at eleven o'clock, so Julie stayed at home to meet him, and asked Evans and Hastings to collect him from the station.

Julie offered him a cup of tea, but he declined wanting to see this contraption, he knew it was possible, but had as yet never seen one. The principle was simple enough, but the programming was complex.

He was up in the attic for no more than half an hour before he climbed back down with a confused look on his face.

"Hum, Inspector, it is hum, complicated, hum," he said as if he wasn't sure about what he was saying, but it transpired that he did, and paused for thought between every word according to Evans.

"Ma'am, he is brilliant, he just stops very often as if thinking, you get used to it," Evans had told her.

"Complicated, Professor?" Julie asked.

"Hum, yes, hum, to hum, to remove it, could destroy it, hum, erm, to even switch it off, hum, could be bad, hum. I think, hum, I think, it would be hum, better if we hum, put some hum, flooring in the hum, attic and hum, worked in hum, situ. If that would be, hum, acceptable?" He asked in his affected way.

"Yes, that would be fine. Evans, go to the wood yard, and get some flooring and nails, please?" Julie asked him giving him some money.

"Ma'am, he will need a keyboard and some other things as well," Evans informed her.

"Evans, I am a lowly Inspector, not the Chief Super, my bank account has limited funds, very limited. Just how much do you need?" Julie asked him.

"To do it properly, about one and a half thousand pounds, for everything we need, but we can pinch from the office and return, if you like?" Evans asked.

"How much?" Julie asked shocked, "Never mind, take as much as possible from the office, and I will try, and get my money back, later," Julie added.

"We will need a high speck computer, very fast, and that is probably the highest cost. The IT investigative team have one, but it is in their office, and we won't be able to use it. I am going to have to build one. I will need a high speck computer, and then add parts to make it faster, erm, more powerful, it's hard to explain to, if I may say, a novice, Ma'am," Evans said trying to be careful in what he said.

"I can accept that, it is a tool to me, and that is all; like a hammer, I use it to knock nails in," Julie said openly.

"Yes Ma'am, but you would not use a sledgehammer, to knock a panel pin in, would you? Here I have what appears to be a panel pin, but it isn't, it is very complex, and I will need a sledgehammer, to knock down the fire walls, well I

252

won't, but the professor and Hastings will," Evans said.

"What do you hope to achieve?" Julie asked.

"We want to get into this computer to read his E-Mails undetected, trace where they are coming from, and locate his money, and that is three things we are trying to achieve, not one, which is why we need the special computer. The one at Humberside cost one hundred thousand pounds and has been added to. We do not need one to that speck, but it will not be cheap," Evans said.

"So you are saying that I need to take out a second mortgage?" Julie asked.

"I thought this was rented, sorry Ma'am, and no. I have a friend in IT, and he will buy it from me, to him it will be cheap, saving labour costs. In fact," he said brightening up, "He may pay for it, but he may also want to be here, if that is alright?" Evans asked.

"Bring him in, just don't let the Chief Super know, getting the extra help was hard enough," Julie said, and smiled at him.

Julie rang Williams, to come and pick her up, and take her to the office.

Evans decided that they could only get two feet wide lengths through the hatch, and had the wood yard cut the lengths of flooring chip board into two feet wide pieces. With Hastings help they started to board out the attic, while the professor began to build the computer from the parts Evans had bought. It took them the rest of the day to lay sufficient flooring for them to work on, and to build the computer. The programs took the best part of the next day to create, before they were ready to start.

Now came the difficult part, they needed to get inside the computer in the attic, and connect their computer to it without disturbing it, this was a long and laborious job, as they checked every detail before doing anything, every minor detail had to be right.

Evans was sweating from the heat, and his concentration, as was Hastings, they were feeling the pressure. The professor and Evans friend, who had joined them from IT Investigations, seemed relaxed, they were not aware of the time limit, and therefore the pressure the team faced.

Julie was sat in her lounge watching the television when she heard the shout, and rushed up stairs.

"What the hell is going on? I thought someone had been injured," Julie asked anxious.

"Sorry Ma'am, it works, and we are connected, four days hard graft has paid off, we are now inside his computer, well this relay part. Tomorrow we can start tracking him, and deciphering the messages, his encryption is very sophisticated, but the professor is very hopeful that we will crack it, quite quickly. It is numeric, and from what we already know it will be just a simple job, but may take some time to get it completely. The hardest part is going to be getting past his fire wall. Colin and I will start on that tomorrow, whilst Hastings and the professor will continue to decipher the encryption," Evans said.

"Well done, what time tomorrow?" Julie asked.

"You normally leave at eight thirty when Williams picks you up. I can be here for then, and let the others in, if you like?" Evans asked.

"That will be fine, would you like a beer before you go?" Julie asked them, they all said yes, and they joined her in her lounge sipping beers and chatting for a bit, before they went home, and to bed, it had been a long exhausting day.

For the next two days the team worked on checking and re-checking files statements, and creating the program for the computer. Hastings was given the job of telling Julie that the computer link could not be unplugged or moved, and they would have to work on it, in her attic.

"I understand, and Hastings you know where the cups are, the tea and the coffee, etcetera. You also know where the hot water tap is, the washing up liquid, and the Marigold's are. If you value your life, you will use them," Julie said smiling at him, with meaning.

"Yes Ma'am, you are low for tea Ma'am, erm well, run out, actually," he said shyly.

"You also know where the shop is, don't you?" Julie asked adding, "And I suppose it was Evans that brewed up last?" she asked.

"Actually no it wasn't, it was the IT officer, Ted, but I will be here bright and early with a full box for your morning cuppa, Ma'am," Hastings said accepting her jocular complaint.

"You have left me some coffee and my chocolate, haven't you, for tonight?" Julie asked leaning in close.

"Hum, erm, yes Ma'am, I-I think, Ted made the last brew, Ma'am," Hastings said taking her scowl for what it was, serious, yet not.

"Hastings, you are in charge, therefore if I do not have a brew before I go to bed, who do you think, will be suffering at my hands, hum?" Julie asked him.

"I will just go, and make sure there is a brew for you, Ma'am," he said laughing as he left her. "Yes Ma'am there is a brew for you, two tea bags and some coffee you don't like it strong, do you?" He asked when he returned.

"Get out, go on, before I propel you through the doorway," Julie said laughing, and shaking her head.

Julie knew they had got so involved in their work they would not have noticed that the tea caddy was empty, until it ran out, likewise the coffee. She considered it a small price to pay, for the valuable work they were doing.

Julie checked her cupboard, and Hastings had been right, there were just two tea bags left, and just enough coffee, if she made it in the jar for one cup, a weak cup, she also checked her biscuits, and found crumbs.

The shop on the corner was still open so she replenished her supplies. She arrived just as he was about to close, but he served her first.

"Good morning Hastings, bright and early as you said. You are going to be here for a bit, so there are going to be rules. In here," Julie said opening a cupboard door, "Are my things, my tea, my coffee, my biscuits, touch them and I will remove fingers. Here we have tea, coffee and biscuits for you, and

256

here, is a jar, it is empty, but by tonight it will not be, as you and your friends put change into it, to buy tea etcetera for you to consume. Do we have an understanding, Hastings?" Julie asked him.

"Yes, Ma'am, it will not be empty by the time you return," He said dropping a two-pound coin into the jar and smiling at her.

"Thank you, I knew you would understand. Good work by the way and how is it going?" Julie asked there was no tension, just good-humoured acceptance of the facts.

"I have almost finished writing the program, and the professor and Evans have made the connections, undetected, so we believe, by tomorrow we should be in and working. Is there any news from the office?" He asked.

"Not as yet, but my profile, is growing, and Mayberry, Atherton, and two of the extra twelve we got, have found a connection, but they are still working on what it means. They suggested that we run facial recognition on all the passengers arriving at the airports, believing that it may find more than one person to match.

We know he uses several passports, identities, but facial recognition will spot the similarities. The problem is, we do not have one face to align it to, so it is a permutation into millions, if not billions, thank god for computers," Julie said.

"Ma'am, just an idea, what if they checked the passports of British citizens, and their address. It just occurred to me that he will, as we know, use derelict buildings or buildings that no-longer exist, so if someone arrives in Mexico, for example, and the UK address does not exist, then use them as a base line," Hastings suggested.

"Interesting concept, yes that may just work, or at least reduce the workload, thank you Hastings, for that you can have one of, my biscuits," Julie said smiling at him.

"Thank you Ma'am," he said and took the one offered, and dunked it in the tea Julie had made for them, as did Julie in her tea.

Julie left him supping his tea, as the others arrived, and she left with Williams who had arrived to take her to work.

Julie went into her office as usual, and sat down, and began to read her mail, her first job, whilst she waited for the rest of the team to arrive.

The Chief Super rang her wanting a report, which she gave him, it didn't seem that she had done much, all she could report was that they were still working on the airport connection, and checking the statements, and reports, but she was hopeful.

"Hopes and dreams are for youngsters, not seasoned Inspectors, when will you get some sort of result, a tangible lead, at least?" He asked.

"When one turns up Sir, until then we will keep looking, and investigating," Julie said.

There was a knock at her door, and she told them to enter.

"Ma'am, we have a Julian Smethurst on the Euro Star, he arrived in Paris the day before the shooting, and returned the day after. It struck me as odd, too short to be a holiday, it was mid-week, and a business trip would again take longer, I believe?

This means that I have a question mark on that being the case, possible, but it just seems a little off, when asked if his trip was business or pleasure, he said pleasure and the passport people flagged his passport, but it was cleared. May be I am clutching at straws, but what else do we have?" Atherton asked.

"We have a face to use for facial recognition, and accept a fifty per cent similarity; these rubber theatrical masks will hide most of the features, but not the symmetry, so don't expect too much of a likeness," Julie said hopeful.

Julie having set up, and given her directions, went for a walk in the town. I was early spring and warm, but there was a bite in the wind, She was well wrapped up against the wind; even so it seemed to cut right through her.

As she walked she looked at all the faces, and wondered if one of them was her killer? They were so good at disguises, she wondered if she would know them, if she saw them. Down the high street, and a look down the alley way where she had helped Williams, when she had first arrived, it was all quiet now, lights had been erected it was no-longer a dark secluded alley way. As she started to leave the town she stopped, a new shop had opened up selling adult toys, and she entered.

Julie was amazed at the range of toys, and the sexually stimulating underwear, it wasn't for her, but she wondered where her killer bought his outfits, the dresses he would probably buy online, or at a dress shop, but the underwear she decided must be special.

"Hello, if I decided to enlarge my bust without surgery, is there anything I can buy in a shop say, like this? I do know that theatres and film crews have them, but are they available to the general public?" Julie asked the shop keeper,

"Indeed there is madam, but it would be by special order, we do offer a bra which can be inflated," he told her.

"Have you ever had such an order?" Julie asked.

"Madam, discretion is our watch word," he said smiling at her.

"I see, but if I said that I was an Inspector with the Metropolitan police, and making enquiries about a murder, perhaps then you may be able, to help me?" Julie asked, showing him her warrant card.

"I would not be able to give you a name, but if one had been ordered then I could say so," he said nervously.

"You have not been open long enough, but it says that you have two or more shops, perhaps in one of those, you had one ordered?" Julie asked.

"Indeed yes several, they are popular with our transvestite customers, they offer good support and shape, and they are virtually undetectable. I must admit though that the silicone bust, is taking over from the bra, it is far more realistic. It was manufactured for women who had, had the misfortune to have to have a mastectomy, so it is very realistic," he told her.

"Now are you going to make me go, and get a search warrant, or can you give me the names of the males who have bought the false bust? Half a dozen big policemen searching your premises, is not that good for business, is it?" Julie asked him.

"Inspector I run a legitimate business, and here let me show you. This box contains a false bust, it can be bought over the counter, so I do not have the names of the people who buy them, and as I said this item has taken over from the inflatable bra, and it is available in virtually all adult stores. This particular one is a, 'C,' cup, but I do have them in cups ranging from an, 'A,' to, 'D,' cup, any larger, and it would then be a special order, and I can assure you I have not had one bigger ,ordered," he told her.

"What is this?" Julie asked picking up a box with the writing saying it was a rubberised mask

"It contains three bottles; you mix two of them, and then paint the mask onto a mould of the face you want. Peel it off carefully, apply the face glue, and then put the mask on your face. It is used again for a male wishing to appear female, or older, or even younger. I don't sell much of it, it is usually used in the theatre," he said.

"I am just surprised it is on general sale, I thought it was only used by theatrical people," Julie said.

"Sex toys are not the most popular items, although they do sell well. That is why I sell to actors and theatrical people. In the back room I have uniforms and other items of clothing, for stage and fancy dress," he said.

"Interesting, hum, so my murderer would find it quite easy to get what they wanted from a shop like this one, interesting," Julie said more to herself than to the shop keeper.

"Thank you for your time, it has been very interesting," Julie said and left the shop.

As she walked out, she was sure she heard him give a sigh, of relief, Julie smiled whatever he was up to didn't interest her at that moment in time. Her interest was more to do with the ease her killer could get the items he needed, select specialist places were not the only place, opening up a whole range of shops and suppliers.

Julie walked back to the office, and called Williams into her office.

"Williams did you know that everything our killer needs is on sale in a whole range of shops. I was hoping that it was specialised," Julie said.

"I was of the same opinion until Alex got the make-up artist involved. Perhaps I should have told you, but the artist arrived at our house with polystyrene, a block of it and carved the face, and bust to fit Jones size, and shape. Then coated it with this rubber stuff, and just peeled it off. The hard work was in carving the face, that took two days, but after that it was an hour if that, to make the face, and for it to set," Williams said.

"Didn't the polystyrene flake away?" Julie asked.

"No, she used a special thing a branding tool, it left the surface smooth, and then she coated it with a varnish that, is what it looked like, and gave her a smooth surface to work on, and hard, erm, firm," Williams told her.

"So once carved, you can make several faces from that one template?" Julie asked.

"Ten to twenty so she told me, and you can adjust it, by adding bits very small, like to make the chin chisel shaped say, and add two bits to make it round, a small nose, add a bit to make it bigger," Williams said.

"So facial recognition is another waste of time," Julie said annoyed at the dead ends she kept coming up against.

"Could be, but the best option so far, like you said, a fifty per cent match will have to be enough. There are certain characteristics that can't be hidden completely, but most of the ones that make identification positive, like scars, and moles all go, even eye colour, as we know," Williams said.

"OK Sergeant, you have managed to depress me enough. I had hoped that they would need a specialist supplier, but they don't. I had hoped that the basic features would identify them, but apparently they won't, so you may go," Julie said.

"It is always darkest before dawn Ma'am, it can't possibly get any darker, so perhaps it is almost dawn," Williams said upbeat.

"That's what I like about you, always the optimist," Julie said, and smiled at him.

"Come," she called out in answer to a knock at her door, Adams entered, and he was smiling a broad beaming smile.

"Ma'am, you know how facial recognition is dubious, can we say, because he is a master of disguise, well I spoke to one of our friends at IT," he began.

"I do not have any friends at IT, they drank all my coffee and tea, and ate all my biscuits, go on." Julie said laughing.

"There is a new system out, it is being trialled, and I managed to get us a copy. It looks at people's gait. We assumed we all walk the same, but we do not, and everybody has a slightly different gait. The length of stride, the speed even we walk at, the shape of the body, some people lean forward others twist, there are several different things we do when we walk. Well, we have found six people who walk the same, facial recognition says a forty to fifty percent match, which is not good enough, but their gait is eighty per cent, which is good, you will never get one hundred per cent, and it needs to be refined yet. Ma'am, we have our killer, I am certain.

Miss Angela Hodgkin, at Mexico, Mister Brian Derwen, at Chicago, Mrs. Brenda Wilson, at Hamburg, Miss Susan Green at the Euro Star, unknown erm no name, at Humberside, and a Mister David Harrison boarding a flight for Paris, who just happens to arrive in Bogota, as Miss Angela Hodgkin. That particular person had a ninety-five per cent match. Ma'am we have him, we are now going over the files again, searching for them at other airports, I have given the list to Mayberry, and she is going to check their addresses," Adams said eagerly.

"Well done Adams, that is good news," Julie said beaming with him.

"As I said Ma'am, darkest before dawn," Williams added also smiling, it was terrific news.

"Indeed it is, but just because we have the person it does not mean we have the conviction. We now have to place the gun in their hand, and we also have to prove they were at the place at the time of the shooting. We still have a lot of work to do," Julie said, but she was upbeat about it.

September announced its arrival in style with a terrific thunderstorm and high winds, property damage was inevitable, torrential rain hammered down, and floods were expected. Julie looked out of her bedroom window and sighed, it was pitch black outside, even though the dawn had broken; the clouds were so heavy. Streetlights were still on, illuminating the roads.

As she stood gazing out a drop of water fell on her head, she looked up at the growing damp patch. Then it struck her, a tile must have moved in the storm, and the computer was above her. Julie dashed to the landing, and put the ladder up, and climbed up into her attic. She had been right, there was a hole not that big, but close enough to the computer to damage it.

She climbed back down, and collected plastic bags, and then climbed back up and put the computer in the bags; hoping to save the work done by the team working in her attic, trying to trace the money. She didn't hear her front door, as Evans arrived, and made his way up into her attic. Julie had given him a key so that they could come and go as they needed to.

"Ma'am, let me help you here," he said offering her a plastic bag and helping put the computer in the bag, "Ma'am, you are soaked, I will finish here; you go and get dried off," he said with concern, "That is not a small hole, several tiles must have moved," he said looking at the hole.

"Thank you, I hope I was in time to save the computer, and yes, I feel like a drowned rat, my hair. That was a waste of money, I only had it done last night, and now look at it," Julie said upset.

"I will put the kettle on Ma'am, whilst you change, and then we need to put bowls up here to stop the rain doing more damage," Evans said.

"A bit bloody pointless now, the ceiling is soaked, and I am sure that will cave in, ruining my carpet, and bedroom. I was more concerned with the loss of the computer than saving my bedroom, silly me," Julie said, and sighed.

"I am sure you did save the computer, if that is any consolation, and the insurance will cover any damage to your bedroom, won't it?" Evans asked.

"Yes, I'm sure it will, but it is just the inconvenience, and it never covers everything," Julie said, as there was a sodden crash. Julie looked down and the bedroom ceiling below her which had just collapsed.

"I doubt that I have a bowl that big," Julie said, and looked at Evans with mournful eyes.

"Tea, Ma'am?" Evans asked.

"No a bloody big Brandy, go on put the kettle on," Julie said resigning herself to the situation.

Julie showered, and dried herself off, and got dressed, and then joined Evans down in the kitchen, and a warming cup of tea.

"Ma'am, bowls will be useless, you need a big sheet of plastic to cover the whole roof, the wind will now get under the slates, and the hole will get bigger. Builders will not go up on the roof in this weather, it would be too dangerous, and I would suggest you book into a hotel, for tonight. You will need to pack a suitcase, is there anything I can do for you, Ma'am?" Evans asked, with concern in his voice.

Julie laughed the laugh of the defeated, "Stop it raining, if not then there is nothing else, is there? To go into the bedroom where the rest of the ceiling is about to collapse would be silly. Ring the rest of the team and tell them to go straight to the office, you will not be working up there today. I will have to go and buy something to wear for tomorrow, as you said; I will have to stay in a hotel tonight. I don't think fondling my knickers as you pack them, is compensation enough for you to go up into the danger zone, do you?" Julie asked looking at Evans through the top of her eyes, and laughed, "It is either that or cry, and I do not cry," Julie said smiling at him.

Evans rang the team, and told them about the situation, and then he took Julie to the shopping centre, and parked. She went into a dress shop and bought some underwear, and a new dress, before he took her to the office.

Julie went into her office, and dumped her new clothes on the floor by her desk, and sat down, there was a knock at her door, and Williams entered smiling as usual.

"Sorry to hear about the roof Ma'am, I have rung Alex, and she agrees you will come home with me tonight, and stay with us. Our eldest is away on a school trip to Austria, and her room is free," Williams said, Julie smiled at him.

"Thank you that is very kind," Julie said.

"Ma'am, we have known each other for a couple of years now, and become friends, as well as work colleagues. Alex will be disappointed if you refuse the offer," Williams said quickly.

"Then I don't seem to have any option, do I? Thank you, it is appreciated, Dan. God knows how much damage will have been done. The rain is pouring in, and there is a hole in my roof about two feet square and getting bigger. By lunch time I doubt having a roof," Julie said.

"It is a bad storm, and there will be a lot of damage. Two streets over from my street there is a bungalow quite new, and it has been repossessed by the bank. You always said that the house you were in was temporary. Why not look at that bungalow, it will be quite cheap, and is in a decent area?" Williams suggested.

"Why not, who is the estate agent, do you know?" Julie asked.

"Actually I do, my wife, rather the firm she works for. Shall I ask her to bring the keys home with her, so that you can view it?" Williams asked her smiling.

"You know more than you are saying, why not, we can view it tonight," Julie said brightening up.

The day went as expected, as the officers looked for the addresses of the people identified, and then contacted local police stations to check if that person lived there, or if the address even existed. The computer work had been halted; they were not allowed to work in the attic because it was considered dangerous, and so they spent their day checking the addresses as well.

Williams took Julie to his home as agreed, it had stopped raining, but the storm had not passed, and more rain was expected. Julie had spoken to her insurance agent, and started to make a claim, and her landlord, who had said that he would make contact with a builder, but was not hopeful of the work being done quickly.

Alex and Dan took Julie after dinner to the bungalow, it was a two-bedroom bungalow, and in good order.

"Julie, these are selling for around one hundred and twenty thousand, as you will appreciate the bank just wants its money back, and it will be put up for sale for ninety thousand. It goes on the market tomorrow; we just got the details yesterday. I am sure I can get it for sixty thousand, the bank will not accept anything less, because that covers their debt," Alex told her with a smile.

"Interesting, yes I do like it, and I think I can afford that price, what about a mortgage?" Julie asked.

"Shall we go back home, and I will do the calculations for you, I do not see any problems. The bank wants to see about one third excess collateral in the property, so with a valuation of ninety thousand, and a mortgage of sixty thousand, they have what they want, and then there is any deposit you can put up, to reduce the debt. You are young enough to get a twenty-five-year mortgage, which means that it will be less than the rent you are currently paying," Claire said.

"Then it is sold," Julie said with a bright smile.

Chapter 23
More Clues and Leads

Julie spoke to her landlord, and he said that the damage was extensive, and would take over a month to make good the repairs, so she handed her notice in, and he accepted it.

She also had another stroke of luck, her bank was the one that had repossessed the bungalow, which speeded up the purchase because the bank knew her credit history, and as the bank manager said, it was more of a formality than a full check, granting her the mortgage. It still took a month before she was able to move in, certain normal requirements were waived, because of her banking with the bank and Alex knowing the solicitor.

Julie took the day off work to move in, and get settled, and then it was back to work, and a new break.

Julie decided to have a coffee, and made her way to the machine in the offices.

"Ma'am, at long last we have found all the addresses, four were as we suspected derelict or non-existent. Two are empty, recently put on the market, and not by the person we have as living there, but one is still occupied, and by one Thomas Alan James, he is thirty-eight, and resides at fifteen Willow Crescent, Wilmslow. He is out of work, yet manages to live in a semi-detached house in an up-market area, and drives a Mondeo, and he is single. His build is, or fits the general description of the person we are looking for, Ma'am we have him," Hargreaves said with enthusiasm.

"Excellent work Hargreaves, but we still cannot put the gun in his hand, or him at the scene, hum, we need to put eyes on him. Let me think about this. I do not want to hand over the case to Manchester, after all the work we have put into it, but that is what will happen if I tell the Chief Super. I need to get him to agree to transfer us, up there, to conclude the case. The question is how?" Julie asked in thought.

Julie went back to her office, and sat down, she appeared to be in a dream world, as she thought deeply about what to do, then she suddenly brightened up, and picked up the phone.

"Roberts, lovely to speak to you, how are things up there in God's country?" Julie asked.

"The same as usual, what do you want, you are after something, I can tell?" Roberts asked.

"There's no pulling the wool over your eyes, is there? OK, we have had a big break in the assassination case. I have spent two years working this case, and I want to put the cuffs on this creep, but it appears that he resides in your neck of the woods. I am loathing handing over the case; my team has worked too hard, for another section to get the credit. I need your support; I want to come up there to finish what I have started.

My team can stay here to do the paperwork that can be done anywhere. I will need a couple of bods to do the leg work, so just one office and accommodation for a few weeks. I am so close, I can taste it," Julie said.

"I will try for you, we have a new Super, and he seems more amenable to ideas, and we have worked together before on the same case. Perhaps if I go with; 'you have led the investigation and know more than anyone,' he might help. Give me a couple of days?" Roberts asked her.

Chapter 24
Manchester

Julie was in her office reading the files, double checking that they were on the right course. She knew that she was, it was in her bones, her gut told her that they had the right person, but there was no actual physical evidence, to make a case. They were a long way from arresting the person. Her gut, and a system that was being trialled would not be enough; she needed hard evidence, to get a conviction.

Her door opened, and the Chief Super entered, "Inspector what do you know about an Inspector Harold Roberts from Manchester?' He asked.

"He is a good Inspector, I met him when he was investigating the murder of the councillor in Manchester, which had a very similar M, O, to my case, and it was decided that it was the same person who had committed both murders, along with the others, as they came to light.

We know we are not hunting a serial killer, the M, O, is wrong, but we are hunting an assassin. The link apart from one murder is that they are all officials, councillors, politicians, government officials. The odd one out, my first case, saw a body dump, whether he knew it or not, we don't know, but that is why, he was killed.

I believe that assassination was the first, the murderer was nervous, after that, hence my murder, but they grew in confidence, and committed the murders in plain sight, and leaving the body to be found, their skills honed, to perfection," Julie said.

"So the request to second you to Manchester, is as a result of what?" He asked.

"That is a very good question Sir, perhaps, because I am the leading authority on the case, and they want my knowledge. My team is the only team with a name, we now know who the killer is, but it is by deduction, from a trial on a new process, so will as yet, not stand up in court, a person's gait," Julie told him.

"A what?" he asked in temper.

"The way a person walks, apparently, we all have slight differences in the way we walk, and this computer program identifies that similarity, or difference, Sir," Julie told him.

"You have spent valuable time watching people walk, a process that has no validity. Really Inspector, what a waste of valuable resources, I am approving the secondment you have one month, and then you can hand your warrant card into me, personally," the Chief Super said.

He didn't see Julie smile behind his back, she now had one month to get the evidence she needed for a conviction, she was confident that she had her man, all she needed was the evidence, to convict him.

By six o'clock that evening, she was in her hotel room expecting Roberts to pay a visit.

"Julie lovely to see you again, we have found nothing as yet, and are still groping in the dark, there just is no evidence, nothing for us to follow. I hope you have something, my neck is on the line here?" Roberts asked her.

"Lovely to see you as well and yes I do have something. London Met, have been trialling a new system with computer recognition. We all know a woman swings her hips to some degree, but apparently we all have a different gait. The length of stride, the body movement, heel first or toe first, there are several differences, so if we see six people all walking the same, then the odds are that it is the same person.

By this process we found six people of interest. My guys then found their addresses, and only one was not a derelict site or had been demolished, and a factory built on the site, or redeveloped. Harry that person lives here in the Manchester area. I know he is our man, my gut tells me, but I need proof. As you will know I need to put the gun in his hand, and put him in the place of the murder, which will not be easy, because he left no clues, as we know.

I do not have enough for a search warrant, so that is out; nor do I have enough to bring him in for questioning. **Harry he is one** Thomas Alan James, he is thirty eight, and resides at fifteen Willow Crescent, Wilmslow, **and as I suspected, he drives a Mondeo, it had to be a run of the mill car, anything flashy would be noticed, like a BMW say, not at his house, but at the crime scene.**

Harry, he wants to blend in as a normal person in his daily routine, so as to throw suspicion, off him, but he wants to stand out when he commits the murder. Not to be caught, but to create a distraction, again throwing suspicion off him, a contradiction.

His neighbours will say he is non-descript, not flashy in the least, which we know the murderer is. His neighbours will say he is an average guy, and couldn't be the killer, he is nice, and friendly, not that they see much of him, he keeps himself to himself, the perfect neighbour," Julie said.

"It may seem stupid, but I like your reasoning," Harry said thinking, and walking up and down in thought, "So how do we nail him? Do you have any suggestions that I can take, to my Super? As you know he will not be happy with a gut feeling, and an untested process?" Harry asked her.

"I am not too sure about that, he may just give us a week to get something substantial. I only have a month before I am asked to submit my resignation, so we need to move quickly, and I do not fancy finishing my career in the Outer Hebrides. You don't really know me, but know of me, and I do have a nasty habit of rubbing my superiors up the wrong way, for some reason, and he wants rid of me; so I have to arrest this murderer, and quickly," Julie said smiling at Harry.

"Julie, telling a Chief Inspector that he knows nothing about policing, is perhaps not the right way to approach a situation. He may not, but he is the boss, try a little bit of tact," Harry said, and gave a giggle.

"When, oh yes, I remember he wanted me to let that creep go because of lack of evidence, and I suggested that it was a stupid idea, I had enough to get a confession, which I did," Julie said.

"Yes, you did, which showed him up as a fool, because it was done in the squad room, not a good idea. I would have asked to meet with him in private. Tell you what, leave dealing with our superiors to me, and you get the evidence and confession in your own inimitable way, preferably before he is arrested, so that he can't claim police brutality, just a suggestion?" Harry said laughing with Julie.

"OK, you deal with the Chief Inspector, and I will sit there all angelic," Julie said laughing, "Thank you for meeting me here, and allowing me to speak my mind. My Chief Super has the rule book strapped to his forehead, and in this case, I think we have to throw it away, and make our own rules.

I want this person, and I am willing to bend or even, break the rules to get him. If I do, it is down to me and me alone. I may be throwing my career away, but there is no need for you to. Now how about a pint in the bar, I am on expenses?" Julie asked laughing.

"Julie, I would be more comfortable in the Golden Hind, just up the road. The atmosphere is more convivial," he said.

They walked up the road, and Julie soon found out why, as several police officers came up to Harry, and were introduced to Julie.

"It is the coppers local, quite a lot of work is done in here, out of earshot of the Super. Brian, have you got a minute," Harry asked one of the officers, "Brian, Willow Crescent, number 15, keep an eye on it for us will you? What can you tell us about the owner?" Harry asked.

"Very little, I have seen him; he stands tall, erect like a soldier, slightly effeminate, but not an out and out queer. Well spoken, intelligent, I got my wrist slapped, my fault, so I ended up walking the beat there for a month. I saw him twice, may be three times, amiable enough, he drives a black Mondeo. Next door was burgled, and I interviewed him, he saw nothing, and heard nothing, which I found odd. He didn't even hear the alarm go off, he said he sleeps soundly, and was in the bedroom at the other end of the house, with ear muffs, I still found it odd, as if he perhaps was not there, and not that he sleeps soundly," Brian told them.

"Did you ask if he was home?" Julie asked him.

"No, I didn't, it was the guy across the street that told me he was home, seeing the lights on, and being the next door neighbour, I decided that he may have seen something, but he didn't say that he was not at home, just that he sleeps soundly," Brian said.

"Thank you Brian, you wouldn't know when, I mean the actual date of the robbery, would you?" Julie asked.

"Not off hand, but I can check tomorrow for you, if it is important?" Brian asked.

"It is, but I am guessing, sorry that sounds bad. We are working a case, and I believe he is our man. Now if that date coincides with a date I have, then it just makes my conviction stronger, but doesn't help as such. Does that make any sense, if not please check for me as a favour, will you?" Julie asked him.

"What is your thinking?" Harry asked.

"What if it coincides with a murder, he would not be home, but would not admit it, would he? The lights would be on a timer, appearing to be at home. Again circumstantial, but important for me," Julie said.

"Another pint Julie, your glass is empty," Harry said.

Julie looked at him smiling, "Why not, my round," Julie said.

Julie bought the next round, and sat back with Harry, "I like this place," Julie said.

"It has its uses, here I am Harry, not the Inspector, and we can talk freely, Brian is not a Sergeant, he is Brian, but we still respect the position of the person we are talking to, it is just, less formal," Harry told her.

At nine o'clock the next morning Julie and Harry were in the Super's office.

"Welcome Inspector, I believe you are the leading authority on the case of the murdered Councillor, which strikes me as odd, because you are from the Met. I understand that there have been several murders of the same or very similar M, O, please explain it, to me?" He asked.

Julie told him about the murders and how she and her team had reached the decision that the person of interest to her was in this area. She gave him the name and address, and all the information she had including her gut feelings and the co-incidences she considered relevant.

"I see, so we got you here on gut feelings, you do not have any evidence, or sound evidence, this is a fishing trip, isn't it?" He asked.

"I would not call it a fishing trip Sir; we have identified the person of interest, but by unproven systems. It does not take a leap of faith to see the connection, and only last night I was handed circumstantial evidence that made my trip worthwhile, if it plays out, as I suspect it will.

Sir, to go to court we have to have evidence, but most cases are cracked on gut feelings, without those, we are lost," Julie said with emphasis, which Harry picked up on.

"Sir, I need Inspector Ashton, as you can see, they have worked hard to get to this point, and our killer is, an expert. They have left no clue or trail for us to follow, only with the tenacity, the long arduous hours the Inspector's team have put in, have they been able to make any sort of break in the case, which I must say is a credit to them. It is circumstantial, but it is all we have. We are not asking for a team, just a couple of Officers to assist us to get evidence. The Inspector's team will continue to work the case in London, adding any evidence we get to their growing pile of evidence," Harry said.

"You said they didn't have any evidence, it was all circumstantial, so what evidence?" he asked.

Julie made to speak, but Harry cut her off.

"Allow me to answer this Inspector," he said putting his hand on hers, to stop her from speaking her mind, and making matters worse, "The evidence is circumstantial, but growing and leading us to this one person. Now focused on a specific individual, we can find solid evidence, instead of looking all over the place. We can stop searching for a straw to begin our investigation; we have that straw, and now need to follow it to the barn. Where with all the evidence we have, irrespective of value, we can find solid evidence, we now have a bail of straw, and it is growing.

Sir, with your open mind, and ability to see that we are closing in on the culprit, we just need a bit of time to get the evidence we need to conclude the case, say one month," Harry said smiling at him.

"Inspector, I am not female, so flattery does not work, with me. You have one week to bring me something tangible.

Off the record, good luck, I fear you will need it. Money is very tight, and I cannot afford any longer, so make it count," the Super said.

They left his office, and went to Harry's office.

"I don't suppose I could have Williams as my sergeant, could I?" Julie asked Harry.

"You will get me shot; I will make the right noises, but don't hold your breath, as for me, I think Brian, he knows the area, and our man, having met him briefly," Harry said, and set things in motion.

Julie went into more detail with Harry, as to how things had materialised, and her feelings on the case, by lunchtime Brian had joined them, and Williams was on his way up from London.

Julie met Williams at the hotel they were staying at, and over dinner she brought him up to speed, ready for the next morning.

After dinner, Julie and Williams set out for the house, and parked the car around a corner, but close enough to watch the house.

"Ma'am, if he is in, what are we going to do, just sit here and watch, for what?" Williams asked her.

"I don't know, if the lights are on a timer, they will come on automatically at a pre-set time, every night, whereas a person switches them on, when needed. Perhaps that is all I need to know that they are pre-set, so we watch tonight, and take the time, and then tomorrow night and so on, and as the days lengthen, will he re-set the timer?" Julie asked.

"You do realise I am missing Holby City, and Casualty, don't you?" Williams asked a gleam in his eye.

"Yes, it will do you good, to miss them," Julie replied laughing, "There, see the lights came on, yet it does not require lights, it is still light, watch the curtains, they have not been closed either," Julie said excited.

"We have blinds, and don't need to close the curtains, perhaps he is the same?" Williams asked.

"You are supposed to be helping me, not hindering. Drive up to the house and stop, I want to have a look inside," Julie said.

"You can also be arrested for being a Peeping Tom, Ma'am," Williams said starting the engine.

"Give me some credit, Williams," Julie said.

He stopped outside the house, and Julie got out of the car, and walked up the drive to the house, and knocked on the door. She waited and waited, and then knocked again louder and waited, and then went back to Williams.

"Drive around the block, and park where we were earlier, this is going to be a long night, Sergeant," Julie said.

They drove back to their original parking place, and watched. As the night progressed Julie began to remove her outer clothes, she looked at her watch, it was now midnight, and the lights went off in the lounge area, and on in the bedroom, again she noticed that the curtains were not drawn, and smiled.

Now dressed in black trousers and top, she applied some black to her face in the mirror, and then made her way carefully to the house, listening to Williams protests, as she left the car.

She carefully went around the back of the house, and used her skeleton keys to pick the lock, she was in, in a flash, and began her search quietly.

She stealthily made her way up the stairs, and into the first bedroom, she smiled it was his bedroom, and it was empty. Julie had been right he was not at home. She opened the wardrobe, not expecting to find anything, but looking.

Then she went to a different bedroom and found just what she had hoped to find, the camel coat hanging on a hanger in the wardrobe, in that room she also found his make-up, and a dressing table where he put the make-up on.

Julie went back downstairs, and out the back door making sure nothing had been disturbed, and the door was locked again, she then went back to the car, and put her normal clothes over the top of her dark clothes, and smiled at Williams.

"Ma'am that was an illegal search, anything you found is not admissible in evidence, so why do it?" Williams asked her.

"Williams, up to now we knew he was our man, not from evidence but gut feelings, no I cannot use it in evidence, but I now have the proof that he is our man, we just need a reason, for a search. We can now focus, on him.

He does not get visitors, so he can leave his make-up out on a dressing table, even if he had a visitor, then he is a transvestite, and easily explained away. We know differently, I am now satisfied he is our man, I saw the evidence with my own eyes, and I expect you, to believe me," Julie said looking at Williams.

"You know I do, I have, like you said, known ever since we found him, but lacked the evidence to convict him, and now we have it, but how to get him, or use the evidence?" Williams asked her.

"That is the million-dollar question. Tomorrow get in touch with Interpol, and all areas in the UK, we are looking for a murder. Abroad it may not happen till tomorrow, or the day after, or indeed yesterday, so say two days either side of today. He will be back for the weekend, an hour difference will be noticed, in the lights going on, and the clocks go forward, this weekend," Julie said fiddling about in her handbag.

"What have you lost Ma'am?" Williams asked.

"My make-up cleanser, I can't go into the hotel blacked up, can I?" Julie asked, smiling at Williams.

"No I agree, it would look bad, I have a clean handkerchief would you like me to spit on it like my mother used to?" Williams asked laughing; his question was answered with a dirty look, and a laugh.

A police car pulled up in front of them, and the officer got out, and approached them, whilst Julie was rushing to remove the black from her face.

"Sir, would you mind telling me what you are doing? We have had a call to say that you have been parked here for some time, is there anything wrong?" the officer asked them.

"Inspector Ashton, and Sergeant Williams, we are watching the house of a suspected criminal, surveillance," Julie said showing him her warrant card.

"I am sorry, we are not aware of any surveillance in this area, who authorised it?" He asked.

"I did, that is why I am an Inspector. I can authorise surveillance," Julie said.

"Which station, are you from, I don't recognise you, Ma'am?" he asked.

"You are right, we have not been introduced. I am on secondment from the Met, as is Sergeant Williams, and we started today at the local station. If you want a formal introduction, I suggest you come to Inspector Roberts' office at nine O'clock tomorrow morning, no wait this morning. When I am sure he will be only too pleased to introduce us to you, now go away, you have blown our cover already," Julie said.

"Ma'am, this is a well to do area, and there have in the past been several burglaries, so we keep a close eye on things, as do the local Neighbourhood Watch people, and I did not blow your cover, you did. I would also like to know why you left the car with your face blacked up. I think we should pay a visit to the local station for verification, would you mind getting into my car?" He asked.

"Just a moment please," Julie said, and took out her phone, "Harry, a slight problem, we have a rather keen officer here, who does not accept my warrant card as being proof that I am Inspector Ashton, and wants to take us to the station, will you confirm who I am, and Williams?" Julie asked.

"What have you done, never mind. I'll meet you at the station," he replied.

285

Julie and Williams got into the police car, and they were taken to the police station, half an hour later Harry arrived.

He entered the room they were in with the night Inspector.

"Well, you have some explaining to do. Why were you observing that house, I know why, or can guess, but Colin here does not, and why black out your face Julie, you did something, didn't you?" Harry asked.

"I saw the proof that he is our killer. How, do not ask? Just accept that I am unorthodox, but I now know he is our man. I saw the camel coat he uses, and his make-up dresser, ex-ray vision," Julie said.

"You broke into his house, didn't you?" Harry asked.

"Indeed not, no, I would never be, so crude. I picked the lock, and locked it behind me. I just entered, and there is no law against that. We cannot use the evidence against him in a court of law, but we now know he is our man, and I will keep saying that until it sinks in. Come on Harry, we knew it was him, but they would not believe us. All I need now is a means of getting inside legally, because the evidence is there," Julie said.

"Your Cavalier attitude will be your downfall; you cannot go breaking into a criminal's house, even if you know he is the guilty party. We need a search warrant for it to be legal, plus the waste of police time acting on a reported incident, of a car suspected of casing the area," The Inspector said.

"Point one, I did not break in, I carefully and skilfully opened the back door. Point two, without evidence, a search warrant will not be issued, so

286

asking for one would be, a waste of time. When was the last time you did a security check on the area?" Julie asked.

"We do not do a security check, we advise when asked to," the inspector said.

"Then it is high time we did one," Julie said.

"Julie, please, let me get permission from the Super, he likes to be kept informed when one of us has a daft idea, and then he can cover his arse," Harry said.

"It is not a daft idea; we are just helping reduce the un-necessary call outs by ensuring the house holders safety. How many of them have five-lever locks on their doors, or locks on the opening windows? Williams and I, with two officers can cover the estate in a day, and then it won't look suspicious, and add credibility to the local nick," Julie said.

"Julie, you are already on thin ice, he will not go for it," Harry said.

"Tell you what; wait till lunch time before you ask, by then Williams and I will have checked his house, ready for some walking Williams?" Julie asked.

"Is this where I develop wax in my ears?" The night inspector asked.

"Yes, it is, and a lot. Julie, how can I hold back, on this?" Harry asked.

"Easy, don't go to see him before lunchtime. If he asks where I am say you don't know, or out in the field, erm, interviewing a witness again, the councillor's agent lives in that area, doesn't he? That will do, we will call on him," Julie said.

"One of these days, Julie," Harry began.

"I know my cavalier attitude or my arrogance, will catch me out, till then criminals, beware, I am coming for you," Julie said, and laughed while Harry shook his head in dismay.

Chapter 25
Dodgy Dealings

"Madam, I am Inspector Ashton, and the local police station is concerned about the number of break ins, in this area, and we are offering a chance to use our expertise; to ensure that the property is secure. It won't take long, if I may come in, just a quick check about your security," Julie said, showing the lady of the house her warrant card.

Julie was invited in, she asked simple questions about the locks, and advised her that the mortise lock on the front door was weak, and really needed updating to a five lever dead lock, she also suggested that locks be fitted to the opening lights in the windows, and filled in a form with her suggestions, and signed it.

Williams, was also knocking on doors, and offering free advice, whilst Julie did her checks on one side, Williams did his on the other side. They started at the start of the street, so as not to raise suspicions. Julie worked her way slowly to the house she was interested in, and after an hour or so, she was knocking on that particular door.

"Good morning Sir, I am Inspector Ashton from the local police station. There have been a couple of robberies in the area, and the Neighbourhood watch has reported several cars parked, as if casing houses. We decided that it would be a good idea if we conducted a check on people's security measures. May I come in, so that I can advise you if necessary, about your security?" Julie asked him showing him her warrant card.

"No, I am a security expert, and don't need advice, good day," he said, and closed the door.

Julie walked away her plan had failed, and she was annoyed at his rudeness, and bluntness. She walked down the drive, and into the next house, and gave her introduction and entered.

"This house is perhaps the best protected, I cannot offer you any advice, five lever locks front and back, impressive. Security cameras on the gable ends, flood lights aimed on the garden. You have a very secure house Madam; I am impressed, thank you for your time. May I ask who advised you, was it a local firm?" Julie asked.

"This is between you and me, isn't it?" She asked.

"Yes, very much so, I am not allowed to suggest a firm, even if it is nice to know the good firms," Julie said not expecting what was to follow.

"The man next door, my husband doesn't like him, and I don't, he seems odd, and there are some odd things going on next door. I am not a nosey parker you know, but I saw a woman leaving the house in his car once. Not odd, apart from a woman had not entered the house, I would have seen her. So my husband decided to upgrade our security, and there were other things, parcels in brown paper," she said giving Julie a suggestive wink, "One night I was sure I had heard a gunshot. He does not work, but has plenty of money, and he hires cars, why, when he has a perfectly good one in the drive. And he goes out late at night, like eleven o'clock. Who goes out so late, and is away for a couple of days, and then returns, so it isn't a holiday, and as I said, he doesn't work," the lady of the house told Julie.

"I see, that is interesting, and I understand your concerns. You wouldn't happen to know when he goes out, like a diary with the dates when he is away for two days say, would you?" Julie asked.

"I don't have a diary, but I can tell you the last time was a month ago. A taxi picked him up at ten o'clock in the morning, and he had an overnight bag with him, just cabin luggage, and he came back two days later," she told Julie.

"So when exactly, if you can remember, was it around the middle of the month, say the fifteenth?" Julie asked.

"Hum, let me see now Bill, my husband, was in Paris, he is a buyer for a clothing firm, and is away a lot, another reason for the upgrade. I can ask him when that was; because it was two days after Bill left that the man next door, went away. The time before that would be six, no eight months ago. I remember that because we had the decorators in, and when I spoke to him, he ignored me, all I said was, 'Off again, have a good trip,' being friendly, but as I said, he got in the taxi, and ignored me, even the decorator commented, on his rudeness," she told Julie.

"Most things have a simple explanation, I am sure there is nothing to worry about, but just for your peace of mind, will you make a note of his trips for me, here my card, contact me at any time," Julie said.

She left, and met up with Williams, it was now lunch time, and they went for a rather late lunch, at a cafe close by the estate.

291

"Well Ma'am, did you get a good look?" Williams asked her.

She gave him a sour look, "You know I didn't; he opened the door a crack, and said he wasn't interested, and closed the door in my face, ignorant sod," Julie said disgruntled, "So you can wipe that smirk off your face, I saw you watching," she added.

"I had better luck, I called on the house opposite, and they told me that he kept odd hours, going out late at night, and going away mid-week for a couple of days, yet didn't work, not evidence as such, but adds to our knowledge of him," Williams said.

"I got even more from the woman next door, they don't like him, and she is not a nosey parker, but sees everything. I want you to go back to the station, and get on to Interpol, was there a murder around the middle of last month, and he was away for two days, so it must be in Europe. I also want to know what taxi firm, picked him up; I didn't ask the woman because I didn't want to raise her suspicions that we were investigating him. She thinks I am suspicious, because of her comments, and aware that there might be something, but not that it is an active investigation. He was picked up around ten a. m. on the fifteenth, no sorry two days after that, so the seventeenth of March," Julie told Williams.

"Would you also like me to check if he uses the same firm all the time, and if they have a record of when he is picked up?" Williams asked her, as they ate their meat pie and chips.

"I doubt him doing that; he will use different firms, just as a precaution, but check anyway," Julie said.

They finished their meal, and went back to the office, and the Super called Julie, into his office.

"We do have a perfectly good detective in charge of advising the public on security, so why did you decide that you needed to waste time doing their job. It is not part of the investigation, is it?' he asked her.

"No Sir, it is not, but it did provide us with an opportunity to meet our man, and collect information about him. We still do not have evidence, but we now know that he was away in the middle of last month, for two days. Williams is checking if there was a murder at that point in time, and again some eight months ago, when we know there was, but it is too vague as yet, to say that he was away at that particular point in time.

Sir, he is very good, and covers his tracks well, I would very much like to put a surveillance team in her house, but they could be there for months, so it isn't viable. But what if we put a camera on her eaves to watch the front of her house, but it had a camera that pointed towards his house, motion activated, so that we don't have to have an officer watching it all the time? Williams and I could monitor it, because it is motion activated, we would not have to watch twenty four hours of blank tape, just an hour at the most, when it was activated for a few seconds or minutes at a time, when it was activated," Julie suggested.

"Next I suppose you will want a phone tap?" He asked.

"We do not have enough yet to get one approved, Sir, but that will come later. From my talk with a neighbour, I am convinced he is our man, but I need evidence, and that is where we are struggling. I need to officially search his house, the evidence is there, so I propose to watch him, he will slip up. I have his car registration number, and my people are now searching the CCTV cameras for its movements. If I can put it in the vicinity of a murder, it will help, and using the walk computer program, put him closer to the murder, I am hoping that we can get enough circumstantial evidence to get the search warrant, we need," Julie told him.

"Walk me to my car," he said.

They left his office and made their way to his car.

"Julie, this is off the record. I know what you did, and I do not approve of acts that can lead us down a disreputable route. I have decided to turn a blind eye to it, but be careful. Was it of any use?' He asked her quietly.

"Not that I am admitting to anything, but I did notice a large camel coat, at least one size too large, big enough to hide a person's actions, say. Sir, he is our man, and I know it, and I know the evidence is in that house," Julie said.

"I will hang you out to dry, if you bring discredit to the force, be careful," he told her.

"Sir, good police work has got us to this point, and that should never be under stated. My team have worked their socks off to get us to this point. We are so close, and yet so far away, and yet I believe that the skills of my detectives will find a solution, and we will bring about a good, prosecution," Julie said.

"Just as long as it is not by hook or by crook," he said and gave her a smile.

The Super got in his car and drove off; Julie went back into the station, and made contact with her team in London, for an update.

Evans told her that they had managed to trace the money to a bank account in the Seychelles, and to a computer in Manchester, it was now just a matter of time before they had the actual location, of the computer.

Mayberry was watching all the footage from the cameras closest to the scenes of the crimes using the gait program, but as yet had not managed to find a walk the same, apart from one fleeting glance, a few seconds, which was not enough to be certain, but it did match.

Hargreaves, had managed to input the Trojan horse, but again it would take time to follow the links around the world.

"Julie, the Super is not stupid, he knew what you had done, the officers who challenged us made a report, and he put two and two together. What now, more illegal antics?" Williams asked her, Julie smiled.

"No, he has approved a camera to be put on the neighbour's house to watch him. Ideally I would like to arrest him before he kills anyone else, but that may not be the case. What about Interpol; was there anything useful there?" Julie asked.

"Yes, around that date a states man was killed in Columbia, from the opposition, a minor person currently, but had great potential, viewed by some as a probable head of state," Williams told her.

"Getting rid of the opposition before they become a threat, interesting, but why didn't the drug lords take care of it themselves? They have never fought shy of murder, before," Julie asked.

"Who said it was the drug lords?" Williams asked.

"Even more, interesting," Julie said, her hand to her chin in thought, "Do we have an exact date?" Julie asked.

"Yes, the twentieth, he was shot with a point two, five bullet, with no striations, using a rifle, they estimate a hundred yards. It was from a tree outside the perimeter wall. Our man is getting clumsy, footprints by the tree, and scuff marks on the trunk and branch, and there was gunshot residue. The victim was attending a meeting at a rich farmer's house, and political activist, with strong links to America, and an outspoken critic of the drug lords, and lack of arrests. Paulo Cortez was to be the front man, backed by the farmer, so we or they believe," Williams told her.

"Time is everything, we know he left the house on the seventeenth; he would then fly to Columbia, so, check flights to Paris, New York and Bogotá, and a connecting flight, use the gait program, and London. Anyone of interest, find out if they used a credit card to book the flight? That may be our way in," Julie said with a smile.

"He could go by train Ma'am, to London that is," Williams offered.

"Indeed he could, so check all transport out of Manchester; I am allowing a day for him to get there, maybe over, say one and a half days taking a roundabout route, Bogotá is where I feel he will arrive, so check El Dorado International airport as an arrival point. Harry, hello, nice to see you," Julie said.

"What do you want me to do, after a greeting like that?" he asked.

"Can't get anything past you, can we?" Julie asked, "I need a couple of your technical guys to install a camera up in the eaves of number seventeen, watching number fifteen, but number fifteen must not know it is there, or that we are watching them," Julie asked him.

"You do have approval, don't you?" He asked.

"Of course," Julie said.

"Julie, you don't sound very convincing to me. Do I take it that the Super did not say, no?" He asked.

"That is correct, and to finish it for you, neither did he say yes, it is on my head. I take full responsibility, for it," Julie said.

"It will be installed by tomorrow lunch time. The Super has some skeletons in his cupboard, which he would rather not have revealed, so he tends to be practical, shall we say? He won't condone what you are doing, but he won't stop you either. Just make sure you are not caught, and that you get a result," Harry said.

Chapter 26
Circumstantial or Fact

Early the next morning, Julie entered her office, the one she shared with Harry and Williams.

Williams was already in the office, and smiling.

"I know you are an optimist, but why the broad smile?" Julie asked him.

"Morning Ma'am, our diligence has paid off; James booked a taxi from his home at ten am on the seventeenth, as we know. And he also took a train from Piccadilly to London.

A Mrs Angela Hodgkin had a flight from Heathrow to Paris that evening, and she was booked on a flight to Bogota the following morning, but she never arrived, then again a Brenda Wilson did arrive, thirty minutes after the Paris flight, in line with a flight from JFK, but she was not booked on that flight.

He mingles in with people from a different flight to throw us off the trail, and as a different person; female to female in the toilets.

This also means that he was in the area at the same time as the murder, this is now proven via the gait program, and weakly, via the facial recognition program," Williams told her.

"That is excellent, but useless, at the same time; one aspect is as yet not recognised by the courts, the gait program, so we can't use it, and the other too weak to be used, as evidence.

"I don't suppose there is any chance of fingerprints, is there?" Julie asked.

"I have asked for CCTV footage, but I bet she is wearing gloves, and in an airport?" Williams asked querying the suggestion.

Julie slapped her head in frustration, "I am a bloody fool, the gun is special, made to order as it were, and so, how does he get it through customs?" Julie asked shaking her head in dismay at missing such a vital part of the plan.

"That I can only guess at, two metal tubes in her hold luggage would not be queried. Just a suggestion Ma'am, especially if they looked like say a lipstick, and the bullet bought locally. Would a sniffer dog pick up one bullet in a suitcase?" Williams asked.

"I like your thinking, and you are right, two tubes could get through easily enough, but the bullet I very much doubt. What about the return does that coincide with our time scale?" Julie asked.

"I will look into that, OH; by the way, they all have credit cards, and bank accounts, which is more good news, because we looked into their bank accounts via a court order. One interesting transaction, and there are more, but in this case ten thousand pounds was transferred from Angela Hodgkin's account to Brian Derwen's account, in the Seychelles two days before he flew out, and another twenty thousand after he had returned. I am presuming that point, it was two weeks later, so I presumed he had got back, by then," Williams told her.

"A good assumption, so we are looking at thirty thousand for the hit?" Julie asked.

"Could be, there is still ten thousand in her account, so that may not be the case," Williams said with a question mark over his answer.

"What is the price for a political hit, these days?" Julie asked.

"Difficult to say, life is cheap out there, but as you said, it was political, so not as cheap as the drug lords dictate. It is only a guess, but I would expect it to be say, ten, to fifteen thousand, over here twenty to twenty-five thousand, may be higher, you were the sniper, not me," Williams said.

"Thank you for reminding me, I just got a week's wages as a lieutenant in the forces," Julie said and laughed, "Have we got enough for a warrant, think about it. We can track his movements, and name changes. When Harry arrives I will ask him for his opinion. I believe we have, but the more I think about it, the weaker it becomes," Julie added thoughtfully.

"We do not have anything concrete, but I think we stand a chance. As you said we can prove the name changes and destinations, and we now have the movement of money to add to our evidence. Yet it all still feels weak, there is nothing like putting the gun in his hand, then we wouldn't have a problem, and this is nothing, like that," Williams said wearily.

"How fortuitous, Harry we were just talking about you, and your excellent connections. All we need is a search warrant for number fifteen," Julie said adding a bright smile.

"Oh, you can put the gun in his hand?" Harry asked.

"Well, not exactly," Julie replied.

"OK, you have photographic evidence of him at the scene?" Harry asked.

"Well, not quite, we have a name trail, we can put him on a train, a plane and in Bogota, at or about the same time, as the murder," Julie said.

"You can put a fictitious person at the scene of a crime in a foreign country. Julie, the judge will require evidence, facts not fiction, as you well know," Harry said.

"Listen to us please, because the fictitious person also bought a ticket to Humberside from Manchester, Brenda Wilson, what is surprising is that she never returned, but a Mr Derwen did," Julie told him.

"How did you know that?" Williams asked.

"I have just received an E-Mail from London. The guys are now looking into any tickets bought by the names we know he used, and around the time of the murders, my good and dear friend Hastings, just told me," Julie said.

"Since when, was he a good and dear friend?" Williams asked smiling.

"Since he sent me that titbit; Harry you have to get me into that house, legally. I do not believe in coincidences, but this is too much of one to ignore it. Williams, list the journey he took to Bogota for Harry, and the movement of money, and then Harry add to it what I have just told you. I'll make us a nice cup of coffee," Julie said, and got up.

"Bribery will not work Julie," Harry said as he sat down at his desk to listen to Williams.

Julie ignored the comment, and left them after making the coffees she joined them.

"Thirty minutes later a Brenda Wilson arrived," Williams was saying, he then went into the cash transaction, and rounded it off with Julies input, Harry had already heard.

"Well Harry, circumstantial, but come on! I have proved how he does it with what weapon and shown my Chief Super that my theory is right, and now so much evidence, albeit circumstantial, but you have to agree, it is overwhelming," Julie said.

"I agree, but I am involved, and know as you do we have the right man, but the judge does not, and it is still not enough to get a warrant. I know the judge he is a stickler, for evidence, hard facts, and indisputable facts. You have so much circumstantial evidence it is overwhelming, I agree, but he will not, unless we have one hard, solid fact," Harry told them.

"Then we have to follow him, watch him kill someone to get the warrant, how fucking stupid, sorry, I am so frustrated with this case, he will kill again, and it is our job to stop him, yet the judicial system stops us from doing our jobs," Julie said, angry at the lack of support.

"Perhaps not, let me think a minute, do we have a means of contact yet, what about us making the approach, a nice target say the Prime Minister, and juicy enough to tempt him," Harry said.

"You mean to contact him, if we have the means, and ask him to kill the Prime Minister. I like the idea, but he won't be online in his actual name, so where do we get the connection and evidence that it is him?" Julie asked.

"Good point and he will not meet us, erm, for payment say, so how does that help?" Harry asked, "Julie, you just ruined my best idea," he added.

"No, it has legs, but needs refining, let me think," Julie said.

"A double in a bullet proof vest, he always aims for the heart," Williams offered.

"I thought you'd never offer, thank you Williams. Now we need Alex's friend, a mask and wig, don't you agree Harry? He is the right build, we just get the Mayor of Manchester to pose for us, whilst Alex's friend makes the mask, and then we are set. I am too small, and Harry is too thin, you are just right. This will take very careful planning, we have to control it right from the start," Julie said, smiling at Williams.

"Am I volunteering for this assignment?" Williams asked.

"I just took it for granted, you would do," Julie said with a smile.

"And I like you too," Williams said in a disgruntled voice.

Chapter 27
Relief

"I made you a coffee, didn't I?" Julie asked.

"Bribery, you heard the Inspector, Sir," Williams said.

"Indeed I did, and thank you for volunteering," Harry said smiling at Williams.

Julie began to plan the ruse with Harry, and Williams help, they were going to arrange a private meeting, putting the Mayor/ Williams in a position to be an easy target, but with limited places for a long-range shot. At each position, a policeman would be stationed, limiting the avenues of attack. Julie selected a place, whilst Harry had the task of getting the Mayor to agree, and the Chief Superintendent.

It took them all day to find a suitable place, with the cover Julie wanted to protect Williams.

The next morning Williams met Julie at the front of the hotel, and drove her to work.

"I do not believe it; you have been let off the hook Sergeant. Check your E-Mails to confirm what I am seeing?" Julie asked him.

"Ma'am I like it, this means I do not have to accept the role. I said Evans and Hastings were good, I like them even more so now, Ma'am. They have got inside his computer, and can print off the communications between him, and the people who booked him. Surely that is enough for a search warrant?" Williams asked her.

"May be, then again, perhaps not, can we prove that Eagle is James, and that the Fox is the person booking him to kill the Bunny. I will ask Evans to prove the names are the people we know they are, but it does let you off the hook.

Code names are not enough, we need real names, and they must be in there somewhere," Julie said, and picked up the phone, "Great work Evans, thank you, now all we need is the actual names for the code names, go back into the conversations to find a real name. I presume that the Eagle is James, but who is the Fox and Bunny, please let it be the local councillor," Julie said, putting the phone on speaker.

"Morning Ma'am, I agree the Eagle is James, but as yet we have not traced the E-Mails, far enough back. We have a problem, which we are looking into, they are deleted, almost as soon as they are received, again leaving no trace. With his computer I can get them back, but remotely it is not as easy, it will take time. What we are doing is monitoring his E-Mails, but that will only warn us of pending kills," Evans told her.

"What if we booked him, if we sent him a message to kill the local mayor? His acceptance of the job would then give us probable cause, and the warrant, a sting operation?" Julie asked.

Julie wanted confirmation rather than anything, using Evans as a sounding board.

"Ma'am, give me a couple of days to see if I can get a name for you," Evans asked.

"Two days Evans, that is all I can afford, I have one week left to my deadline, good luck," Julie said.

"I'll do my best Ma'am, "Evans replied.

"Ma'am," Williams said, as she hung up, "We have the go ahead from the Mayor, but the Chief is not happy," Williams said.

"When is he ever happy? What about the local Chief, he does not have an axe, to grind?" Julie asked.

"He is happy as long as the Mayor is. I will go home tomorrow for the mask to be made, if that is alright?" Williams asked.

"Crafty sod tomorrow is Friday, which means you get the weekend off," Julie said laughing with him.

"Like hell, I will have to sit there for hours whilst she makes the mask," Williams said laughing.

"Go now, you deserve the weekend off, Harry and I can do what needs to be done here. I want you back on Monday bright and early. We have just seven days left, our Super will want me to hand my warrant card in next Friday night, this is going to be tight," Julie said.

"I could stay Ma'am, if you want, and make the trip in one day," Williams offered.

"No, go, go on, I am just waiting for Evans, unless something else breaks," Julie told him.

Williams left the office, just as Harry arrived, after the greetings, Julie told him of the developments, and then viewed the tapes from the camera next door to number fifteen.

She watched carefully as a woman left the house, and got into a taxi, she noted the name of the firm, and rang them asking who had booked the taxi, and where it was going.

Harry listened to her asking the taxi firm, when she hung up he spoke to her.

"Julie, where was she going?" He asked.

"Victoria station, and she had her Camel coat on, Harry, we need to follow her," Julie said, with concern in her voice.

"I'll get the car, you contact the station police, and try and find out where she is going," Harry said.

Julie rang the station police office, and sent them a photo of the woman to observe only, and then she ran down to the car park, and got into the car Harry was in.

He drove fast, the sirens blaring as he ran red lights, racing to the station to try and catch the same train she was on. Julie held on, as he cornered at speed, and then slammed the brakes on at the front of the station, screeching to a halt.

"Morning Sir, there is no rush, is that the woman," He asked pointing to a woman at the barrier.

"I believe it is, where is the train going?" Harry asked.

"Liverpool, it leaves in five minutes, Sir," the officer said.

"What do you want to do, Julie?" Harry asked her.

"He or she, as you wish, has as yet not committed a crime, so I suggest we follow them. Let it play out, but not quite to the end. What is going on in Liverpool that could attract him?" Julie asked.

"That is the problem, nothing, there are no by-elections, or rallies, or controversial proposals," Harry said.

307

"Sir, if I may, there is in Wigan, which is on the same line. I live in Wigan, and there is a visit by the opposition leader, could he be the target?" A station police officer asked them.

"As they say, if that is the only place of interest, then that is where it is, thank you. Harry, get in touch with the local chief, and warn him. I don't want him touched. We need to arrest him. So we have to wait until he is set up, and then grab him, observe him only. Even if he goes for a pee, watch him.

Officer, you know the town, you are with us, he will not be in a high vantage point, like a church bell tower, but above the crowd, so a second story window with easy access, and egress," Julie said.

Julie rang the police station in the station to commandeer the officer, because of his knowledge of Wigan, whilst Harry rang the local police chief, with a description of what their suspect, was wearing.

They watched as he boarded the train, and then got on using the carriage behind his carriage, with the officer boarding in the last carriage.

At each station Julie got up to make sure he didn't get off there, the guard had been told not to start the train at Wigan until Julie indicated that he, could do.

Julie and Harry were sat as close to the door as possible, and watched as he walked down the platform, passed their carriage, they waited for a few seconds before getting up, and exiting the carriage.

By the time they were on the platform, he was already on the stairs leading out of the station, as they passed the last carriage they nodded to the officer, and the guard, who set the train going again.

As Julie mounted the steps her phone went, "Chief Inspector Robertson here, our officers have the target in sight, he is moving north up Wallgate towards the town centre," the chief told her.

"Thank you sir, we believe his target is either the leader of the opposition, or one of his entourage, and we do not want to stop the meeting, it is our best chance to arrest him," Julie said.

"That is for me to decide Inspector, I will go along with you for the moment, but if I feel it is unsafe, then I will stop, the gathering," He told her.

"I have to accept that Sir, but please give us a chance to arrest him, before you cancel the gathering. We know who it is, but we need concrete evidence to make the arrest stick, catching him with the gun in his hand, is the only way," Julie pleaded.

"Is it normal for you to endanger the lives of politicians, just to get evidence, have you thought about using police methods, good old fashioned tried and tested methods, to bring about a conviction?" He asked.

"Yes Sir, that is why we can state with confidence he is here to kill someone, and who to follow, below the dress is a male assassin, but that will not hold up in court, Sir. What I know, and other officers to be true, is not evidence, we need to put the gun, in his hand," Julie pleaded.

"I have gone along with this so far, but you had better be right, and know what you are doing, this is not a practice, it is for real, and a life is on the line," The chief warned her.

309

"Yes Sir, we realise that, but have not had the time to discuss this with you, we only found out this morning, and had it not been for a police officer at Manchester Station, we would not have known where he was to get off, until he did, which would mean that I would be telling you now about the proposed assassination, too late, to do anything," Julie said.

Julie continued up Wallgate to the town centre, where she looked about trying to find a vantage point, she was bumped once or twice by the growing crowd.

"I take it this is where they are to hold the meeting, what is it, do we know?" Julie asked.

"Yes Ma'am, the leader of the opposition is speaking here to rally support for the Labour party for the local council elections, next month. This is a labour area, but their ratings have slipped a bit, and the Local Conservative party plan to what can I say, erm, have their say. A local leader is suspected of dipping into party funds, and the Conservatives want to make sure the people know about it, discrediting the Labour councillors to help win enough seats to control the council," The officer told her.

"That helps me a lot, I thought no-one would be daft enough to try and assassinate the leader of any party, but local politics, he is only too happy to oblige. Harry, I believe the target is the leader of the local Conservative party.

Down that side, and across that side we have banks, which will be secure, he won't get to an upper floor window from those buildings, so that leaves the pub, and the shops, especially that empty shop there, next to the pub," Julie said as her phone rang.

"Inspector, I am calling it off, our men have just lost the subject, and I am not prepared to risk the life of the leader of the opposition, on a whim," The Chief told her.

"Sir don't, not just yet, allow me to try and find him again, give me, well how long have I got, ten minutes, before they start speaking?" Julie asked.

"I can delay them, but you only have ten minutes, if he isn't found by then, I stop the rally," The Chief said.

"Julie, how on earth are you going to find him in time with a town to search?" Harry asked.

"Harry, I was an army sniper, I know what he is looking for, as I said, the banks are out that leaves the pub, which is not secure, and anyone could see him. No, he is in that empty shop, the perfect angle, and trajectory for the shot.

It is daytime and he cannot get in close for the side shot he uses so it has to be from a distance. The shopping arcade is too crowded, the empty shop is ideal.

He will not be disturbed because it is empty, no-one will go inside, and he can escape in the milling crowd, and confusion. I would venture to say that by the time the police are organised, he would be in Wallgate station, on his way home," Julie said.

"I just hope you are right, there isn't time to check anywhere else," Harry said.

Chapter 28
Capture

Julie, with Harry's help, pushed through the crowd to the empty shop, and she picked the lock quietly, she entered, and climbed the stairs silently, she pushed the door open a little, to see inside.

"Shit Harry, he isn't there, where the hell is he?" Julie asked shocked and perturbed at her findings, she was sure he would be there.

Julie entered the room, and looked out of the window.

"He will not get into the banks, where is he, Harry? Look another empty shop, where is the stage? It is below us, I am getting stupid; he will not be in here, but over there. A clear shot, escape behind the crowds, everyone will be focused on the stage, not the rear of the crowds. Wait that is it; that is what he wants us to think. Get behind the door Harry, we beat him here," Julie said, and stood up.

The hairs on the back of her neck were stood up; a clear sign of impending danger, there was a slight creaking sound as the door opened. Julie was ready for his entry, and smiled at him.

"Hello Peter, or is it Petra, you have heard of 'A Bridge Too Far,' well I am here to tell you this is an assassination, to many," Julie said.

She saw his movement, and threw herself into a forward roll, ending up standing right up close in front of him. She grabbed his gun arm, and threw him, using her leg as a lever. There was a pop, and a crack, and Julie was kneeling on him. Dazzled by the speed of everything, Harry moved to join Julie, in the arrest, putting handcuffs on him.

"Bitch, you dislocated my shoulder," He said aggrieved.

"Pay back for you shooting me in my arm, shit that hurt, Harry, can you hold him, whilst I get help?" Julie asked him.

"Let me," was all Harry got out, as he let go of the suspect to attend to Julie, but she was ready, and pushed Harry hard, pushing him into the suspect, and flooring him, and Harry.

"I am alright, you hold him, and I will get help," Julie said opening the window, and calling down for the police.

"Officer, get up here now, with two other officers, Inspector Ashton," she said showing her warrant card.

A moment later two officers entered the room, and relieved Harry of the suspect, they took him out, and put him in a police car.

"Chief Inspector, the assassin is in police custody, he will need to be told of his rights and searched, he will have what may appear as a lipstick case, but it is a gun, and in his bag there will be an extension, and telescope sights to turn it into a rifle," Julie told him.

"Well done Inspector, why are you not arresting him?" He asked.

"Something to do with a hole in my arm, I am off to the local hospital," Julie said, adding, "But if possible, can I interview him?" Julie asked.

"Of course you can, we can hold him for forty-eight hours with what we have, and then there is the illegal gun, so we can hold him for as long as you want," He told her.

Julie knew that was not correct, but there was enough to hold him for questioning, and she would be out of hospital later that day, a night in a hotel, and then she would question him.

By ten o'clock the following morning Julie was stood in the ante room looking at him through the one-way mirror.

James sat in the interview room defiantly, staring at the mirror unflinching.

"Julie, we have him, and forensics are now going through his clothes, and weapons. We can put the gun in his hand. The hospital has been kind enough to get the bullet they removed from your arm to us, for again, forensic analysis," Harry told her.

"A slam dunk case, a confession is superfluous, but nice to have, has Williams arrived yet? I want him with me in there, he deserves to be with me as we close the case," Julie said.

"I have been told he has just arrived, complaining about the road system," Harry told her laughing.

The door opened, and Williams entered.

"Morning Ma'am, is he sweating?" Williams asked.

"No, not in the least, just as I suspected he is far too professional. He may confess, but if he does, don't be surprised if it comes out bragging, he is proud of his skills, much the same as I am, but I put mine to a legal use, he didn't, but we are the same, you would not break me, either," Julie said, Williams picked up on her proud voice at her comments, and the confidence, with which she spoke.

They left the ante room, and entered the interview room.

"Good morning Mr James, I am Detective Inspector Ashton, and this is Detective Sergeant Williams. I won't beat about the bush, I would like a confession, but like me you will not break under pressure. So let us begin with the evidence.

One specially made gun, primitive, but effective at close range, found on you at the scene, one bullet again basic, but effective, which was extracted from my right arm, you will be charged with grievous bodily harm, and attempted murder. I am the victim, and witness.

Inside the bag you were carrying, they found an extension to the butt, and to the barrel, the extension had rifling, and also in the bag we found oversized bullets, the wadding designed to fall away after exiting the barrel, giving the bullet the spin to travel true.

A search warrant is on its way, and I expect to find a smaller gun, again basic, and the one you used to assassinate the local councillor, and low powered bullets for your more popular means, of assassination.

In my past I have been a sharpshooter and sniper, I know what you have used, and how, I now have the evidence to support my belief, formulated from my knowledge of being, a sniper.

Mr James, confession or not, you are going to prison for a very long time, say fifteen years, followed by a trip to America, where they have the death sentence, and I will again, give evidence.

I will make a single offer, which expires once I leave the room, confess, serve your time here, and any extradition case by America will not be granted," Julie said.

He looked at her, his eyes boring into her, as she gave him the same look; she wanted a confession, which he would not give her the satisfaction of, so she made the offer, after ensuring he knew they were of the same ilk.

They sat there silently for several minutes, until Julie won, and he smiled.

"Why ask, if you know the answer?" He asked.

"I didn't, I just made an offer, which I presume you decline, thank you, an animal like you does not deserve to live, but I abide by the law, so cannot do what I would like to do. Believe me; it would give me the greatest of pleasure to put a lump of lead between your eyes, and like you, I do not miss, good day," Julie said, and got up, and left the room with Williams.

"What the hell do you call that Inspector, you were supposed to get a confession?" The chief asked her.

"Sir, as I said, he will not confess under pressure, please be my guest and waste your time, in there. I have better things to do, come on Williams, time to go home," Julie said, and marched out of the station saying her goodbyes, as she left.

An officer was detailed to drive them to Wigan North Western station to catch the train back to London; they arrive at six o'clock in the evening.

"I missed out by one day, so first thing I will go to the chief, and hand in my resignation, it has been my pleasure to work with you Dan, and if you hear of a vacancy for a ruthless killer, please, give me a call that is the only thing I am good at," Julie said.

"Ma'am, that is not true, you are a good copper, and if you resign I will also, and we can start a detective agency, or security personnel," Williams said, to bolster her.

"No thank you, climbing up trees to spy, and take photos on someone having sex; is not my idea of how to make a living, and definitely not babysitting some rich bloke, I am more likely to thump the elitist prig," Julie said, and laughed.

"Before you go, I know Alex would want to say goodbye, so dinner at my place, tomorrow night?" Dan asked her, cocking his head to one side enquiringly.

"Thank you, I would like that," Julie replied, and went inside her bungalow.

At nine o'clock sharp the next morning, Julie, was stood outside the Chief Superintendent's office, her resignation in her hand. He told her to come in, and offered her a seat.

"Six months and one day, so here is my resignation, I won't bother to sit, I have to go job hunting," Julie said bluntly.

"Inspector, before I accept your resignation, I have something to say so please sit, you are still an officer until I accept your resignation," he told her, Julie gave him a look, and sat down, "The Police Commissionaire, in his infinite wisdom, has asked me for my opinion. I told him that you were rude, insubordinate, and overconfident, and that you did not fit into the police force, of today.

Perhaps in Victorian times when the police were more ruthless because of the laws of the times, you would have fitted in, but in a modern, caring force, your aggressive nature was not a requirement, we needed.

He smiled, and said, "She single handed takes out four assailants who were beating a Sergeant to a pulp. She finds the means, and method of an assassin, who we know killed at least eight people, may be more. She tracks him down and affects an arrest, getting wounded in the process, and still manages to hold and detain him, and you believe she has no place in a modern police force, are you mad.

She is ideal, if a little forceful. Find somewhere for her, I will not accept her resignation, unless it is accompanied, with yours." He told me, so I have searched the length and breadth of England, and found the ideal spot for you, Detective Chief Inspector, rural England, it goes with the promotion.

Obviously, you do not have to accept the promotion, and location, if you feel it will be too quiet, for you?" The Superintendent asked her, with a nasty smile.

"Why Sir, after the ordeal I have just endured, it will be nice to find peace and quiet, I accept," Julie said beating him at his own game.

A week passed allowing Julie to say her goodbyes properly, and pack, and then she was on her way to, Little Hampton, the largest of the towns on her new patch.

'What a miserable day to start my new job?' Detective Chief Inspector Ashton thought, as she drove through the pouring rain.

THE END

318

www.ingramcontent.com/pod-product-compliance
Lightning Source LLC
Chambersburg PA
CBHW010822250626
47172CB00004B/972